I'd got what I came for. I headed for the door.

I didn't quite get there. My legs turned to rubber, my heart started to pound. Every sound, every smell exploded in my brain. Someone behind me shouted something I didn't quite understand.

Next thing I knew, I was in Smokey's Joe's fetid elimination place, yorking my guts out, with Velda holding my head over the pot.

"Good thing you didn't take more of that brew," she scolded me. "Don't you know better than to drink something you didn't order?"

"I thought I was used to Joe's brew," was the best I could come up with between heaves. I gasped for air, trying to block the crazy sensations streaming through my head.

"I'll find you a pedishaw," Velda soothed me. "And then Basher and I will get to the bottom of this. No one poisons anyone at Smokey Joe's without our say-so."

She hauled me outside, heaved me into the seat of the nearest pedishaw, with orders to the driver to take me to Foodie Alley, and orders to me to go straight up to my digs and sleep it off.

The last conscious thought I had was, *I must have got someone's attention.* I only wished I knew who…and why.

GUARDIANS

of

LORR

ROBERTA ROGOW

ZUMAYA OTHERWORLDS   AUSTIN TX

2024

GUARDIANS OF LORR

© 2024 by Roberta Rogow

978-1-61271-439-4

"Zumaya Otherworlds" and the griffon colophon are trade-marks of Zumaya Publications LLC, Austin TX
https://www.zumayapublications.com

To Liz Burton, who was willing to publish the book no one else would touch.

ARTIST AND MODELS

I NEVER KNOW WHAT'S GOING TO COME THROUGH MY door.

Usually, it's some citizen of Lorr with a small family problem, something they don't want to bring to the attention of their Guild, or the Administration, or the City Guard. A spouse hasn't shown up for a day or two, coin, or merch isn't where it should be. Someone's being unpleasant about an incident that happened a while back and is threatening to put it on Post Six unless the citizen coughs up coin. They want answers, and I provide them.

That's why they come to me, Pola Drach, Independent Eye. I'm not connected with any of the Guilds, I'm not Admin, and I am definitely not in the City Guards. I specialize in Domestics—family problems. The sort of thing Basher Bob tends to shy away from, and that are too trivial for The Brain to bother with.

On this particular day, a month before Winterfest, I'd just told a male that his young spouse was not seeing another male, but *was* frequenting the casinos on Entertainment Row. His missing coin was probably going into the money-pouches of the card-dealers.

He left, muttering to himself. If his spouse wanted to throw their coin away, that was their lookout, not mine. What the client did with my information? Also not my concern. He got what he laid out the coin for.

I was just tidying up my files, getting ready to call it quits for the day when I got a tap on the outside door,

"It's open!" I don't bother to lock my door when I'm there. When I leave, that's another matter. I have a lock, and most of the time it works.

I almost didn't recognize the client. The last time I'd seen Captain Sara Atterson out of uniform was the day we met at Guards Training Camp over fifteen years ago. Since then, she's always been in some kind of official garb, whether it was the dull khaki of Guards Trainees or the spiffy brown-and-white of the Lorr City Guards. She's tall, fair, trim and always put together, even under extreme stress. Not a hair out of the tight bun at the back of her neck, not a wrinkle in her jacket or trou.

Today she wore a blue jacket with red piping along the sleeves, matching trou with the red piping on the outside seam, red cap pulled over her eyes. As a disguise, it worked. No one who knew her would have guessed she even owned such garb, The only giveaway was the stiff way she carried herself. Fifteen years of Guards posture is a hard habit to break.

It took me a few seconds to assess her appearance. Then, I gestured her toward my wooden chair, the one I keep for clients. It's deliberately uncomfortable—hard seat, back tilted away from me. I want the clients to get on with their business so I can get on with mine.

"To what do I owe the honor, Captain Atterson?" I mentally ran over my last few cases. Nothing came to mind that would attract the attention of the City Guard. True, I'd exposed a particularly convoluted plot involving Vernor Delrey and a negotiator from Contramont who had resorted to murder; but the negotiator was on his way back to Contramont for punishment, and the Banker's Guild had dealt with the Delreys. I wasn't involved with either procedure.

Atterson sat, gingerly, on the edge of the seat. "I have a small problem," she confessed.

I waited.

"It's my sister's child. She may be in some trouble."

I'd never thought of Sara Atterson as having a family. Of course, she had to have come from somewhere, but I'd never seen any of them during my brief stay in the Guards. She was my team leader, I was the rookie, and that didn't make for intimacy. After I left the Guards, we'd meet from time to time, usually when I'd got myself into some difficulty and she had to get me out of it. Not a chance for family chat there, either.

"Tell me more. Who is she, and what makes you think she's in trouble?" I reached into the bottom drawer of my desk for a standard form and a graphite stylus and prepared to take notes.

"Her name is Audra, Audra Martino. Her mother is espoused to Eduardo Martino. He's an auditor for the Construction Guild."

An office drone—one of a multitude in Lorr, scratching away in the Guildhalls and business offices. Respectable, edging on the top of the Tech heap, not quite into the Admin class but aspiring to it.

Atterson got more agitated as she went on. "She was supposed to come home for a family dinner, but never showed up."

"Come home? She doesn't live with her parents? Just how old is this young female?"

"She's finished her terms at Advanced Academy. Past her twenty-first."

"Adult status, then." Meaning she's on her own, if that's her choice. Most young people in Lorr want to get out from under the parental thumb as soon as possible. "Occupation? Guild affiliation?"

"It's complicated. Audra was studying Natural Science at the Advanced Academy, with the option of becoming an Academic, but she changed her mind. Now she's studying at

3

the Rafe Urbine Studio in the Artist's Sector, and she's sharing digs with some of the other apprentices there. She's listed as a Craftsman's Guild Apprentice, pending examination for full status."

Interesting. Started as a boffin, then went to Craftsman's Guild? Something of a comedown. Academics rate with Dark Ones and Admins—middle-tier, but still thinkers, not makers. Craftsmen are more like top-tier Techs; they work with their hands, create things, don't sell them. Merchants do that, which puts Merchant's Guild a notch above Craftsmen in the Lorr pecking order.

"What made her change?"

Atterson shrugged. "No idea, but I've seen some of her drawings. She's really good. Eduardo's in favor of her continuing as an artist, but my sister doesn't like it. She thought Audra should continue her studies in Natural Science. Audra'd made the Top Ten in her class, even been offered an internship with one of the instructors, working toward full Academy membership, before she changed her mind and decided try her hand at Art instead."

"Total break with the family?"

"Not at all. She came to a family dinner not three weeks ago to show off her latest work and announce that one of her pictures was going to be shown in Urbine's own gallery on the Grand Boulevard. I wasn't there, but according to Eduardo, she was really chuffed about it. She sent him and Geri invites to the grand opening.

"Quite a spiffy do, plenty of top-tier Admin and Guildmasters on hand to see what Urbine had come up with, so being chosen to show was quite the honor for a new student.

"That was two days ago. Eduardo went, Geri didn't. He stayed long enough to look around, exchanged greetings with some of the Craftsmen he knows through their work with Construction. He told me he talked with Audra, she promised she'd be home for Winterfest the next day; and the last he saw of her, she was in the middle of a group of young folks talking about going to Entertainment Row to enjoy the Winterfest decorations and have something to eat and drink."

"But she didn't come home." I finished the story for her. I didn't ask Atterson why she hadn't been at this family dinner, why she'd heard about it secondhand. There was something there she didn't want to say. Family dynamics are tricky, which is one reason Basher and the Brain won't touch them, and leave them to me to sort out.

"No, she didn't."

"And the parents don't want the Guards involved," I guessed.

"Geri doesn't. Eduardo came to me this morning with his worries. Audra's living in Artists' Sector now, not Garden, so it's the Artist's Sector Guardhouse that would have to look into her disappearance. Only, Artists' isn't a friendly place for City Guards. They tend to leave the residents to their own devices, let them sort out their problems on their own."

That's an understatement, if there ever was one. Artists' Sector is a magnet for all kinds of loonies and crackpots from all over New Earth. Anyone who thinks they can create something different or new or even just pretty heads for Lorr and finds a home in Artists' Sector. That includes political rowdies, would-be Scribes and Craftsmen, and Entertainers of varying degrees of talent. None of them want to have the City Guards looking into their lives.

Atterson went on. "I checked with the Guards assigned to Artists', and they haven't heard anything about a missing female, and don't want to ask. I went to the studio and asked the usual questions, but got nowhere."

"So, you come to me."

She shifted on the chair. "You can go places the Guards can't. The artists will talk to you." It must have cost her a lot to admit it.

I leaned back. Atterson and I have a touchy relationship. She's been an information source, but keeps me at arm's length. I'm on my own as an Independent, unaffiliated with any Guild, not committed to the Advanced Academy or the Dark Ones. Not usual in Lorr, where everyone knows where they fit in.

But there are only three of us Independent Eyes here, not enough to make a Guild even if we wanted to. Which none of us does—not me, not Basher Bob Basheer, and definitely not Julian Hunt—the Brain—and her able assistant Reg Bonwit.

"Well, Captain, I owe you a life debt or two. You've pulled me out of some nasty situations. I'll take this on, debt for debt."

I pulled one of my standard forms out of the bottom drawer of my desk, shoved it toward her along with a graphite stylus, and pulled out another piece of paper to make notes.

"No." She stiffened. "This is strictly business. I'll pay your usual fee. You'll report to me. Whatever you find…" She stopped.

Neither of us wanted to say aloud what we feared.

I thought of the most likely reason for a young female to go off on her own. "Any males in the picture?"

"No."

I probed deeper. "What about her studies? Was there someone at the Advanced Academy she might have upset? Some reason why she changed direction? Maybe something at her hostel?"

"Audra lived at home, not at one of the student hostels. With her parents living in Garden, she could use a two-wheel to get to classes. When she decided to study at the Urbine studio, she moved into digs near there, well away from Garden."

I could understand why a lively young female might want to get away from parental supervision, but changing career

6

direction? Just to move across town? A little extreme, not usually done. Especially changing from Academic to Craftsman.

I got back to the details. "So, according to what you've heard, the young people went out to Entertainment Row after the festivities at the gallery, and she didn't come back to her lodging?"

"Nor anywhere else. No one seems to have seen her after that night."

I thought this over. "What about this move? Any problems with her leaving the parental roof?"

"My sister wasn't happy, but as I said, Eduardo was in favor of it, thought she might have a talent no one expected. Especially after her Academy instructor chose her to illustrate his latest publication. Eduardo made a few inquiries, showed her drawings around, and got the attention of Rafe Urbine. Urbine agreed, and Audra moved across town. Or so he told me. As I said...I'm not part of the family circle."

There was a bitter tone to her voice. Something to look into, but not now.

"This Rafe Urbine...his school is legit?"

"It's not a school, it's a studio," Atterson corrected me. "Apprentice artists work under his direction, he doesn't hold open classes. He doesn't take on too many apprentices, either; he only picks the ones he thinks have real talent, and the ones he takes always land feet-up, on the primary list for Construction Guild decorating jobs and illustrating mags. Audra considered herself lucky to be chosen to work with him. Eduardo said she was as good as on Gold Moon when he put her drawing up in his gallery."

"What about scandals? Anything worthy of Post Six?"

Atterson shrugged dismissively. "According to my sources, he's totally legit. No commitments, male or female. He does have select patrons who buy his paintings and hire him to decorate their houses, who are mostly female, mostly connected to the top-tier Guildmasters. He calls them his Muses."

"Was Audra one of the Muses?"

"Too young and not rich enough. The Muses are mature females who have the coin to spend and the time to enjoy what they've bought.

"Audra was dazzled to be in his studio. The last time I saw her was when she announced she was leaving the Advanced Academy, moving across town." Atterson hesitated, then said, "My sister and I do not get along, but Eduardo invited me to the family celebration when Audra got her Academy certification. That was back in the early summer. I haven't actually spoken to her since then, but I did see her once or twice, on Entertainment Row with her artist friends. I didn't want to press it, just a wave and a quick greeting. She didn't wave back."

Given the distrust between artists and those who were out to restrict them, I could see why Audra might not want to let her friends know she had a Guards connection.

"I didn't know the Special Squad was patrolling Entertainment Row," I commented. Atterson's latest assignment was investigating the one thing that gave Lorrans the cold shudders. Anything to do with death is to be avoided, especially violent death. Atterson's Special Squad leadership was not a reward for good work, but a punishment for being too good at her job.

"I've been called to examine bodies found in odd corners of Waterfront and Fishmarket. No sign of injury, but internal bleeding and some kind of brain damage. The Dark Ones think it's a new form of stimulant. Victims are mostly youngsters, the kind who'll ingest anything they think will make them stronger or increase their success with females. So far, most of the bodies have been Pangkoti or South Coaster, dockworkers or seamen, a few Street Lizards no one cares about, but…"

"Sooner or later, some lad from Admin will try his luck with it?" I finished for her.

Of course no one would notice if the bodies were only poor Mechs or sailors off the boat, but it would be inconvenient if someone from Striver's Hill got a taste of the wilder side of Lorr.

"No chance this would have anything to do with your missing niece?"

"That's what I want you to find out. I can't get through that wall of silence. Those artists will talk to you." She produced three silvers. "Here's your standard fee. Find out what happened to Audra. Let me know if there's a connection with this new drug. And then let me deal with it."

"What about Fee M'Farr?" The Master Assassin was usually involved in most things violent in Lorr.

"Master Assassin M'Farr has nothing to do with this," Atterson snapped. "It's not within the Fatsos' purview. Besides, he hates the drug traffic worse than I do."

"Mostly because he can't control it." I sniggered. Anything having to do with pharmaceuticals is run by the Dark Ones, and not even Fee M'Farr's Honorable Guild of Forgers, Assassins, Thieves and Swindlers can get into that business.

I looked at the coin on the table between us. "I just said I owe you."

Atterson shoved the coin toward me. "Take it. This is a professional job, not personal. I haven't been welcome in my sister's life for many years. Eduardo came to me as City Guard, not as family connection. Whatever personal debts you feel you owe me, that's your affair."

I picked up the coin and shoved the form and graphite stylus closer to her. "Put it down, in clear Lorran, what you want me to do. Sign it. Then, let me do it."

She wrote and signed, then handed the form back to me. "Three days," she said. "And don't bring the answers to the Central Guardhouse. I'll call back here for information."

And then she was gone, leaving me with the feeling there was a lot more to this situation than she was telling me.

ii

I sat for a moment, organizing a plan of attack. Usually, my first thought is to find out as much as I can about the client, then about the victim. In this case, I didn't have much to go on. Jake and Holly, the clothiers who are also my landlords, know everyone who is anyone in Lorr, but even they don't have a handle on middle-management Guild drones. Holly keeps an eye on the top levels of the major Guilds—they're her best clients—so a mere auditor for Construction wouldn't be worth her time.

On the other hand, Rafe Urbine *was* the sort of person they'd know about, even if they didn't know him personally. Anyone that cozy with the Upper Tier would draw notice.

I put on my new jacket—a lizard-leather number with zip fastenings—tucked a long green scarf around my neck, clipped my small bludgeon to my belt, and locked the outside door. Then I used the inner door to get into Holly's private office.

Holly was in her usual tizzy, surrounded by bits of paper, with her newest drone Zeta hovering over her. Zeta is a large, bouncing female just out of Secondary Academy. She'd been sent by the Clothier's Guild as a pin-girl, but she's proven to be better at office organizing than sewing. I even let her sit in my office when Holly doesn't need her, to take messages if they come in. I just wish she'd stop reading adventure mags. They make eyeing sound more glamorous than it really is.

I spend a lot of time waiting for someone to show up, usually outside some grim little tavern or shop, in rain or wind or hot sun. Not glamorous at all.

Holly waved at me without taking her eyes off the latest set of invoices.

"Not now, Pola, I've got to deal with this shipment of trim."

"Just need a minute," I said, making room on her desk for me to perch my rear. "What do you know about Rafe Urbine?"

She put down the paper. "Is he in trouble?"

"Not exactly. One of his apprentices may be. A female. Her family hasn't heard from her in a bit, and they're getting worried. Any reason to think he might be involved?"

Holly grinned. "Depends on the apprentice. He's usually surrounded by admiring elder females, but as far as anyone knows, he's never done more than paint their pictures."

"What about males?"

Holly shrugged. "If he's more than friendly, he doesn't make a show of it. He's a sociable type. Hangs out at various taverns on Artist's Way between Entertainment Row and the Artists' Sector when he isn't wowing them at soirees on Striver's Hill. The kind where artistic types meet to argue about Art and Philosophy."

"The soirees or the taverns?"

"Females at soirees, males at the taverns. They're not supposed to be all-male, but females are made to feel unwelcome unless they're known as major players in the art world. And even they have trouble getting noticed."

There aren't many places in Lorr that are either all-male or all-female. Total equality is written into the Regs. Of course, there are still a few gender-specific places, like the baths, where separation is considered necessary for sanitary reasons. And there are some waterfront taverns where things can get a little rough for some females.

The taverns on Artist's Way aren't on my usual route—I leave high-flown discussions of Art and Philosophy to the boffins and academics who promote them in their mags. I like my furnishings and decorations simple, without a lot of curlicues and frills. I want a chair to fit my bohunks, a table of the right height to eat off of, and a picture to look like something I can recognize. When I read a mag, I want the pictures to tell me what the story is about. Too many fancy decorations are there to hide the unpleasantness underneath.

"What else do you know about this Urbine? Where did he come from? When did he show up in Lorr?"

Another shrug. "No idea where he came from, could have been Hinterland or South Coast. He was around for years—Craftsman's Guild journeyman, good work but nothing special—until

Selva Delrey latched on to him a few years back. She introduced him around, sponsored his first showing, got him noticed by the Upper Tier."

"And then?"

Holly grinned maliciously. "As soon as he got a few big commissions, he dropped off her map. I don't know if she got tired of him, or he got on to her. Either way, she took up with Ishka Kunine, and Urbine went on alone, picked up plenty of work without her. Now he's got his own gallery, and she's in one of the Delrey hunting lodges somewhere in Hinterlands, well out of Lorr."

"I don't know that I've seen any of his pictures," I confessed. "I'm not one for galleries, and I don't go to Striver's Hill soirees." Especially not those sponsored by the Delrey clan!

"Most of them are in private hands. Portraits of the Upper Tier, that kind of thing. But he's usually got one of his own pictures on display in the window of his gallery on the Grand Boulevard. If you have to ask the price, you can't afford it. He's not one to make multiples, either, and he doesn't do mag covers anymore. The ones he did are selling for as much as his new paintings."

Very exclusive! I could see why he'd attract followers, hoping some of his social magic would rub off on them.

"So, where do I find this paragon?"

"You could try The Lizard's Claw on Artist's Way. His followers tend to hang there with the rest of the artist crowd. His studio's nearby, but I couldn't tell you where. If you're welcome there, he'll tell you, otherwise, not."

That was enough for me to go on, a place to start. I waved to Zeta and set off into the late-fall afternoon.

iii

A chilly, damp wind rose off the river, bringing a dank mist with it that made me pull the jacket tight to my chin. At this time of the year it gets dark fairly early, and the electric street lights were just coming on.

12

The Grand Boulevard is well-lit, as befits the main shopping thoroughfare of the most populous city on New Earth. Every shop window had some kind of ornate display featuring Winterfest and the Solstice celebrations, pushing merch for gift-giving. This year being the four hundredth since the First Landing, the show was especially lavish, with plenty of sparkling lights and lots of shiny stuff to reflect them.

The Urbine Gallery is on the Grand Boulevard between the Guernreich Shoppe and a gallery selling elaborate pottery. Two pictures in the window, with more inside. One picture was supposed to be a vase of flowers. I couldn't tell what kind, because they were all fuzzy, not specific, and all different colors, splotches here and there. The vase was on a brown surface—I assumed it was a table, but that was because you don't have a vase of flowers hanging in mid-air.

The other picture was just plain weird, a bunch of squares and triangles that might have been houses, arranged along what could have been a road, in muted colors on a gray background. At least, that's what it looked like to me. There was no telling what it was really meant to be. But I suppose someone will buy it and put it on their sitting-room wall because it was in Urbine's gallery, and anything here must be fashionable. That's the way it goes in Lorr.

I wasn't going to buy either of them as Winterfest gifts. Not that I had too many people to buy Winterfest gifts for. Basher Bob and Velda were on my list, as were Jake and Holly. I'd give Fletcher a good bonus for serving me meals at odd times over the year, and the various servers at Smokey Joe's could expect extra coin. The only blood relative I have is Commander Regina Polaris, and I haven't seen or heard from her since she arranged for my care at the Temple of Healing when I'd been hauled out of the river several weeks ago, bashed and shivering. I owe her my life, but not a Winterfest gift.

As for Julian Hunt and Reg Bonwit…that was still up in the air. So far, no more communication with either. Maybe I'd get a greeting note from them, maybe not. And I didn't owe them a Winterfest gift, either.

I hesitated a moment, then went into the gallery. I checked out the pictures on the walls. More of what was in the window, plus some graphite drawings of people I recognized, among them my favorite buskers Randi and Kira.

One painting propped up on an easel caught my eye— a female in a black dress, low-cut and held up by shoulder-straps, looking away from the artist, her face in profile. Not a pretty face, but an arresting one, with a long nose, arched eyebrows, firm chin. I thought I'd seen that profile before, but the placard just called her *Citizen of Lorr*.

A neatly dressed female stepped forward before I could penetrate farther than the open gallery; hair tucked back into a braid, jacket and trou set of a refined weave—a cut above the usual office drone.

"May I help you?" I heard a Flatlands accent trying hard to be Upper Tier.

"Just looking around," I demurred. "Nice pictures."

The female drone raised an eyebrow. "Guildmaster Urbine's work is considered the best in Lorr."

"That's what my friend says. Her relation is one of his apprentices. She suggested I look in here, said the deb's picture was being shown."

"Indeed? We do have a selection of Guildmaster Urbine's apprentices' work on display." She pointed to a bunch of pictures on the farthest wall, well away from the electrics.

I peered at the pictures, mostly in pencil or chalk. The usual subjects for student art. People I assumed were models, or maybe friends, some with clothes, some without. Collections of oddments, flowers or tableware, carefully drawn and colored. Scenery, mostly the low hills that frame the City of Lorr, forming its borders. They weren't bad, but nothing special.

Until I came to one picture that held my attention.

No colors, black-and-white. The riverbank, weeds bending over the edge, with the water beyond. Swirls and twirls in the

14

water hinted at something almost visible in the curls of the waves, something with long arms and a bulbous head. I'd once seen something similar, but I hadn't told anyone about it. Interesting to know someone else had seen it, too.

"Who did that one?" I pointed to the river scene.

The drone had to check her list.

"Apprentice Craftsman Audra Martino. A rising talent; she has an unusual style. That picture has attracted a good deal of attention."

"Is it for sale?" I fingered my money-pouch.

"Apprentice work is not considered adequate for gallery sale, but a private negotiation is always possible," the drone hedged.

"Where do I find her?"

"I believe Guildmaster Urbine's apprentices share quarters in the Artist's Sector, but I may not give you the specific address."

Privacy issues, of course. Guildmaster Urbine didn't want other artists poaching his prime followers.

I looked at the drawing again. It was definitely weird, but compelling. There was a hidden menace in those swirling lines. Atterson was right, her niece had talent.

I left the gallery and ambled along the Grand Boulevard past Arriver's Hill to where the Grand Boulevard ended at the Flatlands Bridge. I considered my options.

I'm not all that familiar with the side streets and byways of Artists' Sector once I get past the lights of Artist's Way. This is Basher Bob's territory. He and Velda share digs in Artists' Sector, and he's more familiar with the back alleys than I am.

Consulting Basher would mean hauling myself all the way to Smokey Joe's, and it was getting dark and cold. As long as I stuck to Artists' Way, I figured to be safe enough.

I turned away from Entertainment Row and headed for the taverns where Craftsmen congregated. With a little luck, I'd find someone who knew where Audra was.

iv

The evening crowd was starting to gather at the entrance to the Flatlands Bridge, where the Grand Boulevard turned south and became Entertainment Row. The bridge was already lit, and the lanterns across Entertainment Row were bobbing and swaying in the wind.

On the downstream side of the bridge, Entertainment Row beckoned, all glitter and glamor. Two theaters and the Opera House, food-shops ranging from mere holes in the wall to luxurious restaurants, casinos and cabarets, all ready for visitors from outlying settlements, come to Lorr for Rest and Recreation. Licensed sex workers of all genders strolled along, also ready for action.

Upstream from the bridge is the Artists' Sector, curving around the base of Arriver's Hill. It straggles under the Flatlands Bridge, then along the riverbank and behind Arriver's and Striver's Hills to the inland border between the City of Lorr and the Mineral Mountains of Hinterlands that leads to the infamous mines. Farther upstream, the river leads to scattered villages and Norland.

Artist's Sector comprises a ramshackle collection of buildings old and new, built of whatever materials Construction had on hand at the time. When the Founders arrived, they settled where the river curved around a flat beach, setting up the first prefabs. There was enough space there for shuttle landings from the First Ship, until the fuel gave out and the shuttles were beached and ransacked for whatever could be repurposed.

After the Second Ship arrived and trade started, this stretch of river became the principal marketplace for Landing Operations, Rest and Recreation. Then things changed.

The City of Lorr expanded—over Arriver's Hill and Striver's Hill, across the basin of what the boffins assure us is an extinct volcano. The piers were built, and the barges went farther downriver and offloaded on the far shore in Flatlands, where there was more room for expansion. The factories were built, first in what became Industrial, then across to Flatlands.

The old warehouses, the prefabs, and what was left of the shuttles were taken over by squatters, people who needed space for working in metals and pottery. A few people coaxed veg to grow, raised goats and fowls to sell to the hungry Craftsmen. Entertainers looking for cheap digs moved in, adding to the mix.

Of course, wherever you have free spirits, you have troubled ones, so there's a Dark Ones' Shrine to care for anyone who gets injured in the inevitable disputes. There's a bathhouse, and a selection of small food-shops, tacitly allowed by the Grocer's Guild in conjunction with Entertainment—an admission there are people living in a sector that was originally designated strictly for business.

Artist's Way is the main thoroughfare of the Sector, well-lit with plenty of people moving on it. On either side of the entrance to the bridge, the Craftsmen's Guild had established a pop-up Fair in defiance of the Merchant's Guild, who insisted all sales should go through them.

Rough tables held handmade doodads, jewelry and toys, all kinds of bits and pieces to tempt passers-by into spending a coin or two for a Winterfest gift. Between the tables, a few enterprising Grocers tended makeshift kitchens, dispensing clet and chai, pastries and other nibbles. One was frying fish, another had skewers of meat with veg-sauce on the side. If any Dark Ones were lurking in the crowd watching for violations of the sanitary regs, they weren't showing themselves.

I kept my eye peeled for The Lizard's Claw Tavern. It was as good a place as any to start eyeing.

I sauntered along the road, taking in the sights, sounds and smells. The crowd here was mixed, the garb ranging from standard Mech boiler suits to jacket-and-trou suits to multi-colored caftans in exotic fabrics and even a few kilts, whose time in the Fashionable World had come and gone very quickly. Skin tones varied, from the palest of Norlander to the dark-brown of South Coast, and all shades in between.

Social barriers are even more relaxed in the Artists' Sector than on Entertainment Row. Not too many guild badges in view, no sigils designating rank. The person next to you could be a Tech out for a quick drink before heading back home, or an Admin higher-up slumming.

The tables gave way to taverns, where people could get out of the wind and into a nice, warm room. I stopped to take a good look at the patrons. More refined than the types at Smokey Joe's. No sailors here, and the sex workers were of a higher type than the gaudy joyboys and female licensees who hung around the casinos on Entertainment Row. High-level Techs, I judged, or low-level drones a step up from Flatlands, not quite ready for Garden. Maybe Strivers' Hill wannabes, or Arriver's Hill cast-offs. And a few I couldn't quite place on the social scale.

I considered my approach. Who would I be? An Upper Tier throwaway, down on luck, looking for a handout? A Tech, looking to place a child in a studio? I was a little too old to be looking for an apprenticeship myself.

I rewound the scarf around my head, letting the ends drape over each shoulder, and opened the zip fastening on the jacket to reveal the lace collar on my shirt. Then I sauntered along the row, assessing the tavern patrons with the air of one who was judging each and finding them wanting.

I stopped in front of the Lizard's Claw, distinguished by its sign—a large beast's paw with a curved talon. Otherwise, it was just one in a row of cinderblock structures, relics of the sector's industrial origins. It was a well-lit establishment, reasonably clean as far as I could judge. Most of the tables were already taken, but the one closest to the window was kept open, clearly for a chosen patron.

A youngish male in a canvas jacket and trou jostled me aside in his haste to get to the tavern door.

"Watch it, lad" I exclaimed. "Mind your manners!"

"Sorry," he mumbled. "It's just…I heard Rafe will be here tonight. I want to get close to his table to hear him talk."

"Rafe? Is that Rafe Urbine?" I put on my snootiest Upper Tier accent. "I was hoping to catch him. He seems to be unreachable these days, quite impossible to contact."

"He's got the gallery now," my informant told me. "You're supposed to go through them. He doesn't take commissions anymore. He doesn't have to." I couldn't tell if the lad resented his idol's success or envied it.

"Oh, dear. I really wanted him to decorate my new villa. We've a new place on Arriver's Hill, and it really needs touching up."

"He's far too important these days to do mere decorations." My new friend leaped forward. "There he is! Rafe!"

I didn't know what to expect of this superstar of the fashionable Art World. Perhaps an eccentric, with a wild beard and long hair? Or maybe a dandy, in the most extreme tailoring?

Instead, what I saw was a perfectly ordinary-looking male, neatly dressed in matching jacket and trou, nice but not too fancy. No glitter, no beading, just fine woolen fabric out of Norland, fitted perfectly, with a patterned scarf around his neck, neatly tucked into the front of the jacket. Short beard, well-trimmed, hair cut slightly longer at the sides than necessary, but not so long as to cause comment. It takes coin to afford that look, and confidence to carry it off without seeming pretentious.

Behind him stood a trio, only heads visible over the crowd that surrounded Urbine—tall male in a hat that made him look even taller, short male in Pangkoti turban, female with disheveled red hair. They were swallowed up in the crowd that formed around the Master Craftsman.

Urbine seemed affable enough, nodding to this one and that one, with the practiced smile of one who knew his own worth and was willing to share his glory with friends.

He paused in front of my informant.

"Good to see you, Augie. How has it been going for you? I heard you've set up your own studio since you left mine."

"I've been well enough," the lad stammered. He remembered me. "Um, this female says she's been trying to reach you with a commission."

19

I stepped forward. "I've heard so much about you," I gushed. "I saw the pictures in the gallery, and I knew I had to have something just like them for our new villa on Arriver's Hill." I emphasized it again, pushing the image of someone moving up in the social ranks. Striver's Hill rich is one thing; it takes more than just coin to get a place on Arriver's Hill.

Rafe brushed me off. "See my agent at the gallery."

"But I am a particular friend of Selva Delrey!"

That cut even less ice with the artist than my social standing. He flinched, and pushed through the crowd to greet someone just behind me.

"And I heard such wonderful things about Audra!" I called after him.

That stopped him in mid-stride. He turned back to me.

"Audra? Have you heard from her? I missed her after the gallery party. I went back to the studio to congratulate the students, but she wasn't there."

"That's odd. She was most enthusiastic about her studies when I saw her at her parents' social gathering. That's why I went to your gallery—to see her work. They were looking forward to having her home for Winterfest."

Rafe frowned. "She told me she was going home to Garden right after our gallery opening. Then she joined the rest of the young folks when they went off to celebrate on Entertainment Row. Is there some problem?"

"There may be. If she's not at home, and she's not with your students...?" I let my voice trail off.

Rafe's frown deepened. "This is very disturbing. I am sure she said she was going to see her family. She was not especially pleased, but she felt it was her duty to show up at their Winterfest gathering. As her Craftsmans' Guild sponsor, I'm responsible for her behavior. I don't want any trouble with the Guild over this."

"Perhaps one of the other young people at your studio knows where she is. If I can talk to them, perhaps I can solve this little problem for you."

"That would be very kind of you, er..."

"Pola Drach."

He took another look at me, eyes narrowed. Maybe he'd heard the name before? I'd been in a few notices on Post Six, and there was that song still being sung by buskers that mentioned me as an Independent Eye.

"I provide my apprentices with lodgings at the end of Riverwalk," Rafe said. "Turn at the end of Artist's Way and go towards the river. It's past the paved road, across from the goat farm. If you're in the river, you've missed it."

"Thank you for your information, Guildmaster."

"I hope you find Audra, Friend Drach. She is a most talented young artist."

He waved me off and made his way into the tavern.

I had a lead. Now to see where it took me.

υ

Riverwalk is one of those meandering paths left over from the Settlement Time, before the Founders organized Lorr into a proper grid. The ship's Mechs built what suited them, wherever it was convenient, often using bits and pieces of the grounded shuttles for construction material after the trees gave out. Once there was permanent housing for the Fishmarket, people were moved out and goods moved in. By the time the electrics were set up in Lorr this area, situated close to where the barges from the Norland settlements docked, was mostly warehouses.

As time went on, some of the old structures were replaced, but most of them were just repurposed. People moved into them, but no one in Admin wanted to spend coin to expand the outside lighting. The lamps reached only to the end of the paved road. Beyond that, whatever light there was came from alcohol lamps that flickered beside doorways and the moons.

On this night, neither Gold nor Silver Moon rose over the horizon. Clouds scudded across the sky, blotting out the few stars that twinkle over New Earth, a reminder of how far we are from the center of the galaxy. Somewhere in that blackness was Sol, the star of Old Earth, indistinguishable from all the other tiny sparks in the sky.

I walked along trying to get a sense of the buildings on either side of the paved path. It was hard to make out more than the outlines with the few lights showing and minimal electrics. Then the paving stopped, and I was on plain dirt, damp but not quite muddy. I could feel stones turning under my feet as I walked slowly towards the river gurgling ahead of me. I passed several former warehouses now presumably being used as living quarters, doors closed against the damp wind rising off the river.

That wind made me shiver. I stopped to close my jacket and wound the scarf over my ears.

Something behind me clicked. I realized I was being followed. I took a tentative sniff, but Ficus's gift was wearing thin, and whoever was behind me had no distinctive scent.

I reached under my jacket and unhooked my bludgeon from my belt. I could hear heavy breathing somewhere in the darkness. Ficus's pheromones still worked on my auditory nerves well enough for me to pinpoint how fast my unwanted companion was moving. The steps were heavy, so I assumed the pursuer was male, probably larger than me. A direct attack wasn't advisable.

Instead, I went on as if I hadn't noticed, checking each house until I came to the very end of the path. I could just make out two buildings, set back from the berm. On my left stood a small house surrounded by a wooden fence. On the right, a taller structure, lights flickering in the windows providing just enough illumination for me to make out the shadow of someone behind me.

I whirled around, bludgeon at the ready. "Who are you, and what do you want with me?"

The response was a jarring whack to my bludgeon. I ducked, parried, and dodged another blow. I backed up against the fence and was startled by a sudden "Baaaa!" in my ear.

Something poked me in the rear. I dodged, forcing my attacker to turn his back to whatever was behind the fence.

There are times when Ficus's gift of extra sensitivity to olfactory and auditory stimuli is a blessing, and times when it's a curse. This was one of the curses. I could smell the goat behind the fence. I didn't have to hear it or see it to know it was there.

Not that I have anything against goats. They're one of the few mammals that survived the journey from Old Earth. They eat almost anything, they give milk that makes tasty cheese, and goat meat is stringy but edible. They can even be trained to pull small carts.

Some of the first goats to land got away, went feral, and now can be found from the mountains of Norland to the desert between Pangkot and South Coast. Like humans, goats have found a home on New Earth. And as long as the owners keep them penned up, the Dark Ones have no objection to their being within Lorr's boundaries.

Goats do have a few bad traits. They are smelly, loud and very territorial. I was grateful to the nasty-looking buck with the huge twisty horns that bounded forward to defend his yard, even if I was the one he had attacked first.

Another loud "Baaaa!", and the attacker was impelled forward. I leaped aside, whacking downward with my bludgeon. I hit hard flesh, heard a grunt. Someone was going to be very sore tomorrow morning, for sure!

Then, heavy steps, running away. I was alone again, wondering who I'd annoyed recently, and whether this attack had anything to do with Audra Martino.

"Don't worry, he won't leave his pen," a large female in typical Norland knit tunic and wool trou yelled cheerily from the doorway of the small house. She lifted a lantern high above her head to light the way from the door to the road.

"Are you sure?" The goat in question was making angry noises and pawing the ground.

"It's feeding time," his owner explained. She proceeded down the path with a pail of grain and leaves in one hand and the lantern in the other. She set the pail down before the goat, who accepted the offering. Two smaller goats I assumed were his females joined him in the feast.

While the critters had their feed their owner looked me over. "You're new here, aren't you?"

"I'm looking for the Rafe Urbine studio," I explained. "Guildmaster Urbine told me some of his apprentices live at his studio. I'm trying to find one of them. A female, Audra Martino. Do you know her?"

The goatkeeper's expression changed from amiable to wary. "I can't say much about those people. They keep to themselves, as do I. They don't bother the goats, and I don't bother them."

I tried to recall if I'd seen any pictures of goats or their keeper at the gallery, but I didn't think I had. If the artists didn't want to depict their nearest neighbor, there might be some friction there.

"I was told their studio was at the end of the path. Is that it?" I waved at the house on the other side of the road.

"That's the house, but I don't know who's to home right now." The goatkeeper shrugged. "They come and go, those artists. One day here, next day off somewhere else. But Hildy the cook buys my milk and cheese, so I can't say they're all bad souls. The males are foolish, of course, and the females let them get away with it, which is more foolish, but that's Lorr for you."

In other words, male apprentices tried to intimidate females in ways no Norland female would allow. Considering her size, I doubted any weedy artistic types would get anywhere with this particular Norlander.

"I tell you what, I've got to deliver the dairy order. I'll light you across the way. You can ask your questions, and maybe one of those artist types will lend you a lantern to find your way back to the taverns."

She went back to the open door, reached inside and picked up a large basket. Once again, she lifted the lantern, joined me at the fence, and the two of us crossed the road to the two-story cinderblock structure dating from the days when this was the mercantile center of Lorr, before the Central Plaza took its final form and the Guildhouses were built.

Two small windows on either side of the front door showed flickers of light within, indicating someone was at home. I only hoped I could find some answers to my questions.

vi

The goatherd knocked and was welcomed in by a rotund female. She wore a combination of Lorran trou and Norland knit tunic, her hair tucked under a Pangkoti-made scarf.

She burst into speech as soon as she recognized the goatherd. "Inger! Thank the Goddess you've come. I've got the chowder almost ready, I was waiting for the milk."

She hustled the goatherd through the house. I followed the pair past a dimly-lit workroom into a vast kitchen, where a large iron stove held several pots. Tantalizing odors tickled my sensitive olfactory nerves, reminding me I hadn't eaten in several hours.

Inger the Goatherd handed over the basket. The cook took out a glass jar with white liquid visible inside and two rounds of cheese. Coin changed hands.

The cook then realized there was another person in the room. "Who's this?"

I took charge. "I'm Independent Eye Pola Drach. I have a few questions to ask, and this person..."

"Inger Thorasdatter," the goatherd identified herself. "Citizen of Norland, with connection to Grocer's Guild. I have a permit to deal in dairy products, I am cleared by the Dark Ones."

25

"What's your business here?" the cook snapped at me. "I don't have time for questions."

I didn't see any badge or sigil, so I assumed the person in the kitchen was a Mother's Guild caretaker.

"Friend Inger, Friend Mother, I'm looking for Audra Martino, said to be apprenticed to Craftsman's Guildmaster Rafe Urbino."

The hefty female corrected my assumption. "I'm Hildy Vargas, *Servant's* Guild, Cook, qualified in all culinary crafts." She sniffed her disdain of the Mother's Guild as a gather-all that included caretakers of youngsters from infancy to Secondary Academy, as well as those who managed lodgings for the indigent, infirm, or aged. "If you're looking for Audra, she's not here. She went to her parent's house in Garden Sector."

"That's interesting, because she never got there." I sniffed the air. "Something smells delicious."

"Fish chowder," Hildy said. "My own recipe. What do you mean, Audra never got there? She packed up her clothes, went with the rest of them to the gallery opening. She said she would leave from the gallery party, would send someone for her satchel…" She paused. "She didn't send anyone for her things. I wondered about that."

"When was that?"

"Two days ago." Hildy's round face creased in a frown. "I thought it was odd. Maybe I should have said something, but things get busy around Winterfest, what with people coming and going and making ready for the Great Feast…"

Before she could speak again, three people burst into the kitchen. A loud female voice rang out amid the stomping of feet on the wooden floor as they crowded around the table

"Hildy, where's the food? We're starving!".

"I thought *all* artists are starving," I said, looking the lot over.

26

One of them certainly looked famished, a scrawny specimen in Pangkoti baggy trou and a South Coast lizard-leather jacket, topped with a Pangkoti turban. The loud voice belonged to a red-headed female, taller than me and much rounder, in tight wool trou and a colorful tunic that could have come from a Desert Folk encampment.

Looming over them was a tall male, made taller by a high-crowned felt hat. He had dressed for a night on Entertainment Row in a beaded blue jacket with pale-yellow trou, the latest style from Guernreich.

I pinned them as Urbine's apprentices, who'd been with him at the tavern. Apparently, they'd decided to leave Urbine to his other devotees and come back here for supper.

"This is Independent Eye Pola Drach." Hildy waved a hand at me. "She's looking for Audra."

"Whatever for?" That was the redhead, with an accent I couldn't quite place. Not exactly Flatlands, but trying to sound like it. "Audra went crawling back to her nice safe Garden Sector as soon as she could get away from this hovel. She'd had enough of the Boho life—no private bathing or elimination place, no heating in the sleeping quarters. Nothing so grand as her house in Garden."

"Marta, you're just jealous because her work got into the gallery and yours didn't." That was the big fellow, clearly the leader. He turned to me. "Craftsman Dowad Edard at your service. I've been put in charge of this unruly lot. Guildmaster Urbine trusts me to see they keep the peace and learn their craft."

"Guildmaster Urbine is far too important these days to come into his own studio more than once a week," the Pangkoti groused. "Maybe if he stayed longer, we'd learn more."

"Maybe if you spent more time in the studio, Chezan, instead of at the Green Dragon, you'd learn more," Edard chided him.

"I have friends at the Green Dragon," Chezan retorted. "And my work got into the gallery, right there next to yours."

"I've seen some of the apprentice work at the gallery," I offered. "Who did what? Paintings, drawings?"

"The paintings are mine," Edard admitted. "New colors, from a factory in Hinterland. There's a boffin there, he's working with coal to find ways to get the colors out of the slag left after refinement. I wanted to show the different ways light plays on plants in the summer sun."

"Which of you did the riverside scene? The one in black-and-white. I suppose it was done with a pen, in ink, not graphite stylus? That was…" I tried to find the right word. "Magical!"

There was a sudden hush. "That's Audra's," Marta said. "She claimed she saw something in the river."

"And did she?"

The Pangkoti shrugged, then winced. "She might have. She only draws what she sees."

I passed this off as spite. "Where did she go when she wasn't here in the studio?"

Marta and Chezan exchanged meaningful looks. Marta spoke first.

"I have better things to do than look after silly young females. I told her not to follow me about, but she *would* trail after me when I went to Artist's Way to meet friends."

Chezan chimed in. "She came with me once when I went to Fishmarket for worship of Kali Mara. She says she is looking for something…I know not what. She is a most difficult person to pin down. One minute she's staring at the river, then she's chasing pteros across the hills. And she never stops prating about the Norland legends of the kraken."

"She even went to a Third Shipper's Meeting," Marta said. "Now, *that* is pure garbage. There is no Third Ship, and anyone who thinks so is insane, no matter what that so-called Prophet says. Entertainment Row is where he belongs, for sure."

"You mean the one who's taken a stand across from Foodie Alley?" I'd seen him setting up his stand, but never considered going closer to hear his pitch.

Chezan turned on her. "He makes a good case for it. The First Ship got here by following the instructions of the Big Black Box. Buda-Ganesha and Mata Deva led the Second Ship here. Why would the Third Ship not find their way?"

"Because the Second Ship changed the markers so they couldn't." Marta was very sure of this. "They didn't want to be contaminated by whatever destroyed the Third Ship."

"'And somewhere in the Cosmos, a ship sails on, filled with mutated rodents and other vermin'." Edard intoned in the measured cadence of a Conservationist lector. "Here endeth the lesson. We've all heard it, over and over, from our first day in Primary Instruction. The lectors at the Meeting-House repeat the story. It makes sense. No one has heard from Old Earth since the Second Landing, and that was a good three hundred years ago."

That much was true enough. The First and Second ships certainly reached New Earth, whether under direction of the Big Black Box or the Gods of Pangkot. If there ever was a Third Ship is still being debated, let alone that it is somewhere out among the stars, seeking New Earth and revenge.

I brought the discussion out of the realms of theology and back to Audra Martino. "Audra never arrived at her parents' house. When did any of you see her last?"

Marta looked at Edard. "I can't really say."

"Think!" I urged. "According to Guildmaster Urbine, she was at the gallery opening. Were any of you there that night?"

"I was at the gallery opening," Marta stated. "I assisted with the refreshments and sales. I saw Audra there, preening, taking credit for that one drawing."

"As well she should," Chezan put in. "That drawing had the Post Four crowd in ecstasies." He sneered his opinion of the fashionable art critics.

"I saw her at the gallery opening party, too," Edard said firmly. "She was showing off her work to her sister's spouse. I know him—Eduardo Martino; we've met at meetings of Construction and Craftsmen's Guild committees.

"As for the Post Four critics, it is only to be expected that they would ferret out something new and exciting. Audra was very much in demand."

"You'd think the Post Fours would have better taste," Chezan groused. "Guildmaster Urbine put my painting out, and Edard's, but did they notice it? Not at all. They homed in on that black-and-white object."

"It was good of Guildmaster Urbine to include us apprentices at all," Edard chided him. "Our work is not supposed to be on public view until we get full Craftsmen's Guild status. Audra's drawing..." He paused to formulate some measured response.

"A very weird subject for a mere drawing" I reminded them.

"It drew a lot of attention," Edard said. "I wanted to tell her about the Post Four mention, but when I came around after breakfast the next day, she wasn't here."

"That was the day after the opening? Yesterday?" I tried to keep track. "Not here? Then where?"

"I don't know. I don't live here, I have lodging down the road." Edard looked at the other two. "Didn't she come back here after the opening? I thought she went with you two when you left the gallery."

Marta and Chezan eyed each other. Then, Marta said, "We were feeling a little...um, merry...and Chezan wanted to celebrate with some people he knew..."

"At the Green Dragon?" Edard didn't like that connection at all.

"Oh, no, you don't blame me!" Chezan was having none of it. "You wanted to go along with the crowd of punters who were heading for some other dive at the end of Entertainment Row. Audra just tagged along, the way she always does, whether you ask her or not."

They looked at each other, suspicion deepening.

I picked up on this. "Audra tagged along? Wasn't she welcome to join your friends?"

Marta grimaced. "Audra was such an innocent! She'd been so carefully brought up, she was eager to be part of something—I don't know—racy? She had no idea how the world really works outside Garden Sector. You'd think, having gone through the Advanced Academy, she'd understand, but she was like a child in some ways. She wanted to be liked, like one of those baby felines that follow you about, waiting for treats from the table."

"She insisted on tagging along whenever we went to Entertainment Row," Chezan put in. "Didn't wait to be asked, just came."

"And she drew a river scene with something odd in the water," I mused.

"She's done a few of them," Edard said. "She showed me her preliminary sketches. The one at the gallery is the one Guildmaster Urbine thought the best. He had her finish it in ink before he had it framed for the showing."

I made a mental note to take a good look at her drawings in daylight and got back to the subject at hand. "So, she went to Entertainment Row with the two of you. Where did you go?"

"Different places," Chezan hedged. "I may have gone to the Green Dragon, but I'd had a bit of rice wine, so I'm not too sure." He looked at Marta. "I don't think you were with me."

Marta scowled at him. "I saw you with your…friends. I went on to some other places, I'm not sure where. It was foggy and crowded, and I'd had a bit of jack to celebrate the gallery opening."

I didn't let up. "What about Audra?"

"I think we lost her somewhere in the crush," Marta said. "There were a lot of people out that night in spite of the fog. The wind had died down, so it was almost pleasant to be out with the crowd, celebrating before Winterfest."

"When did the two of you get back here?"

"I don't know…late, very late." Chezan shrugged. "It was almost dawn, I think. I was a little dizzy."

"You were blotto," Marta sniffed. "If it wasn't for Edard putting us into a pedicab, you wouldn't have got back at all. You'd have wound up sleeping it off in the back room of the Green Dragon again with some joyboy for company."

I turned to Edard, who quickly said, "I wasn't part of their group, but I followed them to Entertainment Row, just to make sure they didn't get into trouble."

"What he means is, he doesn't want anything to happen that would make the Craftsman's Guild unhappy with the Urbine studio," Chezan sneered. "He's worse than my amah back home. He has a fit if he sees me anywhere near the Green Dragon."

"When and where did any of you see Audra last?" Trying to make sense of this lot was like herding pteros. "Edard, you say she was at the gallery, and on Entertainment Row. Did she stay there, did she head back here…?"

"I couldn't say when and where I last saw her," he admitted. "There was a Third Ship lecturer, and I think she may have stopped to listen to him. And the old fellow, the sailor who's unhappy with the way he says the oceans are being spoiled. He was at it opposite the Third Shipper. They'd set up stands at the entrance to Foodie Alley and were yelling at each other, drawing plenty of attention."

"Not from me! I certainly didn't want to hear that crap!" Chezan sniffed. "There were buskers on the next corner, and they were much better. And it was starting to get chilly, and I wanted to get somewhere warm"

"We must have lost her there," Marta realized. "I saw Chezan go into the Green Dragon. I'm not fond of that crowd, so I went on to one of the better taverns, I'm not sure which. " She turned to Edard, who shook his head.

"I thought I saw Audra among the people listening to the speakers, but I wasn't looking for her."

"More worried about my friends at the Green Dragon?" Chezan jeered.

"You should be more circumspect about your acquaintances," Edard chided him. "If you want a full Craftsman's Guild Journeyman's certificate."

"And that was the last time any of you saw her?" I made a final effort to nail them down to a timetable. "On Entertainment Row, in a crowd, listening to some lecturers?"

The three of them nodded.

"I don't recall seeing her again," Marta said. "Of course, I wasn't looking. She's a grown female. If she wants to cozy up to some ranting fool, that's her business, not mine."

"He was more interested in her than in you," Chezan sniped "He stared at her, picked her out of the crowd, and she hung on his every word."

"The Third Shipper or the sailor?" I asked.

"Both."

"You don't happen to remember their names?"

Chezan shrugged. "Who cares what loonies call themselves?"

"The Third Shipper was something like the Prophet of Doom...or was it Disaster?" Marta waved off the orator. "And I don't remember the sailor."

I can't help noticing the Prophet of Doom when I go in and out of Foodie Alley on my way to and from my digs. He is loud and flashy and has a squad of females around him.

Sailors, though, are all over the place in Lorr, what with the fleets from both South Coast and Norland in. The Waterfront and Entertainment Row were full of them, but I didn't recall any setting up stands to protest how the oceans are treated. Still, Winterfest brings out the crowds, and I may well have missed them in the crush.

"I'd like to see Audra's room now," I said. "She might have left something there that would point to where she went, if she didn't go to her parents' house in Garden."

"We have separate rooms," Marta explained. "Audra and I sleep upstairs. Chezan had to move out of the second room and doss down here, in the workroom."

Edard forestalled my next question. "I have a small house of my own down the road, leased from the Guild. One of the few perks of Journeyman-level membership."

"Something for us to aim at. Respectability!" Chezan left no doubt what he thought of that!

"While you prefer to live like a vagrant, and smell like one, too!" Edard retorted. "Your work is good, but not that good. You have to earn your place, Chezan, like the rest of us."

Once again, I had to step in before the argument got personal. "Apprentice Marta, show me where Audra kept her personal things, and then I'll be on my way. I don't mean to keep you from your evening meal."

vii

Marta picked up one of the lit lamps from a row lined up on the table, and led me up a flight of stairs to the sleeping quarters at the back of the house. Two rooms had been made out of an attic space. Each had the same furnishings—a simple slat bed with only a thin mattress, covered with a woven blanket; a table and chair; pegs on the walls to hang clothes. One looked scrupulously tidy, almost as if it had never been occupied. Even the table was meticulously clean, pens and graphite styluses lined up, ink vials corked, no loose papers.

The other room was a mess of discarded clothes draped over the wall pegs, papers scattered over the table, and disheveled bedclothes. The table was covered with scraps of paper, vials of colored inks, steel-nib pens, graphite styluses—all the paraphernalia of a student artist.

Marta had lifted her lamp at the door to the tidy room. I looked it over. A draft whistled through the one window, setting the mesh curtains flickering.

"Not much to look at," I observed. "What's this?" I'd noticed a leather satchel on the floor next to the bed. I heaved it up onto the bed and opened it. Carefully folded garments nestled within. I lifted them out, one by one—cotton shirts, a woolen skirt, the usual underpinnings.

Something rustled under the clothes. I found a sheaf of pamphlets and a mag with a plain red cover.

"When did she get these?"

"No idea," Marta shrugged. "Audra was always reading something odd. I think she got those when she attended some lecture."

I scanned the pamphlets. "'*The Kraken are Real!*' '*Save our waters!*' These aren't Third-Shippers; these are from some group calling itself The Guardians of the Oceans. What do you know about them?"

Marta shrugged again. "More of Audra's weirdos. I think she got into their company when she was at the Advanced Academy. They're convinced there is some kind of intelligent being in the ocean, and it's being hurt by whatever we throw into it. She was full of information about sea life. She'd even illustrated some boffin's tome, as if that was enough to get her full recognition as an artist."

The beings the Norlanders called the kraken had been reportedly spotted in the ocean from time to time, but no one had been able to capture one; and the official line from Admin is that they don't exist, they never existed, and we're the only intelligent lifeform on this planet. Of course, some of the boffins argue about whether or not the walking trees and sensation plants are intelligent, but boffins are always ready to argue about anything.

I wasn't about to tell this female about my own experience not so long ago, when something emerged from the river

35

and helped me get out of a nasty situation. I keep that information to myself. I owe that being a life debt, and the best way I can pay it is to let it go its own way, without interference from boffins or anyone else who might do it harm.

"What do *you* think?" I asked, stuffing the clothes back into the satchel. I kept the pamphlets and mags for later examination.

"Humans have been on New Earth for four hundred years," Marta replied. "The Founders made sure there was no intelligent lifeform here before they landed. If there is one, it's kept itself well away from us, which proves how intelligent it is.

"And sure, the Exploiters were careless about throwing waste into the river, but that's been taken care of, and all the bad stuff now goes into the ocean instead. That's big enough so it shouldn't matter. I don't see what the fuss is about. Audra was one of those people who get involved in saving this or that. She didn't understand what's really important."

"Which is?"

"The basics of real living. Keeping a roof over your head, putting food on the table. Getting along with people you don't like."

"Such as Audra?" I thought this over as I stared at the satchel. I didn't want to haul it with me down that dark road back to Entertainment Row. "This should go back to her parents. You should get someone to send it to them." I picked up the printed matter. "You said she was very much taken with this Prophet. A good-looking male?"

Marta shrugged. "If you like the type. Black hair and eyes, musical voice. He was after females, I could tell, and there were plenty of them around him. Not me, though. I know better."

"What about Audra? Would she have been likely to fall for his charms? Or was there any other male in her sights? Or maybe females?"

"Audra?" Marta sniggered. "I don't think she got past the lesson on 'these are the male parts, these are the female parts' in Primary Instruction. She nearly had a fit when we had a male model for figure study…unclad. Still, she tackled that lesson the same way she did the other assignments Guildmaster Urbine set us. Reproduce what you see, accurately, whether it was a collection of random objects on a table or the scenery outside the door."

"She worked at her craft," I summed it up, "and she didn't waste time with romance. What did you think of her artistic talent?"

Marta's face went blank. "I am not the one to judge. Guildmaster Urbine thought enough of her to place that drawing in his gallery."

I checked the table for anything besides pens, styluses, and blank paper. "Is this all she had? Don't you artists usually carry paper with you? Sketching books, that sort of thing?"

"Guildmaster Urbine told us to take a notebook with us when we went out, to sketch what we saw. Audra had a fine sketchpad made up. Reptile leather binding, rag paper." In other words, very expensive, beyond the reach of most Mechs and quite a few Techs as well.

"It's not here." I checked the items in the satchel. "Did she have it when she went to the gallery gala?"

"I don't think so. She wasn't carrying a bag, and she was dressed for show. Slinky dress, not jacket and trou. No pockets. I think she had one of those little pouches, with a coin or two, but nothing large enough to put her sketchpad in."

Something else for me to find. What was it with students and apprentices and notebooks? I'd had a bad experience recently with one of them. Was this going to be another ptero chase?

"Who has been in here since the gala?"

"No one. We're supposed to clean our own quarters. Hildy's a cook, won't pick up trash or scrub." Marta grimaced.

"Too proud of her kitchen skills to do anything outside her own little domain. Audra took care of her personal space. Didn't mind doing it, she said she always tidied her own room at home."

"So, no one picked up Audra's satchel? Didn't you wonder why no one had come for her clothes?"

"She had others, at her parents' place in Garden," Marta said. "Why bother with these rags? Just to shock the stiffs in Garden with her boho garb"

I was getting a whiff of something that didn't take Ficus's gift to figure out. Marta's jealousy was obvious, but jealous of what? Audra's talent? Her family wealth? Urbine's attention? Something else for me to work on.

I took one last look around, shoved the pamphlets under my jacket, and followed Marta back down to the large workroom. A table and chairs were set up in the middle of the room, with bowls and spoons in front of each chair. Chezan was already seated, Edard stood behind him. Marta followed me in and took a seat at the table.

I looked around. Easels with paintings had been shoved aside to make room for the table and chairs. A wooden pedestal held a lumpy figure that might have been a human. I examined each picture carefully.

"You've been using each other as models," I commented. "Did any of you make a picture of Audra? A small sketch, not something the size of this." I gestured toward the largest painting, a representation of a house made up of colorful square and triangular shapes.

"I did one of my caricatures," Edard said. He pulled a small notebook out of his jacket pocket and showed me a drawing of a young female with a beaky nose and dark hair winding around her face like vampire vines. Not quite the face in the startling portrait at the Urbine Gallery, but very like it.

"Clever, but I need something that looks exactly like her," I commented.

Marta got up from her chair, went to one of the easels and flipped through the papers, then handed me a small sketch in graphite. "Here, take this. One of our exercises in facial representation."

I could see the resemblance to Edard's caricature—the dark, intense eyes and long hair. "Very nice. You have a good eye for faces."

Marta shrugged and winced. "You can keep it, if you like. I'm not really interested in linear. I'm working in three-D now." She indicated the clay lump.

"Thank you, this should do nicely. I can take this around Entertainment Row, ask a few questions. It's possible someone will remember seeing her."

Marta sat down again as Hildy emerged from the kitchen with a large tureen.

"That smells yummy." I waited a few more moments, but no one invited me to stay. "I'd best be on my way."

"I'll go with you." Edard offered. "I have a lantern. It's dark out there, no electrics this far from Artist's Way."

"I can make my own way," I said. "And you don't want to miss this chowder."

"I have to go back to my own digs anyway," he said. "Ally's got the evening meal waiting for me. I only came with the others to make sure they were settled in for the night."

Chezan stopped slurping long enough to make a derisive noise at Edard. "I've got some people to meet on Entertainment Row."

"At the Green Dragon?" Marta sniped.

Chezan just grinned and dove back into his soup.

Edard retrieved a lantern from just inside the front door, a kind I hadn't seen before, with a glass globe inside a metal frame with a wick inside, hanging from a wooden handle. He used one of the long spills on the table to light the wick from the flame of the alcohol lamp hanging over the big table.

My nostrils contracted as I caught a strange metallic scent. "That's something new. What is it?"

Edard beamed. "The very latest from the boffins at the Construction Guild, by way of South Coast. It's fueled by a byproduct of coal. It makes a brighter light than alcohol, and it's kinder to the plants."

"Coal? Not petroleum?" There was a rumor someone had found a source of this magic material somewhere near South Coast. It was the basis for a lot of the stuff they had on Old Earth, including the fuel that had lifted the ships off the planet in the first place. Something produced by ancient creatures, long before we ever got to New Earth. It was one of the things the Founders were looking for when they did the first surveys; and they found it, but not anywhere they could get to it, which is why they couldn't get off New Earth once they landed. Or so I've been told.

"Something like it. There is a person at the South Coast kiosk on the Central Plaza who can explain it better than I." He hefted the lantern as we set off, illuminating the path ahead of us. "I'll see you as far as the paved road. Once you're on that, you'll be able to get back to Artist's Way."

"And from there I can get to civilization," I joked. "Thank you, Journeyman Edard, for your help."

viii

The wind had picked up off the river. I could smell weeds rotting in the retreating tidal bore, a sure sign of coming winter. I heard something skittering in the dead leaves under the trees skirting the lane. Not reptiles—they'd mostly gone underground to escape the cold. And the pteros had made their way to South Coast and the Southern Continent, where they would be able to soak up radiant heat.

The only wild mammals in Lorr are feral felines and rodents, brought with us on the First and Second Ships. If there are any other critters, they aren't large enough for me to worry about.

As for human predators, I didn't think Edard was the one who'd attacked me earlier—I'd landed a good whack on my attacker's right arm, and Edard held his lantern with his right hand. Anyone who wanted another go at me would have to deal with him.

The lantern threw out a circle of yellow light, larger than the blue flicker of an alcohol lamp. Edard held it high enough I could make my way along the dirt road toward the cluster of lights ahead of us.

"You can get back to Artist's Way from the paved road," he told me.

"Thanks for the light," I said. "While we're walking, you can tell me more about Audra Martino. You were her teacher —"

"Not precisely," he interrupted me. "I am not qualified to be an instructor. I just organize the apprentices, review their work to make sure it is up to the Guildmaster's standards before I submit it for his approval. And I make corrections, when necessary."

"Then you were the one who got Audra accepted into the studio."

He paused. "I suppose…yes, I suppose I did. That is…I know her parents, through the Construction Guild. My family has been in that Guild since before the Merchant's War, and it wasn't such a stretch when I moved from Construction to Craftsman. Craftsmen and Construction often work together—one builds, the other decorates.

"I ran into Eduardo Martino at one of the joint Guild meetings. He mentioned his daughter's desire to find a place to further her study of art. He showed me some of Audra's sketches, made for her natural science studies, said she might even be asked to illustrate a book."

"Without Guild approval?"

Edard shrugged. "Not my concern. I thought the sketches showed promise, and said so to Guildmaster Urbine. He spoke

41

with Constructionman Martino, met with Audra, checked her work, and accepted her as an apprentice. She joined the studio when he came back from his summer in Hinterland."

"Is that where he comes from? Has he family there?"

Edard hedged. "I can't say much about Guildmaster Urbine's family. I know he has a smallholding somewhere near Delray Lodge, and he spends the hot months there. He returned at the Equinox, when the weather was better, to set up the new showing at the gallery."

I thought that over. "Did you ever meet Audra in person before she came to the studio?"

"Not socially. My family are Tech, from Flatlands, but not on the same tier as Martino. I interviewed Audra when Eduardo presented her to me as an aspiring apprentice. I wanted to be sure she was serious about changing her direction from natural science to art.

"She showed me what she'd done for a book to be issued by the Advanced Academy." He hesitated, then added, "Guildmaster Urbine does not take many apprentices. At the moment, the only one is Chezan."

"What about Marta? Isn't she an apprentice?"

Edard hesitated again. "Marta is more than an apprentice, but has not qualified for the Craftsman's guild. She has been with Guildmaster Urbine since he arrived in Lorr. From Hinterland."

But they don't live together, I thought. *The Guildmaster has a place on the wrong side of Striver's Hill, while she's still taking care of things on Artists'.*

I got away from the personal and back to the professional. "What is *your* opinion of Audra's work?"

"She was accurate, almost to a fault. What her eye saw, her hand recorded. An excellent touch with the graphite."

"What about that river scene. That was done in ink, wasn't it?"

"Originally in graphite, I suggested she emphasize certain aspects with ink. A striking example of the art form. Guildmas-

42

ter Urbine was truly impressed when he saw it, which is why he put it into the gallery show. He doesn't usually show apprentice work—the Craftsman's Guild prefers to highlight their own. Although there are amateurs, self-taught, who occasionally rate an Auxiliary Membership—nonvoting, of course."

Interesting insight into Guild politics, but not relevant. "Where do you think Audra is?"

"I don't know. If she is not at home…" Edard sounded worried.

I felt the dirt turn to paving under my feet. Electric lights marked the beginnings of what passes for civilized living in Lorr, although these were spaced far enough apart there were deep pools of shadow between them.

I summed it up aloud. "Audra Martino left the Advanced Academy, moved clear across town, and set up here as an apprentice Craftsman." Silently, I wondered, did Audra plan to go back to the Academy with her drawings to prove there was something intelligent in the river?

Edard had stopped in front of a small cinderblock house at the dividing line between dirt and paved roads.

"This is my home," he said. "I'll leave you here. Just stay on the road, you'll get back to Artist's Way soon enough."

The door to the house opened. Someone looked out and beckoned.

"One more thing," I said. "What did you think of Audra? Not as an apprentice, as a person. Do you think she's the sort who'd just take off on a whim?"

"When I met her, I was struck by her serious attitude. Intense, I think, is the correct word. Her work is meticulous, careful, exact. She claimed to have seen something in the river and drew what she thought she had seen. If, as you say, she did not come home when she said she would…" He stopped. "I find that very unlikely. She always struck me as one who fulfills what is demanded of her. I hope you find her alive and well, Eye Drach. I really do. Audra Martino is a great talent."

He headed for his house and the welcoming arms of his spouse. I plodded along until I reached the corner, where I turned onto Artist's Way.

I considered what I'd learned about Audra Martino, and decided I'd done enough to make a start. I continued to Entertainment Row.

ix

By this time, the crowd had thinned considerably. People were on their way back to their homes, whether across the river in Flatlands or across the city in Garden Sector or in the hovels of Fishmarket at the end of the Waterfront piers. The wind had picked up, and the various vendors had packed their wares and left for warmer quarters. The taverns and eating-houses were jammed. I sniffed the aroma of roasting meat and fish, and realized it was long past my own meal-time.

I followed the few walkers still outdoors from Artist's Way to the Flatlands Bridge, the line of demarcation between where the Grand Boulevard ended and Entertainment Row began. The two theaters had opened their doors. Signs outside Theater One advertised their latest farce, while Theater Two was showing an action-packed melodrama. I'd seen the farce, which was worth another visit, but not tonight. I decided to pass on the melodrama.

Two of my favorite buskers, Randi and Kira, performed in front of Theater One, doing their best for the few passersby who stopped to listen to them. I dropped a coin into their box.

"How's business?" I asked politely.

Randi shrugged. "We're working till the end of Winterfest, then we're heading to South Coast. I hear Port Chicago is ready for street music, and no fees charged."

"No Guild protection," I pointed out.

"The fees aren't worth the protection," Kira groused. "After the fight at Smokey Joe's, we were banned from a lot of the taverns. And those characters over there are taking all the crowds."

44

She waved at the entrance to Foodie Alley, where opposing speakers were setting their stands up, ready to do verbal battle, one warning about the danger approaching from the sky, the other decrying the horrors in the oceans.

"There's a puffer-ship leaving for Port Chicago right after Winterfest closes, and we'll be on it."

Randi nodded, then drew me aside while Kira tuned her gittar. "Another winter here in Lorr will be too much for Kira," he muttered. "She's not doing too well."

No one wants to mention disease in Lorr. It's almost as bad as saying the words for death. It's one reason the Dark Ones are so feared—they deal with things no one wants to think about.

I pulled Audra's portrait from under my jacket. "Ever see her in the crowd? She was supposed to be with some of the art students that came around two days ago. Her friends said she stopped to listen to you, but left to listen to those two." I tilted my head toward the two stands, which were already drawing crowds.

Randi peered at the drawing, then passed it to Kira.

"I don't know...we get a lot of listeners," Kira said slowly. "But yeah, I think I remember her. Mostly because she asked if we knew any songs about the kraken. Which we do, and we sang it for her. She left a bit of coin, too."

"I didn't know there were songs about kraken."

"From Norland," Randi explained. "About a kraken male and a human female who can't be together because they are so different...but fall in love anyway." He nodded to Kira, who started to strum her gittar.

"I'll hear it next time," I said, before he could launch into song. "What happened after she left your stand?"

"No idea," Kira said. "Those two started yelling at each other, and we couldn't be heard over their preaching. We had to move on, and that was the end of it."

"Thanks for the info," I said, dropping another silver into their box. What they said matched what the art students had

45

told me. Audra had come to Entertainment Row and was caught up in the kraken myths.

I glanced across the surging crowd to the entrance to Foodie Alley. While I'd been busy, two new speakers had set up shop. I drew closer to see what was drawing the attention of the passers-by.

"My friends, you must trust me!" a voice boomed out, amplified by a cone-shaped speaking device. "They are coming for us! No one will be spared their wrath!"

"The oceans are being destroyed!" That was the other speaker, using his own lungs. "We must save the sea creatures from Exploiters!"

I moved closer, edging through the growing crowd.

The first speaker was a male of my own age, well-formed, with dark, wavy hair that fell to his shoulders and a penetrating gaze. He stood on a small platform, dressed in a flowing white kaftan and headwrap like those used by the Upper Tier of Pangkot.

He seemed to focus on first one, then another person in the crowd, as if speaking only to that individual. Two young females in similar robes but without the headwraps stood next to him, handing leaflets to anyone who passed by. Some took them, others waved them away.

"Listen to the words of the Prophet of Doom! A firestorm is coming. It's taken them four hundred years, but the Third Ship will find us! They will burn Lorr to the ground, destroy any human creatures they can find. We must flee to Hinterland, away from the terror that is coming! Your coin will buy a place in the bunker!"

I could smell a swindle here. If Fee M'Farr and his Fatsos hadn't caught on to it yet, that wasn't my concern. As for the followers of this Prophet, they were on their own. If they wanted to go into the Mineral Mountains with this character, I wasn't about to stop them.

I turned to the other speaker—leathery-skinned, darkly tanned, well past middle-aged, hair white with a bit of beard showing gray. Not tall or commanding, but something in his voice demanded attention. He was attended by three younger males in seaman's garb—canvas trou and jacket, knitted caps on their heads. Another young male in basic trou and jacket stood near a small table loaded with what looked like mags, but thicker, with red covers. Had I seen one of those in Audra's satchel?

"We have been here four hundred local years," the older man called to the crowd, "and in that time we've managed to wipe out whole species of creatures. The great sea reptiles are gone. The huge land reptiles are decimated. We have introduced our own animals and plants, and disrupted whole ecosystems. The boffins who care can't do anything, and not a lot of them care. We have to stop the Exploiters and give New Earth time to regenerate!"

I drew closer. I knew this male. "Jox Custo!" I cried out.

He was a lot older than the last time I saw him, but I still remembered my father clapping him on the shoulder, telling me, "This is Jox, the best First I ever had." Back then he was Drogo Drach's right hand, the one trusted to run his ship for him. I'd thought Jox was gone by now, along with everyone else who'd sailed on that last voyage.

"That's me. Who are you?" He scanned the crowd, finally focused on me, in the back row.

"Remember Izveta? Drogo Drach's youngster?" I elbowed my way to the front row of his listeners.

He gave me the onceover.

"Izveta...the one he got from Commander Polaris?"

"The same. But I go by Pola Drach now."

"Honoring the Captain." Not a question, but a statement. "Where is he?"

"Long story."

"I have the time for you to tell it."

"Read the book." He pointed to the pile of red-backed mags on the table.

"Better for you to tell it to me direct."

Jox hopped down from the stand to take a better look at me. "Izveta Polaris…Pola Drach. You've grown up."

In more ways than one. Izveta Polaris went to Norland, Pola Drach came back to Lorr. Not the story to share with this old-timer.

"And I have a lot of questions to ask. Come, have a meal with me, and give me some answers."

Jox looked grave. "You may not like the answers, Pola Drach."

"It's better than not knowing," I told him.

"Hannes!" he called to the young male at the table. "Take over! I've got a fish on the line. I'll be back, soonest!"

Hannes nodded, mounted the stand, and took up the spiel, while the other two tried to pass the red mags out. They got fewer takers than the Prophet's fetching females.

I led Jox through the crowd to Fletcher's Food Shop. How had I missed him!

"I've got digs upstairs," I explained as I marched in without waiting for the server and took a seat at the table at the far end of the room, facing the door. Fletcher didn't need to take my order. He just sent a server to set a mug of brew in front of me and went into the kitchen to slice something off whatever beast was roasting that night.

"Anything for you, Jox?" I asked. "Name it, you got it."

"I've eaten," he said. "But a brew would do me fine."

I waved the server down, ordered the drink, and prepared to listen.

"Allright, Jox Custo. What happened to my father?"

Jox glanced up at the server, accepted the mug of brew, and tried not to look me in the eye.

"It's been nearly twenty years since Drogo Drach left Lorr," I reminded him. "Where did he go? What did he do?"

"Read the book," Jox said.

"I don't have time for that. Where is Drogo Drach?"

"At the bottom of the Middle Sea," Jox said. "A sea reptile got him. Very big, Twice the size of the ship, and vicious with it. One with a huge body and a little head at the end of a neck like a snake. A hundred times bigger than any fish would ever be, and a mouthful of teeth in a gaping jaw to go with it."

"Was that before or after you made landfall?"

Jox paused. "After. We got across the Inner Sea…read the book to find out how. And between the currents and the tides and the rocks, the ship beached.

"The ship wasn't totally lost. It just took some time to repair the hull. We had to go inland to get supplies, see what we could find to eat, maybe cut down a tree for wood, for fuel and to fix the hull." Jox went on. "Some of the crewmen were taken by the big lizards. Another got some kind of ailment. Some of the plants were toxic, we found out the hard way. When we finally finished repairs, we had a small boat, with one sail, good enough to go over the reef.

"There weren't many left of the crew, just me and two others. The Captain did what he could, but those winds were fierce, and then the sea reptile showed up…" He took a swig of brew.

"It was up to me to get us home, bring the Captain's logs and charts back, like he told me. I let the current take us north and east, back to the ice and south again. Once we got to the other side of the Inner Sea, we abandoned the craft on the shore and set out on land. We hiked south, to the Contramont settlements, me and Rachel."

"Rachel?"

"The female boffin who'd kept the Captain's logs for him, made notes on the plants and animals we'd seen. She was the one who insisted on getting the information back to the South Coast Advanced Academy in Port Chicago. When we finally got to Port Chicago, she and I parted company. She'd met

49

another female boffin, and the two of them took to each other. No room for me!

"She stayed in Port Chicago with her new friend, took Captain Drach's logs and notebooks to the Advanced Academy, and wrote a book about what she'd seen and done. Even put my name to it, as 'consultant', because she'd asked me to help her remember what got lost in the wreck."

"Nice of her to include you." Most boffins don't pay much attention to the underlings. A book about Drogo Drach's discoveries would be a huge coup for whoever printed it—especially in Lorr, where Drogo Drach was an icon, the image of the Bold Explorer. Hard to live up to, which is why I prefer not to mention my relationship unless directly asked.

"The Advanced Academy published it." Jox grimaced his disgust. "Rachel got a position as Chief Instructor on the strength of it. A copy had to be put into the records of the Scribe's Guild in Lorr, and someone must have noticed it, because the next thing we knew, she'd got a copy of what they published, re-edited. Rewritten, is more like it!"

"How? And when? Was that what brought you back here to Lorr? I don't know much about the book business, but I do know these things take some time."

Jox frowned into his drink. "Let me think...I'd just come back from the trip South. Karlo Fuchs, one of the South Coast Junta, he financed a ship to see if there was any truth to rumors of a new settlement, maybe some of the crew off South Coast wrecks.

"There wasn't, but the young boffins were shocked at the state of the beaches, where bits of debris were scattered around. That's what got me interested in what we're doing to the oceans on this planet. If we're not careful, we'll wind up worse than Old Earth, because this time, there's no escaping. Maybe we could build another space-going craft, but we can't fuel it to leave New Earth without petroleum, and we can't get to enough petroleum to make the fuel."

This was interesting, but not what I wanted to know. "When did you find out about this book being published?" I persisted.

"I'm not sure. Maybe a year ago? Time tends to slip away when you're at sea. But when I got back to Port Chicago, Rachel came to my digs, told me she'd got a nice payment for her book, and gave me a healthy cut of it."

Rachel seemed to be a righteous sort, sharing her good fortune with someone like Jox.

"And was the book actually published?" You'd think a book about Drogo Drach would get a notice on Post Four, and I hadn't seen any.

"Oh, they printed it, allright, but not the way she wrote it. I've seen what they're selling at the Scribes' Guild table in the Central Plaza, and I tell you, it's not the same book. Oh, it's got pretty new covers, but some mucker in the Advanced Academy got his hands on it and changed it. Left stuff out, put other stuff in, and got someone to make pictures that don't match Rachel's.

"I tried to see the boffin who put his name to it, to tell him what I thought of his messing about, but he blew me off. I'm not that easy to get rid of. He'll find out. I've got the real deal, that's the one I'm giving away. I don't take coin for lies! Mine is the true story."

"But they sent a copy to Port Chicago," I pointed out. "Rachel must have given her approval, or the Admin wouldn't have allowed the Scribe's Guild to go through with publication."

"I don't know what she signed, and by the time I saw the book, she'd used the coin to take off with her friend on another voyage, so I decided to come to Lorr, to have it out with the Academics, and set the record straight. And to alert people to the dangers we face here on New Earth if we don't clean up our oceans!"

I didn't need enhanced hearing to catch the note of desperation in his voice. Whatever he may have been in the past, Jox Custo was now a real fanatic about cleaning the ocean.

"So, that's what you're doing here? Trying to get the fishermen to stop using their nets? Good luck with that!"

"It's not just the nets. It's the rest of the stuff that gets thrown overboard. The wasted food, the ropes. The puffer-ships are spewing coal dust into the air. Don't people realize how bad that is?"

"They did back before the Merchant's War," I reminded him. "Admin put through a whole lot of regs, about how much fuel could be used, and where the factories had to be located, away from the residential sectors."

"Lorr is only one city, one part of a whole planet." Jox leaned closer. "Admin thinks they can run things, but they can't enforce their regs. Each settlement makes its own rules. The fishermen out of Pangkot don't care what they throw into the ocean, or how much they take out. They just want as much as they can now, they don't think of tomorrow. South Coast, same thing. It's greed, pure and simple, and if we don't do something, we'll destroy New Earth, just like we did Old Earth." His voice rose to a screech. People started looking toward us.

"How long have you been here in Lorr?" I cut off his rant before someone had to call the Guards to stop a riot.

"I pulled in last week, checked in with the Seaman's Guild to see if I was still on their books, and got a room at the Guild Hostel on the Waterfront. I reported what happened to Captain Drach to Admin Security, and got grilled good and proper by Security Chief Polaris.

"Then, I went to the Advanced Academy, tried to get to the boffins in charge, but they wouldn't listen to me. I was sent away, with the warning not to cause trouble. That won't stop me. I mean to cause trouble! If the boffins won't listen to me, maybe someone else will. If I make enough noise, some-one will listen, and maybe do something before it's too late."

"You set up a stand on Entertainment Row," I said. "What does the Guild think of that?"

"I didn't ask them, One of Hannes's youngsters is a student at the Advanced Academy. He got permission to set up a stand, said it was to teach about the oceans. Not Entertainment, Academic."

"Nothing entertaining about dirty oceans," I agreed. I remembered what I was really after, and pulled out the portrait of Audra Martino. "Ever see her in your audience?"

"We've attracted a number of folks," Jox said, barely glancing at the drawing. Then he took it from my hand and squinted hard at it. "Wait a bit…yes, I remember her. Not a face you can forget," he added, handing it back to me. "She kept asking if I'd ever seen a kraken."

"And have you?"

Jox grinned. "I thought I might have once. I was trying to swim underwater to see what was in the tide pools near our landing-site. I have an idea about how to stay under longer. If I could put air into some kind of container, and tap into it somehow…"

"The young female," I urged him. "When did you see her?"

Jox came out of his reverie. "It must have been, oh, two days ago. I remember she was with some other young folks, and they tried to drag her away. She wanted to know more about krakens, so she stayed while they went off. What's wrong?"

"She didn't go with her friends," I said slowly. "The last they saw of her was when she was listening to you."

"It was Hannes talked to her," Jox protested. "She asked foolish questions, and when he didn't answer the way she wanted, she turned to listen to that other fellow, the Prophet of Doom.

"Now, there's a fool if there ever was one. Third Ship! Hah! We don't need rodents to destroy us, we're doing it to ourselves!" Jox finished his drink. "It was good to see you, Pola Drach. I'm sorry I had to give you the bad news. I told Security Chief Polaris what happened to Captain Drach. Now, there's a cold female! She only said she'd assumed he met a sorry end, and that was all."

I didn't doubt it. My mother had used Drogo Drach to get what she wanted. Once she got it, she'd had no need for him.

Jox set his mug down and rose. "I've got to get back to my stand. Go well, Pola Drach."

He left, and I decided to go to my digs upstairs. I needed to consult with Ficus.

x

Fletcher had a lantern already lit for me, along with a pail of water for Ficus. I climbed the stairs to my rooms. The heat from the cooking below made them tolerably warm, so I didn't have to deal with the small heater. Better to leave that alone until the real chill set in.

Ficus was getting larger every day, but it was still only half what it had been when it was torn out of its pot and stomped on by Selva Delrey in the summer. It had put out new shoots and leaves, but it was spreading outward, not upward. I didn't know if that was good or bad.

Not much is known about sensation plants, and what is known isn't spread around. Boffins tend to keep that kind of information to themselves.

I checked Ficus for insects or other critters that might have gotten in while I was away. The window was closed, but it's not sealed; and there are some creepy-crawlies that manage to make their way through the cracks, looking for a place to nest over the winter.

Ficus greeted me with a rustle of leaves, eager for its portion of bone-meal and powdered clet. I fed and watered it, and was rewarded with a spray of pheromones.

"Good plant," I cooed. "Good Ficus. You're doing well. I won't let anyone come in and shred you again. I promise."

Ficus rustled again, the green veins in its leaves turning purple.

I put the lantern on the table across from Ficus and deposited the various pamphlets I'd picked up next to it. More rustles from Ficus, and the purple turned darker.

"I've got a case. Missing girl," I explained as I took off my jacket and sat down to read the pamphlets. "She had these in her rooms. Last time anyone saw her, she was listening to the speakers on Entertainment Row who give these out."

Ficus bent a few lower branches toward the pamphlets. The purple turned to blue again, a sign of curiosity. Ficus likes me to read to it. I don't know if it's responding to the sound of my voice or the chemicals in my breath, but it puts out more leaves and gives me more pheromones when I do.

I picked up one of Jox's leaflets. "This is about the oceans. An old shipmate of my father's, Jox Custo, has come back from the sea with a mission. The missing girl was interested in beings under the water."

Mostly, the material recapped what Jox had told me, that the oceans were becoming polluted, and humans were responsible. He'd set up a fund with the Seamen's Guild to help with the cleanup, should anyone care to donate.

I read that to Ficus, and added, "Conservationists will eat this up. It's what they've been saying all along—resources are finite, we must not waste them. Don't discard anything, keep what you have. That goes for coin, too. Jox may have their moral support, but he won't get a copper bit to finance any cleanup he has in mind."

I turned to the other leaflet. The Prophet of Doom had a good artist on his staff. The cover showed a huge rodent menacing a small human female, depicted in bright colors. Inside was the story of the Third Ship, as it has come down since the Second Landing. A horror story, to be sure, but who knew if it was even true? Whatever signals the Founders had sent back to Old Earth were never answered. We don't even know if they were received.

The Second Ship got here fifty years and three generations after the Founders landed. No one else has come since. As far as we know, we humans on New Earth are the last of our species.

According to the Exploiters, we're here to use everything we can find to expand our population. The Conservationists say we've got to take it slowly, let the planet get used to us, for the native species to adapt to ours, and for humans to adapt to New Earth.

Most people leave these discussions to the boffins and Admin. We just go about our business, staying alive and coping with what's here. Whoever put the data into the Big Black Box was guessing about what they'd find when they got to wherever they could land. As it turned out, some was right and some was wrong.

It's all very well to have information on how to make things, but it's no good if the basic materials aren't available. The Founders had to scavenge what they could out of the ships, and made up the rest out of what was already here.

I read the vivid description of the Third Ship Mutiny to Ficus, whose leaves turned red in terror.

"Are these super-rodents coming for us now? Not likely," I soothed it. "The markers were changed, so if there *was* a Third Ship, it's completely lost in the universe somewhere far away from here. And if these mutated rodents did get here…there's a lot of this planet that hasn't been explored. The whole Southern Continent is a mystery. No one's managed to penetrate the green barrier of plants that protect the interior. You're safe enough, Ficus. I won't let anyone hurt you again."

I rubbed its leaves until they turned a healthy green.

I stacked the leaflets on the table and sighed. "I could wait until morning, but I'd better go over to Smokey Joe's."

Ficus rustled at me, its leaves edging to purple again.

"I'll be careful. I'll ask a few questions and come right back. Besides, Basher will be with me. He takes care of me. Nothing will go wrong. I'll be back before you know it. I'll leave the lantern on for you."

Ficus's leaves turned darker purple.

"No, I won't get into another fight." I didn't tell Ficus about my encounter in the Artist's Sector. "You're fussier than a Mother's Guild caretaker. I survived the street lizards, I survived the river. I'll come back and give you another spritz as soon as I can. I just want a word with Basher and his buddies. Maybe one of them saw Audra when she was on Entertainment Row."

I put my jacket on again, swapped my small bludgeon for the large one with the extra weight in the handle, and made sure I had the portrait of Audra tucked into my inside jacket pocket. I didn't really want to go out again, but I'd taken coin, and I owed the client my best efforts.

Besides, I wouldn't want Basher Bob to think I was moving in on his territory. Bob's a good friend. I don't want him as an enemy.

xi

The two speakers had left their posts when I got back to Entertainment Row. Most of the crowd had retreated to the warmth of theaters, casinos, or other places of interest to anyone seeking refreshment of mind or body. The lanterns strung across the street swung crazily in the rising wind, sending weird shadows up and down the buildings.

I poked my nose into a few places, looking for anyone who might have noticed Audra. No luck—the licensees weren't interested in females, and neither were the joyboys. I reached the end of Entertainment Row, where Smokey Joe's marks the boundary between it and the Waterfront.

The carrier station across from the tavern was vacant, lit by one electric light. Overhead, stars were hidden by scudding clouds, blown by the chilly wind off the river. The air was scented with river weeds and rotting fish. Under the piers, the feral felines prowled, looking for whatever they could find, while the lizards scuttled away from them.

Something slapped at the water, making a splash that wasn't the tide coming in. Was it whatever had helped me escape a nasty situation a few weeks ago? I didn't want to speculate.

Instead, I headed for Smokey Joe's, a long, low wooden building dating from the very beginnings of Lorr, when wood was available and cheap. There's no sign outside. If you know what it is, you belong there. If you don't, you don't.

The doorman, Sneaky Pete, was on duty just outside the front door, chewing a bit of weed.

"Oyo, Pete," I greeted him. "How's business?"

Pete spat weed-juice. "No more of them uppers," he reported.

"Just the usual crowd?" I was glad to hear slumming was no longer fashionable among the young lads of the Upper Tier. Not after what happened to Gorgeous Gyorgi Delrey, now exiled to Port Chicago. They would have to satisfy their itch for adventure somewhere else.

"Norland fleet's in. So's South Coast."

That could be good or bad, depending on how the fishing had gone. Norland sailors with coin in their pockets were good news for taverns and licensees, bad news for anyone who got in their way. That included South Coasters, just as large as Norlanders and twice as touchy. I made sure my bludgeon was handy, in case I had to bash my way out of a brawl.

I strolled into Smokey Joe's main room, and regretted Ficus's pheromones. My olfactory nerves were assaulted by the odors of unwashed bodies, bad jack, and weed-smoke. My ears winced at the roar of many voices, in several languages and dialects, mostly male, with a few shrill female entertainers added to the mix. The stage was empty for the moment, but I expected a singer or storyteller to appear sooner or later. After the success of Liko Batom, Smokey Joe's had become a venue for buskers trying to move up the Entertainment Guild ladder.

The joint was jumping, as the song says. Norlanders in knitted tunics, Pangkoti in blue cotton jackets, South Coasters in striped and printed shirts, all yelling at the top of their lungs in assorted Lorran dialects. Licensees and joyboys circulated around the tables, looking for trade. More noise came from the door leading to the gambling room, where all sailors could lose their pay without the elegant froufrou of Entertainment Row's casinos. It was all jolly good fun, with Winterfest just weeks ahead.

I located Basher Bob Basheer, a big dark-skin male, at his usual station at the end of the bar. His popsy, Velda, snuggled up to him, and a couple of characters in black leathers hovered behind them. Basher had picked up a following in the latest Fatso recruits from Pangkot after he'd got one of their number out of a tight situation. With my help, I might add.

"Oyo, Basher. How's business?" I looked the leather-clad males over. "Oyo, Brutus."

Basher answered for both of them. "Not bad, Pola, not bad. Brutus made good on his promise to Master Assassin M'Farr. He's kept out of trouble and earned a badge and sigil from the Assassin's Guild."

"I'm off the factory watch, and on bridge duty," Brutus declared with a note of pride in his voice.

Basher patted him on the shoulder. "Brutus saw the error of his ways. He's a stalwart citizen and a Guild Assassin in good standing."

"Glad to hear it," I said, and I was. I'd had a few encounters with Brutus when he was working for Selva Delrey as muscle-for-hire, and I didn't want to risk any more of them.

"How's business with you, Pola? Anything interesting?" Velda asked.

I fished the picture of Audra out of my inner pocket. "This young female, gone missing these two days. Last seen on Entertainment Row. Any of you lot recognize her?"

Basher squinted at the picture and passed it on to Velda, who frowned at it.

"Interesting face she's got." Velda handed the picture to Brutus. "She looks familiar...not a licensee, though."

"Craftsmen's apprentice," I told her. "Working out of the Urbine studio. She was supposed to go home to Garden for Winterfest, but never did. I've been hired to find her."

Basher nodded. "You think she got into some kind of trouble on Entertainment Row?"

"I was told she was on Entertainment Row two nights ago with the rest of the apprentices, celebrating a gallery opening. You sure you didn't see her?"

Brutus moved to the lamp hanging over the bar to get a better look at the picture. "Maybe I did see her. On the Fishmarket Bridge, it was. At first I thought she might be a jumper. Folks get melancholy at Winterfest. Bad karma, no friends to celebrate with. But she just stared at the river, didn't jump."

"Was anyone with her?"

"Not on the bridge." Brutus's brow furrowed in thought as he handed the picture back to me. "At least, I didn't see anyone. But the fog was rising, and the moons were setting, so I can't say for certain there wasn't anyone there." He hesitated, then went on. "I might have seen something moving on the other side of the bridge. One thing I know, if there was footsteps I'd have heard them. That bridge rings like crazy."

"But you didn't hear footsteps." I pressed him. "Someone else on that bridge, besides this female?"

"Hey, it was two days ago," Brutus protested. "And I'm on the Flatlands side, to see no one gets over the bridge without they pay the toll. It's an important post."

And he'd also have been on the lookout for anyone coming from Flatlands, not the other way around. Especially someone who hadn't paid the Fatsos for permission to work the Lorr side of the bridge.

"If this female turns up, let me know." I retrieved the picture. "Her family's worried. She didn't turn up at the Winterfest gathering."

"Important people, are they?" Basher hinted. "Admin?"

"Construction Guild," I said, dismissing any thoughts of a fat reward. "But they've got Guards connections, so any help will be appreciated."

Brutus snarled, "Guards are no help. They haven't found who's passing the pinkies around Fishmarket."

"Pinkies?" I echoed.

"Pink pellets," Basher explained. "Going around among the youngsters in Fishmarket and Waterfront. Word is they're some kind of pepper-upper, make you stronger, keep you going longer."

"And do they?"

"Maybe, but they do it by taking more out of a body than it's supposed to put out. Two lads were found last night, brains practically shredded in their heads. Nasty stuff!"

"Nothing on the posts about it," I noted.

"You think the Dark Ones are going to let the rest of Lorr know what they're up to? Not a chance. My guess? Some boffin found something in one of the Southern Continent plants that matches something in the Big Black Box. Admin is keeping the Guards in line, and between Admin and the Dark Ones, they don't want anyone to know the stuff exists."

"Except that it does, and it's being handed around," I pointed out. "I don't see the connection with my missing female, though. Thanks for the tip, Brutus. Keep your eyes open, and if you spot her again, let me know."

I saw a mug of brew in front of me. I hadn't ordered it, but Bartender Joe knew me and what I like to drink. I took it as a Winterfest offering.

I dropped a coin on the bar, took a swig of the brew, and wished I hadn't. Smokey Joe's brew ranges from drinkable to barely, and this wasn't one of the drinkable batches. It tasted vile. A few drops got down my throat before I spat out the mouthful I got.

"Founder's Faith, what did you brew that from? Sundew pods?"

Bartender Joe, at the other end of the bar, didn't hear me.

I'd got what I came for. I headed for the door.

I didn't quite get there. My legs turned to rubber, my heart started to pound. Every sound, every smell exploded in my brain. Someone behind me shouted something I didn't quite understand.

Next thing I knew, I was in Smokey's Joe's fetid elimination place, yorking my guts out, with Velda holding my head over the pot.

"Good thing you didn't take more of that brew," she scolded me. "Don't you know better than to drink something you didn't order?"

"I thought I was used to Joe's brew," was the best I could come up with between heaves. I gasped for air, trying to block the crazy sensations streaming through my head.

"I'll find you a pedishaw," Velda soothed me. "And then Basher and I will get to the bottom of this. No one poisons anyone at Smokey Joe's without our say-so."

She hauled me outside, heaved me into the seat of the nearest pedishaw, with orders to the driver to take me to Foodie Alley, and orders to me to go straight up to my digs and sleep it off.

The last conscious thought I had was, *I must have got someone's attention.* I only wished I knew who…and why.

xii

My heart and head were more or less back to normal when I woke up the next morning. My stomach wasn't. I fought down the heaves while I tended to Ficus, then donned the most inconspicuous outfit I owned—dark gray trou, a plain off-white linen shirt, and a knitted Norland tunic in undyed wool. Warm, drab, loose enough for action, tight enough not to get caught on anything.

I settled my stomach with a bowl of warm grain mush instead of my usual browned bread, and chai. I wasn't sure whether last night's experience had been a deliberate attack or just an accident. I could have grabbed someone else's drink in the ruckus around the bar at Smokey Joe's. After all, who knew I'd be there? And why try and poison me now?

I drank chai, ate mush, and went over my plans for the day. Brutus had seen Audra at the Fishmarket Bridge, the second of the two bridges that crossed the river from Lorr into Flatlands. I recalled the little cave under the bridge where the homeless youngsters called street lizards used to congregate before they were put under Fatso control. It was as good a place as any to start my search for the missing female. I only hoped I wasn't too late.

I made my way through the morning crowds coming over the Flatland Bridge to their jobs in Lorr, threading around two-wheels and avoiding pedishaws. The food-shops on Foodie Alley already had their Winterfest decorations up, glittering in the morning sunlight—stylized eight-sided snowflakes and white and silver electric lights from Lorr, green boughs from mountain conifers brought south from Norland. One casino had a sign up announcing a sing-along of "old ship songs", led by Moggy the Busker. Red and yellow streamers with Pangkoti characters clashed with the snowflakes—Buda-Ganesha and Mata Diva weren't going to be left out of Winterfest celebrations.

The tide was up. Fishing boats that had come in overnight were offloading their cargoes, making ready to leave on the outgoing surge. Dark Ones inspectors were looking over the catch to make sure the fish were whole, while vendors from the Fishmarket that gave the district its name waited to take their selections away. All nice and normal, and what you'd expect on a fine day in Lorr with winter coming on.

I drank in the sights and smells...and caught a whiff of something vaguely "wrong." Something not fish, not weeds, not water.

I followed the scent to the Fishmarket Bridge, where the piers ended and the Fishmarket Sector began. The Guardhouse at the Lorr end of the bridge was open for business, the door ajar. I recognized the Guard outside, a tough old bird, her eyes alert for anyone who might be thieving without a license from the Fatsos.

"Oyo, Nattie. How's business?"

"So-so, Drach. Eyeing today?"

I showed her Audra's picture. "Ever see her?"

Nattie shrugged. "Can't say. A lot of people going in and out of Flatlands for Winterfest. What's her pitch?"

"She hasn't been seen in two days," I said. "Her family's worried."

"Probably run off with some lowdown male," Nettie commented. "She'll find out what he's like, and run home when she comes to her senses."

"I only hope you're right," I muttered.

Moving on, I got another whiff of something rotten. I followed the scent to the bridge. According to Brutus, Audra had gone halfway across. Then what?

I slowly crossed the bridge, hanging onto the railing. I peered into the river. The water surged outward, toward the ocean. Dark eddies swirled around the concrete pilings on the shore. I thought I saw two large eyes and a bulbous head bobbing under the waves, but they disappeared before I could focus on them.

I leaned over the railing, trying to see what Audra saw in that river. Got another noseful of death.

I went back to the shore, to the small cave under the bridge where the youngsters with no homes had once gathered for warmth and comfort. Master Assassin Fee M'Farr had set up a dormitory for the gang in one of the Fishmarket warehouses, to lure them into signing on with the Honorable Guild of Forgers, Assassins, Thieves and Swindlers, and most of the street lizards had taken advantage of the offer.

The cave should have been empty at this hour. I edged around the pier to see what was inside.

It wasn't pretty. What had once been a young female lay stretched out under the overhang of the cave. Various critters had been at her, but they hadn't taken her long, dark hair. I noted the ring-shaped marks on her arms and legs, what was left of them.

I backed away from the cave and yelled for the Guards. It was up to them, now. I'd done what I'd been paid to do.

I'd found Audra Martino.

xiii

Captain Atterson's Specials arrived by skimmer, with Dark One Kelvin and his crew close behind. Atterson took me aside while the Dark Ones examined the body.

"Did you know she was…gone?" She couldn't say the evil word.

"I'd hoped not," I said, "but it was always a possibility. I've got a witness saw her on the bridge two nights ago, staring into the river. And she was interested in water-life. According to another witness, she wanted to know more about kraken."

"Kraken don't exist," Atterson declared firmly.

I wasn't so sure. Something had helped release the knots that tied me to the underside of the bridge not too long ago. Something was watching from under the water. If it wasn't a kraken, what was it? Whatever it was, I had let it go its own way then, and I wasn't about to draw attention to it now.

"Audra thought they did," I said. "She drew a picture of something in the river. She was fascinated by it. And she just might have tried to join it."

Dark One Kelvin emerged from the cave, wiping his hands on a bit of cloth. "Dead at least two days," he stated. "Marks on the body indicate a struggle, but I'll have to do a further examination to determine if she drowned or was gone before she hit the water."

"Do it." Atterson turned to face me. "Drach, you've fulfilled your contract."

"I only spent one day on it. I owe you two silvers."

"Keep them. I'll deal with this from here."

"I'll send you my report. I've got a witness…"

"Don't tell me how to do my job." Atterson brushed past me. I could see tears lurking in the corners of her eyes, but she couldn't show them to her squad.

I slowly returned to the end of the pier, where I flagged down a pedishaw and rode to my office in Clothier's Alley. I wrote a full report of my findings, including what Brutus had told me, and sent it to Captain Atterson at the Central Guardhouse. Audra Martino's case was finished.

Only it wasn't.

FRIENDS AND FAMILIES

TWO DAYS PASSED. I CHASED DOWN SOME CHARACTERS who were reluctant to pay what they owed, picked up some coin. Checked the posts to see what was happening. Mostly I sat in my office and stewed over Audra Martino and her unfortunate end.

I wouldn't, couldn't, didn't believe she'd jumped into the river for no good reason. Was she trying to contact whatever was in there? Or had she been helped into the river for another reason, one I hadn't discovered yet?

It really didn't matter. Like Moggy's song about the old female who did everything backwards, "'T'isn't my affair, 't'isn't your affair." I was off the case, It was in the hands of Atterson's Special Squad, and that was that.

I sat in my office while my head cleared and my tum went back to its normal function. I waited, while Life went on in Lorr. Nobody came in. No one needed an Independent Eye, which was good for them, bad for me. On the third day, I checked the newsposts to see if there was anything useful that might help me drum up some business.

A notice on Post One from Admin, warning shipping about pirate activity along the South Coast. Old news. South Coast pirates and Pangkot merchants have been fighting an undeclared sea war since before I was born. It's one reason why both settlements sat out the Merchant's War in Lorr; they were too busy with their own affairs to bother about anyone else.

A list of candidates for the Lorr City Council on Post Two. Nothing new there, either; same names from the major Guilds always appear. Councilors of previous years or offspring of Councilors, all vetted by Admin to make sure no one clan or Guild puts too many fingers in the public treasury. No Delreys in the mix—Vernor and Selva were lurking in their lodges in Hinterland, Gorgeous Gyorgi was still in Port Chicago. Devon Delrey, the only member of the clan still resident in Lorr, must have been advised by his Vikk connections to sit this cycle out.

Also on Post Two, a warning from the Dark Ones regarding certain pink pellets confiscated by the Flatland Force during routine inspections of herbal stands at the Thieves Market there. Said pellets were not acceptable analgesics and should not be ingested. Anyone desiring analgesics for relief of pain should get them at the Dark Shrines. Anyone with information about such pellets should immediately contact the Dark Ones at the Temple of Healing. Whether anyone would inform the Dark Ones about them, doubtful; but at least the Dark Ones said the pinkies existed. It's hard to control something if you don't want to admit it's there.

The ratings of commodities on Post Three, the Financial News, don't concern me. I don't invest in anything, and I don't have a large enough income to worry about being over-taxed. I did see a large notice regarding an increase in South Coast coal production. New mines open in Contramont meant more coal shipped out of South Coast. Good news for the manufactories in Flatlands, bad news for anyone worrying about coal dust in the atmosphere or the oceans. Again, not something I had to worry about.

Post Four had the listings of Winterfest public events, starting with the lighting of the Winter Beacon on the Waterfront in a week's time and ending with the Grand Finale and Concert in the Central Plaza on the night of the Solstice. In between were plenty of musical and theatrical performances, all free to anyone who'd brave the cold wind on the Central Plaza. Good pickings for Fatso Thieves, with all those people squished together, not paying attention to eager fingers reaching under capes and into jacket pockets. Fee M'Farr would be ecstatic.

Chief of Security Regina Polaris, on the other hand, would have her hands full protecting visiting dignitaries from the Settlements from the disorderly elements of Lorr, but that was what the Guards were supposed to be for. Hopefully, none of the dignitaries would need the attentions of Atterson's Special Squad, but if that happened, it would be The Brain's services they'd seek, not mine.

Post Four also had a list of art galleries open for Winterfest, including a review of the Urbine Gallery's exhibition, with a particular mention of the distinctive work of Audra Martino. The reviewer was impressed with the use of line, but not so taken with the subject matter. Aside from that, the review was mostly a diatribe against the use of stimulants by youngsters in a vain attempt at touching their inner psyche.

According to the reviewer, the outcome was tragic. The resulting artwork was sloppy, incoherent, and not unexpected as the dire results of indulging in jack, weed, or any other enhancement. Better to allow one's inner self to emerge naturally.

I don't disagree. I'm not one for addling the brain with stimulants, whether it's jack or weed or these new pinkies. Brew is enough for me.

Post Five had the sports ratings. I don't care whose ball-carriers are scoring highest or who hits who hardest in a fighting-match. And the pedishaw races are called off during Winterfest so drivers can rake in as much coin as possible. Passengers are more important than kudos.

Then my eye was caught by a small notice on Post Six, the one reserved for personal communications and gossip.

> Found, on the riverbank, the body of a young female, presumed to have fallen off the Fishmarket Bridge.

No name given, no information as to how she fell or who found her.

I thought about this as I made my way through Clothier's Alley to my office. A stocky male, of middle height, older than me, clad in a standard Tech boiler suit, garish orange with the Construction Guild sigil on the left chest, was waiting for me. I unlocked the door and beckoned him inside.

"Sit down, Guildsman." I indicated the wooden chair. "What can I do for you?"

"I'm Construction Guildsman Eduardo Martino." He lowered his posterior onto the chair. "It's about Audra. Sara says you're the one who found her."

I looked him over. I could see a resemblance to the portrait of Audra—the same dark, thick hair curling around a square-jawed face, the same beaky nose. "You refer to Captain Atterson?"

He nodded. "My spouse's sibling. She came to the house yesterday to tell us what happened to Audra. She said..." Martino hesitated, then went on. "She said she'd consulted you because you were Independent."

"Many people do," I said, and left it at that. No explanations necessary.

"Did you know she was...gone? Before you found her?"

"I suspected it," I admitted. "Two days, and no word to her family? I followed her trail, and it led to the bridge. One of the Fatsos saw her on it but didn't see her leave. According to Post Six, she must have fallen or jumped of her own volition. Either way, unfortunate."

"She didn't fall into the river," Martino stated firmly. "And she didn't jump off that bridge. Someone pushed her in."

"I found her on the bank," I reminded him. "Why do you think she was in the river?"

"The Dark Ones sent us back her clothes. They were wet through. You don't get that wet on the riverbank."

"That's where she was when I found her," I repeated.

"Then she must have got out somehow. And she...she d-died. All alone, in the dark."

"A terrible way to go," I agreed. "But what, exactly, do you want me to do about it?"

"Find out how it happened. Sara says that's what you do. Find things out."

"That's her job, too," I reminded him. "Captain Atterson is the head of a squad specifically designated to find things out about those who have...deceased."

"She's writing this off as a tragic accident. She told us Audra took some kind of drug, or pellet, or something that made her see things in the water that weren't there, and that she went in after this vision, or whatever it was. That's how it's going to be written up, and that's why the Guards aren't going to go any further. It won't do, I tell you. It won't do!" He banged on my desk to emphasize the point.

I gave him the onceover. A tough type, typical Tech one step up from the Mechs who did most of the dirty work in the factories in Flatlands. No office drone, not with those hands and shoulders. Someone who'd worked his way through the Guild. And not someone who'd be put off with Admin blather, either.

"How can you be sure?" I persisted. "From what I learned at the studio, Audra had taken an interest in the arcane. She had pamphlets from someone who calls himself the Prophet of Doom, she'd been to a Pangkoti puja."

Martino shook his head. "That's not like her. She was practical, no-nonsense. We're strictly Conservationist. If she said a thing was real, it was. And anyone who thinks she went into the river after something that wasn't there is full of reptile-poop."

I took one of my standard forms from the bottom drawer of the desk, laid it in front of him with the graphite stylus I keep for clients.

"Understand this," I said. "I can look into the circumstances of Audra's demise. I will do my best to find out exactly how and why she went into the river. What I cannot do is take any action against any person or persons who may have urged her to go in or may have attacked her. That's for Captain Atterson to handle. I can give you facts. What you do with them is up to you."

Martino nodded. "I don't ask for more."

"The facts may not be what you want to hear," I warned him. "Write what you want me to do, sign it, and I'll countersign the contract."

"I can take whatever you come up with. I just want to know." He scrawled a brief statement on the form, signed it, and took out his purse. "Sara said you charge a silver a day" He laid out five silvers, nearly a week's pay for a Tech. I was ready to mention I had a sliding scale for some clients, but the set of his shoulders and the glint in his eye told me he wouldn't like that. I took the coin.

"Five days," I said. "I could do it in three."

"I want answers, not maybes. Take your time, Eye Drach, and don't be afraid to give me the truth. Sara said you're straight. I'm on the Frauds Commission for the Construction Guild, I know how much digging it can take before you get to the bottom of things."

"If I do this, I'll need all the information you can give me about Audra. What she liked, who she was friendly with, male or female connections. I'll have to speak with your spouse, too. When can I see her? I know it's not a good time, what with Winterfest and a consolation gathering for Audra, but…"
I let it dangle.

Martino nodded again. "Understood, Eye Drach. We'll be expecting you this afternoon, before sundown." He wrote down the number of his house in Garden Sector on the back of the contract. "The Service of Consolation is being put off until the Dark Ones have finished their examinations. Once they do, she'll be reduced to components, as the Founders decreed."

That placed Martino firmly in the Conservationist column, attending Founder's Faith meetings, not puja or other arcane rites. Interesting, considering Audra's interest in Third Shippers, Pangkot gods and krakens.

It also meant that I'd better get a wiggle on, before Audra's physical remains were destroyed in the reduction vats.

I smiled at Martino and stood, indicating the interview was over. "I'll get on this right now," I assured him. "Expect me this afternoon at the third hour. I'll see what I can find out from the Dark Ones. They don't always tell the deceased person's kin the whole story, Especially if it's a bit, um, gruesome." I didn't want to go into the damage done to Audra after two days of exposure to river critters.

Martino gave me a hard look, waved, and said, "I'll be waiting. I'll tell Geri to expect you." He muttered a quick "Be safe, be prosperous," and left me with the coin and the contract to consider what to do next.

ii

I heard a faint cough behind me. I turned to face Zeta, who had been standing in the doorway that led to the boutique office listening to the conversation.

"Does this mean you're going against the Guards?" Her blue eyes gleamed in anticipation.

"Don't get any exalted ideas," I told her. "I'm going to do the job I always do. Follow the facts, see where they lead, and find the truth, no matter who it hurts. That's what the client pays for, that's what the client gets."

"I wasn't prying, but I saw the male in the alley, and I thought you might need someone to take notes for you..." She trailed off, wilting under my glare. "And then I heard the name Martino."

"Someone you know?"

"Not exactly, but it's a name known in Flatlands."

I looked her over. She had exchanged her uniform of pink smock with the Clothier's Guild sigil on the collar and matching trou for a dark-green woolen jacket over a slightly grubby linen shirt and dark-blue woolen trou. It looked as if she was copying my style, even to the detail of pulling her hair back into a loose knot at the back of the neck instead of the neat braid affected by Jake and Holly's staff.

"Thinking of training as an Independent Eye, Zeta?"

Her face turned red. "It's more interesting than sorting bills and receipts."

"Also more dangerous. Don't even think of taking over for me until you've had some training in combat, armed and unarmed. Remember, I had a year in the Guards before I went Independent, and before that I was in Norland, where all females do physical training."

Her flush paled.

"And remember where I ended up after my last adventure. The Temple of Healing isn't as restful as the Dark Ones make it out to be."

Zeta backed into Jake and Holly's office where she'd be safe. I stopped her before she could make her escape.

"One more thing. You say you know the name Martino. Who are they?"

"Martinos are a big thing in Flatlands—Construction Guild connections. And they were on the Admin side in the Merchant's Wars. A lot of people still remember."

I hadn't considered that. The Merchant's War ended twenty years ago, but old hatreds run deep. Eduardo Martino had left Flatlands, gone clear across Lorr to Garden Sector. That could be a matter of economics and status, showing how he'd risen from the squalor of a shared block in Flatlands to a single house in Garden, or it could be a sign of something else. It bore looking into.

"I'll be out most of the day," I said. "If anyone comes in, take their name and business, and tell them I'll be in around nightfall."

"I suppose you'll want to interview Guildsman Martino in Garden," Zeta mused.

"I might," I conceded. "But it's no business of anyone's where I'll be, or when."

Not that I expected anyone, but if I was going to have an office drone, paid or not, at least I could get some use out of her.

Zeta bolted, leaving me to plot out my course of action. There was still plenty of time before I had to face Audra's parents. I hitched a small bludgeon to my belt, made sure I had enough loose coin in my pouch to cover expenses, and left the office.

iii

The morning chill had faded, and the sun was edging toward noon. I took the carrier as far as I could, then trudged up the hill behind the Admin complex to the Dark Ones' compound where the dead are processed. I needed some answers, and I knew I wouldn't get them from Atterson.

I went though the usual guff with the Dark Ones before I was let into the chamber where Dark Kelvin was waiting.

"I suppose you want the particulars on Audra Martino," he said without a perfunctory "How's business?" or any other greeting.

"I know what I saw," I said. "She was on her back, her hair spread out under her head. Various bits had been taken by river critters. It was dark under the bridge, but I had the impression there were marks on her skin."

75

"There were," Kelvin admitted. "Most unusual marks. Round impressions, lined up, as if something had been wrapped around her arms and legs."

"Interesting. Any ideas as to what?"

He frowned. "I would not like to venture a guess. There are examples given in texts, but nothing quite like these."

"Anything else? Marks of a struggle? Signs of violence? Bruising, scars?"

"A bruise on the back suggests violence. Not connected with the circular marks on the limbs. But that is not what caused her demise."

"She drowned?"

"She did not. There was no water in her lungs."

"Then...how?"

Dark Kelvin grinned smugly. "I very nearly missed it. A small, sharp object, inserted into the back of her neck, near the bruise."

I thought this over. "Someone whacked her, then stuck a pin into her."

"Tipped with a most unusual substance. I have sent it to the boffins at the Temple of Healing for further analysis, but it seems to be an alkaloid of some kind. It killed the experimental rodent in seconds. It might have taken somewhat longer for a human, given the greater distance between entry and bloodstream.

"The alkaloid affects the brain, causing a sensory overload that essentially overheats the sensory nervous system. The result can be...unpleasant."

In other words, this poison tells the brain to go into overdrive, and most people can't handle it.

"Where did this poison come from?"

"Unknown at this time. Pangkot is suspected—"

"Pangkot always is."

"But this alkaloid does not correspond to anything originating in Pangkot." Dark Kelvin frowned. "In fact, this alkaloid does not seem to belong to any plant species found and classified by anyone on New Earth."

I considered this for a moment. "Could this stuff be from one of the places humans are just reaching now? I've heard of an expedition to the Southern Continent, gathering samples of plants and animals for the Advanced Academy at Port Chicago. According to my source, the plants were more vicious than the animals."

"Your source being…?"

"An old sailor, one of the survivors of Drogo Drach's last voyage."

"Oh. Him." Dark Kelvin sniffed. "Jox Custo? He's been making a pest of himself at the Advanced Academy and the Temple of Healing, claiming to have proof the kraken exist, and that they are sentient. Quite impossible, of course. The Founders were very thorough in their survey before they sent the shuttles down to New Earth. There are no other sentient beings on this planet but ourselves."

I wasn't too sure, but I kept that to myself.

"Then you think Audra was gone before she hit the water?"

"Most probably. Or on the way. In any case, not breathing, therefore, no water in the lungs."

"But her clothes were soaked, which means she was in the water for some time. So, Dark Kelvin, how did she get out, above the tideline?"

"That, Eye Drach, is something on which I do not speculate. Perhaps one of the street lizards pulled her out. Perhaps she was cast out by the tide."

"Street lizards would have robbed her, then thrown her back into the river to drift away downstream. And she was above the tideline."

"Then you have a puzzle to solve, Eye Drach. I leave you to solve it. You are certainly clever enough."

I smirked at the compliment. Then something else occurred to me.

77

"Dark Kelvin, maybe you've heard of a new stimulant that just appeared on the Waterfront and in Fishmarket? Some kind of pink pellet that explodes in the brain? Could this alkaloid on the pin or needle you found be related to that?"

He nodded sagely. "It is a consideration. I have examined some of the victims of the so-called pinkies. Quite appalling, what that substance does to the brain cells. However, I did not find any remnants of such a pellet in her stomach contents. Only fish cake and fermented fruit juice."

"That's stimulating enough."

I've been laid out a time or two by that so-called "fruit juice". Cider or perry, fruits of Old and New Earth respectively, picked, pureed, fermented, then distilled to double the alcohol strength. It's so sweet, it sneaks up on you. At least with jack, you know you're drinking something strong enough to knock you out. You don't know what hits you with the hard cider until you wake up with a head pounding from the inside and no memory of what you'd done the night before.

Which is why I stick to brew.

Cider might have been served at that gallery party, but fishcake suggested a snack at one of the food-stalls along the Waterfront. I could try asking around, see if anyone remembered her, but it would be a very long shot if anyone did. Not after a week with so many visitors clogging up Entertainment Row, and both Norland and South Coast fleets in port, sending sailors into the licensed taverns and pleasure houses on Entertainment Row and the cheaper, illicit places in Waterfront and Fishmarket.

"I see I'll have to examine the remains more closely," Kelvin continued. "Luckily, the body has not been taken to the reduction vats yet. I shall administer the correct tests. These pinkies are not recommended by the medicos at the Temple of Healing. Their use goes contrary to the teaching of Saint Hygeia. The formula is a recreational drug, used only for stimulation, not for healing purposes."

"Where did it come from?"

"No one is quite sure. The pellets appeared on the Waterfront soon after the unpleasantness with Pangkot was resolved. There are rumors that the medication originated with boffins in Pangkot, but there is no proof."

And by the Regs of Lorr, you can't bring legal action against anyone without proof. So, until something turns up nailing a specific person to these pinkies, no one gets accused, and the pellets are handed around.

All very worrisome for Atterson, but I didn't see any connection to Audra. And the one thing those pills didn't do was leave round marks on the arms and legs of victims.

I took my leave of Kelvin and left the compound. I had a lot to think about while I made my way back to the center of Lorr. I wasn't looking forward to the interview with Audra's parents, and I wanted to have another look at the studio in the Artist's Sector. Something was nagging at my brain, something someone had said; but I was still dealing with the after-effects of whatever had laid me low the night before.

Maybe a stroll in the Central Plaza would unwind my mind.

iv

I left the carrier at the Guardhouse Plaza and made my way to the green swath in the middle of Lorr where the Admin had decreed there should be an open space for public meetings and cultural events. No permanent structures were permitted within the boundaries of this park, but that didn't prevent the major Guilds from erecting their Guildhouses on Plaza Road, the main thoroughfare that ran around the Central Plaza.

The Merchants' Guild dominated, five stories high plus a cupola on the roof, glittering in the noonday sun. Flanking the Merchants' Guild stood Construction and Transport, one responsible for buildings and infrastructure, the other claiming jurisdiction over moving anything from one place to another, animate or not. .

Across the plaza from those Guilds loomed the gray bulk of the Honorable Guild of Forgers, Assassins, Thieves and Swindlers, better known as the Fatsos. The Entertainment Guildhouse was at the entrance to the Central Plaza, the Scribes' Guildhouse at the other end, close to the Advanced Academy.

There are other Guilds, of course, but they're not on the Central Plaza. The Grocers' have their Guildhouse at the end of Foodie Alley, where the river barges discharge cargoes of foodstuffs fresh from the farms between Lorr and Norland. The Seaman's Guild has one house here in Lorr on the Waterfront, and another larger one in Flatlands. Craftsman's Guildhouse is at the end of Artist's Way, behind Striver's hill, where they can do what they like without disturbing the more sedate citizens of Lorr. As for the Mothers' and Servants' Guilds, they keep their records in modest offices on the Avenue, behind the other Guildhouses.

All the Guildhouses facing the Central Plaza were decked out for Winterfest with electric lights flashing and bits of greenery here and there. Even the Fatsos had got into the Winterfest spirit with a string of electric bulbs over their entrance. Merchants' Guild was the gaudiest, with more lights than any other; but Transport wasn't far behind, incorporating greenery from as far away as Hinterland. Construction had erected a replica of the First Ship on their roof.

This was going to be one memorable Winterfest, marking four hundred local years of human settlement on New Earth, and the major guilds were determined to make sure every human in Lorr knew it.

Construction Mechs clad in bright-yellow boiler suits swarmed all over the plaza erecting temporary kiosks for the Winterfest Fair, where each Settlement of New Earth could tout its particular virtues, scenery, and products.

I strolled past the Entertainment Guild's double platform at the open end of the plaza. The side facing the Grand

Boulevard was for buskers, singing for the casual passers-by on the Boulevard. The larger stage facing the Central Plaza would be used for concerts and staged plays that needed electric amplification and more lights. Between the two stages was the tech area, closed off by wooden screens. No point letting everyone see how the magic was made.

I looked up and down the plaza, taking it all in. Each of the major settlements had its own temporary stand or kiosk facing the Guildhouses, staffed with their own citizens, eager to tout their own products.

Norland had set out a table with typical Norlander products, mostly homegrown and handmade. I spent a year in Norland, one I'd prefer to forget; but I saw someone I recognized staffing the kiosk—a tall, fair female in typical Norland knit tunic and woven wool trou. What was a student from the Advanced Academy doing staffing a kiosk?

"Oyo, Britta!"

She looked around, then greeted me with a smile. "Hail, Kinswoman Drach!"

"How's business?" I asked politely. "I thought you were going back to Norland after your certification."

"I decided to remain in Lorr for a while. And since I am here anyway, I decided to take part in the Norland Winterfest activities." She hesitated. "And there is the matter of compensation for my time. I am now a certified Academic, and must find a position, either with the Advanced Academy or one of the lesser schools. I have hopes of an internship with Instructor Segretti. He had offered it to another person, but she declined."

"Really?" I scanned the table's wares to see what was on offer, not all that interested in Britta's chatter.

She rambled on. "Although why she would leave such a post to settle in the Artists' Sector is beyond belief."

That got my attention. "A female called Audra Martino?"

Now it was Britta's turn to be interested. "That was the one. How do you know of her?"

"She was found next to the river three days ago. Deceased," I added. "According to the Guards' report, she fell into the water. I've been asked to confirm this report."

Britta gasped in horror. "How extraordinary!"

"You knew her?"

"We were well acquainted."

I could sense there was more to it. "How well?"

"She was looking for companionship, and I was willing to give it. We had several classes together. She was curious about life outside Lorr. She had been carefully brought up, sheltered from contacts outside her immediate family and their friends.

"But I think it most unlikely that she would fall into the river accidentally. She was always careful during field exercises, whether on the beach or beside the river. And I know she could swim. She took part in one of our contests at the Academy Games."

Someone behind me poked me in the side, "Move on, this is no place to chatter! I want to see the goods!"

A large Norland female came up beside Britta, glared at her, shoved her aside and demanded of me, "Is there something you want, Friend? We have good preserves, fine cheese and honey, all fresh-made. And if you buy all three, we will add this lovely woolen carry-bag."

"I'll take them all," I said, handing over coin. To Britta, I added, "I'll talk with you later. Will you be here tomorrow, or at the Stranger's Hostel?"

"I have my room at the Stranger's Hostel, since I am still associated with the Academy," Britta said. "You can find me there most mornings. But…"

"Tomorrow," I told her.

I went on my way, now burdened with a large llama-wool bag containing a round cheese, a glass jar of berry preserve, and a small crock of honey. They'd do nicely for my evening snack.

I continued my stroll, mulling over what Britta had told me. I was startled out of my reverie by a carrier whistle. I stepped out of its path right in front of the Pangkoti stand.

Pangkot had the gaudiest kiosk—not one, but three separate stands. The Construction Mechs were just adding the finishing touches, painting red-and-yellow trim on the upturned roofs. I sniffed the enticing aroma of exotic spices and added a hard-paper box of chai to my purchases. I noted the new fabrics draped around the walls and made a mental note to tell Holly to check them out.

In the back of the stall, a wizened bald person who could have been either male or female hovered over a selection of small vials.I suspected those held medications. The Dark Ones would be around to check up on them, but that was no business of mine. I saw nothing that looked like a pink pellet in any of them.

I also noticed the sharp-eyed youngsters lurking behind the kiosk. The Pangkoti street lizards were on the lookout for prey. I opened my jacket in case I needed my bludgeon, took a tighter grip on the carry-bag, and headed for the far end of the plaza where the Scribes had set out a table with mags and books.

I scanned the selection. Heavy-looking tomes with hard-paper covers from the Advanced Academy. Colorful storybooks meant for youngsters beginning their Basic Instruction. Adventure mags with shiny covers depicting exotic vegetation and even more exotic males and females, clad and not. I considered adding some of the puzzle-story mags to my collection, then decided against it. The bag was getting heavy, and I had other errands to do before I got back to the office.

Raised voices drew my attention to the other side of the stand. Jox Custo stood nose-to-nose with a supercilious male specimen, holding a book in his hands. I moved closer to hear what the fuss was about.

"This ain't right!" Jox shook the book at the Scribe.

"*The Voyages of Captain Drogo Drach.* That is the title, as you see," the Scribe sneered.

"It may be the title, but it ain't the book! I've got the original, printed in Port Chicago, and this ain't it!"

"This is the authorized edition, as published by the Advanced Academy of Lorr."

I stepped forward, picked up one of the hard-backed books, and turned to Jox. "Is this the book your friend wrote?"

Jox opened his copy and read from the title page. "That's what it says, but it ain't what she wrote. It says they edited it, reprinted it, put it into proper Lorran. Only, what it don't say is whoever did all this editing left a lot out and changed some of the rest.

"It's not the same as the ones I brought with me from South Coast. I've got those at my stand on Entertainment Row. You want to know what really happened to Captain Drogo Drach, you come to me, and I'll give you one, and I don't charge coin, neither. This here's a fraud, and I'll take it to the Merchant's Guild if I have to!"

I scanned the title page. "Says here it's written by Rachel Craston, edited by Academic Instructor Segretti, illustrated by A. Martino." That last citation caught my attention. A full credit in a book? Unheard-of for a mere Academic student, never done for a Craftsman's Apprentice. And a possible source of jealousy from someone who might have been passed over for the job. Something else for me to look into.

"How much?" I asked the supercilious male Scribe.

"Two silver."

I whistled. That was a steep price for a book, two days'-worth of Eyeing.

"It's not right," Jox insisted. "Come to my stand, get the real book. Not this piece of reptile dung."

"No, I'll take this one," I fished coin out of my purse and added the book to the collection in my bag.

"You wasted your coin," Jox insisted. "That's not the real book, and it's a pack of lies. You want the truth, you come to my stand." He peered over my shoulder. "Hey! You!" He darted into the crowd. "Wait up, I want to talk to you?"

I turned to see who he was yelling at, but he had disappeared into the growing throng.

I shrugged and quickened my pace. It was getting late, almost time for my meeting with Eduardo Martino. I knew I was just trying to delay what was going to be a painful interview for them and me, but it had to be done.

I paused at the next set of kiosks. South Coast and Contramont sat directly across from Pangkot, and what a difference! Pangkot was all color and flash, smells and bells, lots of trinkets and nibbles for sale. South Coast was where the big stuff got made from the iron ore and coal that came out of the mines of Contramont. Pictures of complicated machinery stood on stands next to a long table with a stack of mags at one end and a selection of bulbous crockery-and-glass objects at the other. In between were ore samples and pamphlets extolling South Coast industry.

I took a harder look at the pottery. It was a squashed globe mounted on a metal base, painted with a design of blue flowers and green leaves on a white background, with a kind of upside-down glass beaker on top. "What's this?"

The South Coast female in gaudy wraparound and head-wrap gave me a smile that showed perfect white teeth in an ebony-dark face.

"It's a lamp," she explained. "There is fuel in the base, a wick that can be lit, and this is a clear chimney that focuses the light and sends the smoke from the wick directly upward, so it does not disperse throughout the room."

"What fuel?" I sniffed the glass chimney. It smelled metallic, not the usual tang of alcohol.

"A new fuel, one just developed from the leftover chips from coal mines." She lifted the glass chimney to display the wick, lit it, and replaced the glass.

I remembered the young boffin in an earlier case whose notebook I'd tried to find. He'd come to a sorry end, but apparently someone had taken over the work he'd done.

"Are these for sale?"

"These are samples, which will be sold when the Winterfest is over. We are currently in negotiations with the Vikk family for exclusive rights to sell these lamps and their fuel through their shops," she recited. "After the close of Winterfest, you may purchase this one for five silvers, with a guaranteed supply of fuel for six months. Once you have depleted the fuel in the lamp you must make arrangements for more with the Vikk-shop nearest you."

Aha! Another coup for the Vikks, going around both Merchant's Guild and Admin. One payment for the lamp, the other for the fuel. I didn't ask who profited at the South Coast end, but there was plenty of coin circulating, between the ones making the pottery and glass and the ones putting the deal together. And whoever was producing the fuel was going to make a healthy pile of coin as well.

Under the table was a row of larger lanterns, similar to the one used by the artist, Edard. I pointed. "What about those?"

"They are for outdoor use. Not suitable for decorative purposes. These are already requisitioned by the Construction Guild for their worksites."

I considered the pottery lamp, with its new coal-based fuel. Even though many of the newer houses in Lorr were being built with electric wiring already installed, older places like mine weren't, This lamp might have a brighter light than the alcohol lamp back at my digs, but did I really want to go into debt to the Vikks for the sake of a brighter light? I'd have to give it more thought.

I glanced at the next kiosk. where the black-clad Contramonters touted their religious tracts. After the revelations of misdoings by some of the Contramont Trade Delegation a few weeks back, those didn't get as much attention as the lamps at the South Coast table, and the shouted sermons of the Contramont clerics were drowned out by the chatter of the crowd.

It was the hour when many offices let their workers out from their labors for a midday break before their afternoon labors. Construction Mechs had to dodge the office drones who'd escaped from behind their desks in the offices that lurked in the alleys off the Avenue between the Central Plaza and Entertainment Row. Lads and debs from the Advanced Academy were out of classes, ready to spend some coin. City Guards and Dark Ones hovered here and there, making sure nothing happened that wasn't strictly according to Regs. Registered Thieves were lurking about, too, watching for the chance to snatch a coin from an unwary buyer.

I felt a twitch at the side of my trou and a tug at the bag with my purchases. Young thieves, of course. Shame on me for letting my attention wander!

I swung the bag to catch the one on my right in the face while I snatched at the hand exploring my trou pocket on the left. The trou expert tried to wriggle out of my grasp. He nearly succeeded, but I got a firmer grasp on him while the other one ducked into the crowd.

There was a general outcry of "Thieves!" People scrambled to get out of the way of the escapee, who dodged here and there, only to bump into his mentor, a scrawny elderly male with a scraggly beard who had been overseeing the operation.

I handed the skinny youngster over to a Fatso while scolding him.

"You should be more careful. I could feel your fingers. And your buddy just left you to take the fall. Not smart!"

I knew they'd be punished, not for stealing but for getting caught. If you're going to be a thief in Lorr, you'd better be a good one.

I glanced at the sun. It was time to get back to work.

v

I headed for the far end of the Central Plaza, where a carrier station marks the junction between Academy Way and Garden Road. There was a line waiting for the carrier, mostly students at that hour, let off from their classes for Winterfest. Two pedishaw drivers stood beside their vehicles, hoping for a fare when the passengers left the carrier.

I debated whether I should take a pedishaw to my appointment, then decided to walk. Better to take some time to consider my approach, and get a feel for Audra's natural habitat—how she lived before she braved the rigors of Artist's Sector.

Garden Road travels along the edge of the cliff that slopes down to the Estuary. Before the Merchant's War this was a district of small farms and the few shops and stores that served them. Once the war was over, and the differences between Admin and the Guilds had been straightened out, the farms were sold off and the land taken over by Construction Guild. The farms were split up into small plots, one per house.

Up on the hill overlooking the rows of houses, the wind turbines clicked away, providing electric light for the lucky souls who could afford those neat little homes with their private amenities. Each house had its own kitchen and elimination place, just like Striver's Hill and Arriver's Hill across town. A house in Garden was a sure sign of success for a rising Tech or mid-level Admin, or one of the Advanced Academy instructors who couldn't quite get into the plum places in Industrial.

These were the "middles," fiercely aware of their status, ready to condemn anyone who didn't match up to their standards of morality. No wonder Martino didn't want to draw attention to Audra's demise—it would upset the neighbors!

I glanced at the newsposts at the intersection of Garden Road and Academy Way, but didn't stop to check them. A row of small shops lined the entrance to Garden on either side of the road—a Grocer's Guild outlet selling fresh meat and veg, a kiosk with mags and snacks, a pastry shop, a clothier's stall, and a personal grooming place.

And, of course, a Vikk-shop. Those things were everywhere, purveying odds and ends, manufactured goods from all over New Earth. Spices from Pangkot, preserved fish from Norlands, and the unavoidable dried-and-ground clet. Gadgets, pots and pans, cooking and eating utensils. A few cheap garments, not designed by Jake and Holly. You can get almost anything at a Vikk-shop.

Facing each other at the end of the row—the Garden Sector Guardhouse and the Shrine to Holy Hygeia. Garden Sector would be protected against evil-doers, both external and internal.

Next to the Shrine stood a small square brick building with the linked ovals of the ISA over the door. Garden wouldn't be complete without its own Meeting House, where the lectors could remind Lorrans of their origins on Old Earth and praise the Founders who got us here, built the City of Lorr, protected us from disasters, and managed to establish this tiny outpost of Humanity in the vastness of the universe.

Up the hill from the shops I saw the school, a large building in the stark style favored just after the War. Garden had both a Primary and Secondary Academy, run by the Advanced Academy under Admin guidance, as well as a number of Basic Instruction locations for the very youngest.

The residences began where the shops ended, facing out over the estuary. I strode down the street, a lone figure, my bag swinging from my arm, my small bludgeon handy at my waist At first glance, all the houses looked alike, but there were small differences—at tree or shrub on the patch of greenery in front of the house, or a decorative bit of wood over a

89

door. Each house was clearly marked with large numerals, from Number One next to the shrine to whatever the largest number was at the very end of the road. Presumably, more would be added as more houses were built, until the road petered out in the wasteland between Lorr and the Pangkot border.

More houses perched on the hillside, and I could see even more in the distance. Construction Guild was hard at work exploiting the available land. Plenty of people seemed willing to pay for the privilege of living in Garden.

The Martino house was Number 15. Eduardo Martino had wasted no time claiming a choice plot when the land was earmarked for domestic construction. It matched the others in shape and size—a brick box, one story, set back from the road, with a patch of greenery between the road and the front steps up to a small landing. A puzzle-tree stood in the middle of the greenery, and a row of sundews had been planted beside the front door as a deterrent to housebreakers. The open door of the shed next to the house revealed a pair of two-wheels. The Martino family budget didn't run to a pedishaw and driver.

I looked around once more. No one on the street. I thought I saw a window drape flicker in one of the houses across the road, but that meant curious neighbors, not enemies. I hitched the bag over my shoulder and rapped at the door.

Guildsman Martino opened it at my knock. No obsequious servants in Garden.

"How's business?" I greeted him. "I may be a little early, but I wanted to get this interview done. I have a few more places to go before the light fades."

Eduardo led me to the main room, a large well-lit space furnished with big chairs, upholstered in pink nubbly fabric, and a long matching sofa. A low table in front of the sofa displayed three mags—*Construction Guild Annals, Notable Persons of Lorr, Current Science*. No adventure tales or political screeds or religious pamphlets, no personal items scattered about in random disorder. Impersonal and correct, very good taste as decreed by the Uppers of Lorr.

A sharp-faced fair-haired female sat on the sofa, her back straight, her legs clenched together as if she was ready to leap up and flee at a moment's notice. Her face was taut with emotion held back. I saw the resemblance to Atterson in the set of her jaw.

Behind the sofa stood a black-clad male, his face a mask of concern. His eyes were the giveaway, hooded and wary. I pegged him as a Counselor, a Dark Ones' psych assigned to deal with the emotional overload caused by the demise of a family member.

"Geri, this is Independent Eye Pola Drach." Martino introduced me. "Sara's friend."

Not exactly a friend, I wanted to say. Instead, I amended, "We served together in the Guards."

"Why is she here?" Geri Martino croaked. "I told you..."

"Guildsman Martino hired me to find out exactly how your child came to be in the river," I said.

"Sara said it was an accident. That she fell in and was drowned."

"That's so much reptile-poop." Eduardo snorted. "I don't believe it for a minute. Audra knew how to swim. She wouldn't just jump into the river for no reason, and if she fell in, she should have been able to get out."

"It doesn't matter now. She's...gone." Geri blinked back tears. "Why drag this... this..." She tried to find a suitable epithet. "...Independent Eye into our private matters?"

I glanced at the Counselor, who said nothing. He was a long-nosed, long-faced drink of water, the kind with a mouthful of banal phrases and a head full of theories, none of which were going to be useful.

"Because if someone or something sent Audra into the river, I want to know what it was," Eduard said. "If it was a person, I want that person punished. Sara says Independent Eye Drach can be trusted to keep private matters private, and that's good enough for me."

They glared at each other. I coughed gently, to break the silence.

"If it matters that much to you, Friend Geri, I assure you I *can* keep a confidence. My business depends on it."

Geri closed her eyes and nodded briefly. "Do what you must, then. But be quick about it."

I turned to Eduardo. "May I see your child's sleeping-quarters? It might give me a clue as to her state of mind."

"Her state of mind?" Geri blurted. "She ran away from us. She went to live with those...those...artists! Craftsmen!" From the tone of her voice, her child might as well have espoused a Pangkoti pedishaw driver.

"That was her decision," Martino stated. "She was of age, she'd put in for her stipend, she knew what she was doing. And she already had a toe in the door. She had the illustrations to show her capability. She had talent, she could make her way on that."

"She was barely out of Advanced Academy," his spouse countered. "She had no idea what the world is really like. She had some notion of making a name for herself in the Crafts-man's Guild, away from Academics or Administration, where she belonged. The illustrations were her class assignment from Instructor Segretti. He had no right to put them into that book."

"She took the coin," Martino reminded her. "That makes her eligible for Craftsman Guild apprentice status."

I tried once again to get through that wall of hostility.

"Friend Geri, Captain Atterson asked me to look into Audra's disappearance. She was worried when she learned Audra didn't appear at your family gathering. I followed certain information, and I was the one who discovered her... her remains. I feel I have some responsibility toward the captain, as well as my professional commitment to Guildsman Martino, to find out how she got into the river and then out of it. And to do that, I need to see where she kept her belongings. May I see the room she used when she was here?"

"You dare to pick over her belongings!"

I might have been one of the Dark Ones' scavengers.

"Eye Drach is only doing what I've paid her to do," Eduardo insisted. "I'll show you Audra's room. She didn't take everything with her when she went to the studio. She left some clothes, and her books from the Advanced Academy."

I followed him to a small room towards the rear of the house. I could see the difference from the rest of the décor as soon as I walked in the door.

This was no bastion of Good Taste, but a room that reflected Audra's personality in a way her room at the studio had not. The walls were painted in vibrant blue, with white borders along the ceiling and floor. Her bed was narrow, with a blue coverlet. Two pillows had been set at the head of the bed, and two more decorated the foot, all embroidered with sea motifs. Her books were lined up neatly on a shelf next to a small table that served as her desk. There was an electric light on the ceiling, and an electric lamp on the table. The solar heating unit under the window gave off pleasant warmth.

I wondered why she'd left this cozy nest to live in the bleak cell at the Urbine Studio. What had driven her away from her safe, secure place in Garden for the uncertainty of Artists'?

I checked the bookcase. The bottom shelf held the stuff you'd expect: Secondary and Advanced Academy mathematics, science and literature texts. *History of Lorr, Words of the Founders*.

The top shelf was more interesting. Puzzle-mags. The bulletins from the Scientific Society of Lorr. A program from a lecture given by some Academic I'd never heard of. A tract from the Ocean Preservation Association.

No romance mags, no adventure mags. Nothing fictional of any kind, except for the literature texts. All that was standard stuff—repeats from Old Earth, poems and stories from before the Merchant's War. Nothing current, nothing radical. No sammies written by non-Guild scrawlers, handed out at illicit gatherings in Artists'.

I moved on to the table that had served as Audra's working area. Like the one at the Urbine Studio, it was almost compulsively neat. Paper, pens, ink-jar, graphite styluses, all carefully lined up.

"What's this?" I picked up the large book bound in leather sitting in the middle of the worktable.

"That's Audra's sketchbook," Eduardo explained. "The studio sent it over with her satchel yesterday."

"How did it get here? Messenger, or did someone from the studio bring it?"

"I wasn't here when it came," Eduardo said. "Geri didn't say who brought it, just that it was here. I put it with the rest of her things."

I flipped through the pages, judging Audra's talent. At least I recognized what she was drawing. A collection of vases and glasses, a branch with flowers and leaves. She had recorded the landscape around the studio, the riverbank, even the goats across the road. She'd drawn Cook Hildy, Chezan, a nude male model, even a few of the buskers from Entertainment Row. All meticulously realistic, nothing of the swirly-whirly style of the picture in the Urbine Gallery. Her stylus recorded exactly what her eye saw.

I reached the end of the book and looked closer. There were a few slivers of paper in the stitches of the leather binding. Someone had removed the final pages of the sketchbook before returning it to the bereaved parents.

I noticed another, plainer sketchbook. Not leatherbound, just hard paper.

"That's some of her early work," Eduardo pointed out. "She left that here when she went over to Artist's."

I leafed through it. Audra had been able to get a likeness, that was sure. The first pages had images of Eduardo and Geri. Then, drawings of plants found along the path, pteros that nest on the cliffs along the estuary, even a sketch of her Auntie Sara Atterson.

A page with drawings of critters with several limbs attached to a bulbous body, with what looked like eyes...or maybe, eye-spots?

And one drawing that had me raising an eyebrow. She'd known Britta Drach very well indeed!

She'd drawn her lying down, hands behind her head, and included the hair under her arms and on her crotch.

I closed the book before Eduardo could see. I didn't know what his views were on same-sex unions, but I felt sure Audra hadn't told him about this one.

Whatever was on the missing pages from her working sketchbook must have meant something to someone. I had no idea what it was, but it was one more thing to find out.

I moved to the stack of papers on the desk, turning the pages over, one by one. Some printed text, some crude drawings, and some that looked suspiciously like the photos preserved in the Big Black Box.

"Those images are from the original text of the book she was asked to illustrate." Eduardo indicated the rough drawings. "There were some problems with the South Coast printing, and Instructor Segretti thought highly enough of her classwork to ask her to devise new illustrations. He gave her his personal copy of the revised text, along with some of the images from the initial surveys. It's been so long since they've been used, they were considered unfit for modern printing."

I thought this over. "Makes sense. It's been quite a while since those first images were taken. But...nothing more recent? What was wrong with the diagrams in the South Coast edition?" Jox had really been upset about the changes. Had Audra got in the middle of some weird Academic feud?

"You'd have to ask Instructor Segretti about that. He seemed quite satisfied with her work, enough to include it in his final draft for the Academy Press."

"No problem with the Guild?" Craftsman's Guild is notorious for insisting on artistic standards, refusing permission to use work they deem unsuitable to be distributed. It's a sore point with artists who want more creative freedom, leading to lively exchanges on Posts Four and Six. The Scribe's Guild is worse, which is why the sammies and their writers get no respect from the Guild.

"Not for this work. As long as the Advanced Academy agreed, Audra's drawings could be printed. She even got a credit on the front page. It was one reason Urbine accepted her into his studio. She'd already proven herself as an artist."

"But she hadn't been entered as a Craftsmen's Apprentice, as per Guild custom. She was at the Advanced Academy." Definitely not the usual route for a Tech. Most are sorted out when they leave the Secondary Academy. Only a few of the top tier go on to the Advanced Academy, with the goal of moving into Admin status.

"That was Geri's idea. She's got Academy connections. Audra was studying natural science," Eduardo said slowly. "She was slated to follow Geri's family into Academics. Her drawing was supposed to be a pastime, a hobby, not to be taken seriously. Not good enough for Craftsman status."

"Did she always have an interest in science?"

I checked the mags again. Two of them had cover illustrations showing the huge sea-reptiles that were supposed to have inhabited the oceans beyond the reach of most ships. Are they still there? No one's sure. Only the heavy cruisers and steam-driven puffers can get through the cross-currents and heavy winds that batter smaller vessels, and they're strictly cargo carriers, not about to stop and observe the wildlife. Unless it got in their way, and then, goodbye wildlife!

"She used to often go down to the Estuary to look at the sea-creatures when we moved to Garden. She kept it up through Secondary, and when she entered Advanced Academy, she worked her way into the senior class with Instructor Segretti. Quite the coup, that. He's one of those Academics who's made a name for himself as the expert in cephalopod species, and his classes are always overbooked."

"When did she decide to switch over to Art?"

Eduardo frowned in thought. "I'm not sure. She may have already decided when she was assigned the illustration project, but she didn't confide in me."

"And when was that?" I tried to work backwards. I don't know how long it takes to actually print something as complicated as a book, but there's more to it than just the printing. There's the binding, and the covers, and placing it with booksellers. Like anything worth doing, it takes some time.

"She was working on the drawings last year around this time, just before Winterfest, handed them in after she got back from the break. Segretti was pleased, sent them on, gave her an 'Outstanding' and promised to promote her to an Assistant Instructor position once she finished her final examinations and got her Academic Certificate.

"Geri was impressed by Audra's progress, but Audra had other ideas. After the work was accepted, and she got her first payment, she asked me to find a place for her to study drawing seriously.

"That's when Geri got upset. One of her parents was a boffin, running the assays at the mines. She wanted Audra to follow that family line into the Advanced Academy. I reminded her that Audra had already made more coin for those book illustrations than most Academics made in a season, but Guilds are Tech, and Academics rank with Admin. Rank counts more with Geri than coin." He couldn't keep the bitterness out of his voice.

Family dynamics. Which tier "ups" whose. I could see why Captain Atterson kept her distance from her sibling.

Eduardo went on. "So, I told Audra if art was what she wanted to do, I'd back her. As Founder Fergus Mac Farlaine tells us: 'Do what you will, and do it well'. When she said she wanted to go study art instead of sea-creatures, I asked around the Guildhall to find out who was taking apprentices. Urbine's name came up.

"I'd met him at some of the building sites I'd been assigned to examine, I knew his work. I heard he'd take on apprentices from time to time, oversee their work and ease their way into the Craftsman's Guild. So, I talked to his assistant—"

"Edard?"

"That's the fella. I showed him Audra's sketches, he showed them to Urbine, Urbine approved. If Urbine and Edard thought she had talent, that was good enough for me. I saw to it she had a stipend, paid her tuition, and let her go. I didn't know it would end like this." He swallowed his grief.

I considered the timeline. "Just when did she make the move to Artist's Sector?"

Eduardo thought it over. "Advanced Academy classes end at the beginning of summer. The offer from Segretti came soon after. She went over to Artist's Sector at the beginning of autumn. Does that make a difference?"

"It might." Whatever led to her decision to switch from Science to Art might have also led to her demise. I needed more information, but I wouldn't get it here. "What did she do between leaving the Advanced Academy and moving to Artists'?"

Eduardo shrugged. "Nothing much. Went to the Estuary, went to the Waterfront, did a lot of drawings of sea-critters."

Like the ones in her sketchbook?

"Any meetings with friends?"

"You mean, male friends?" Eduardo got the hint. "Nothing like that. At least, not that she told us," he amended.

I said nothing about the drawing of Britta. Either he hadn't seen it, or he didn't realize the implications.

The Conservationist position on same-sex unions is equivocal. All right for fun and games, but inherently sterile, nonproductive of offspring. Therefore, not to be taken seriously. Either way, Audra hadn't confided in her parents, and she hadn't had enough contact with Atterson to trust her. I'd have to have another chat with Britta.

"Do you want this?" Eduardo jolted me out of my reverie. He handed me the leatherbound sketchbook.

"Not now. Maybe later. Keep it safe, as a remembrance of Audra." I said nothing about the missing pages. Whoever took them had a reason, but whether it was because of their content or for profit I'd find out when I found the pages.

We went back to the main room. Geri hadn't moved, but the Grief Counselor now sat beside her, holding her hand.

"Well, Eye Drach, did you find out anything you didn't know before?" She obviously didn't think I had.

"Maybe. When, exactly, did Audra decide to change from being a boffin to being an artist? Was it before or after she finished at the Advanced Academy?"

Geri frowned at me. "Do you think that matters?"

"It's a break in the pattern," I said. "Guildsman Martino said she was supposed to start a career in Academics, and instead, she went into an artist's studio. Can you tell me why she made that choice?"

"No. She just announced it," Geri said. "We were so pleased at her progress. She was making great strides in her field. And then she just…gave it up!" She waved her hand. "For nothing! For a legend…a rumor…"

"Of what?"

Eduardo glanced at his spouse. "She was obsessed with the idea of the cephalopods being sentient," he muttered. "One of her friends from the Advanced Academy, a Norland female, told her some of the legends about sailors saved from distress by intelligent beings—kraken, they called them. She was convinced they were real, that there was some kind of intelligent lifeform in the oceans, and that the kraken were that lifeform.

"Nonsense, of course. The Founders made a thorough survey of New Earth before they ever landed. They wouldn't be wrong. They couldn't be wrong." He repeated the phrase, trying to convince himself.

They could, I thought. The Founders weren't like the Great Gods of Pangkot, who exist outside Time and Space. They were humans, fallible and frail, ordinary people who had done the extraordinary, surviving the vast journey across billions of kilometers of real space to find the one place that would support them in the immensity of the universe.

But everyone has blind spots, and if you're convinced something isn't there, you don't look for it. And even if you find it, you don't believe it's really there.

"That's something to go on," I told Eduardo. "I'll talk with the Norlander female, see where this trail leads. I'll report tomorrow and tell you what I find out. Will that do?"

"That'll do," Eduardo agreed.

I left them there, wrapped up in their misery, with the Grief Counselor. I headed back towards the Central Plaza, the carry-bag swinging from my arm.

Garden Way had come alive while I'd been indoors. The youngsters were out of school, running towards their homes, where snacks and love awaited them. A couple of two-wheels jockeyed for position with a trio of tri-wheels, probably students from the Secondary Academy let off for Winterfest. A vendor peddling fruit and veg pushed a handcart, loudly announcing the freshness of the wares. A second vendor with a pedi-cart veered away from the tri-wheels.

The fruit-vendor swerved, jostling me with the handcart. As I turned and staggered, the vendor grabbed my arm. I got a brief look at a shock of reddish hair as something whizzed past my neck, just under my ear.

At first I wondered if there were insects in Garden. Then I felt a burst of energy in my head, my vision blurred, and my knees buckled, sending me onto someone's greenery.

I heard a jumble of voices over my head while I tried to breathe. Hands pulled me upwards, someone hauled me onto a moving vehicle.

Then blackness closed in.

vi

I woke up in a cold room, lying on a hard bed, with a stout female Med-tech bending over me. I made a sound that was supposed to be "What happened?" but came out "Whaaaaa?"

"You're awake," the Med-tech announced.

I struggled to speak. "Whooo?"

"You are a very fortunate female," she scolded me. "If you hadn't turned when you did, you would not have survived."

She was pushed aside, and a stern male in Guards uniform took her place. "According to Construction Guildsman Eduardo Martino, you are Independent Eye Pola Drach. Is that correct?"

I nodded, the best I could do.

"I am Guardsman Conroy, assigned to Garden Sector. Can you speak?"

The Med-tech handed me a beaker of fruit-flavored beverage. I managed a swallow, cleared my throat, and said, "Sort of."

Conroy consulted a small notepad. "Witnesses say you fell down."

"I must have."

"Why?"

"Ask the Med-tech." I put my hand to my neck where I'd felt the sting. "Something bit me. Strange bug?"

The female frowned. "Not an insect. There is a slight bruise on your neck. Something sharp must have nicked you. If it had hit you directly, you would not be speaking to us now."

"Poison?"

"A potent alkaloid, we think, considering its effects on your nervous system." .Guuardsman Conroy checked his notes again. "You were found in front of the home of Guildsman Martino. He stated you had just visited him. Why?"

"Business," I said.

"What business?"

"A private matter." I swallowed spit, took another swig of liquid, formed words. "Nothing that would make anyone want to kill me."

I swallowed more of the liquid, gagged on the taste, and got the rest down. It cleared my throat enough so I could speak clearly.

"I'm not even sure I was the target. There were a lot of other people on the street. For all I know, someone has a grudge against one of Guildman Martino's neighbors, and I just got in the way."

"I'll look into it." Conroy put the notepad into the front pocket of his jacket. "You know this must be reported to the Administration as an attempted murder. This poison was meant to be lethal."

"Was it? Maybe a warning?" Or maybe someone wasn't sure of the dosage, or I *was* just lucky enough not to have taken a full shot of whatever it was.

"You might notify Master Assassin Fee M'Farr as well," I said. "If I've been Sanctioned, he should know his people are doing a rotten job. This is the second time in two days someone's tried to poison me, but I'm still here."

I got upright and swung my legs off the bed. My head felt huge. I wobbled a bit, but I got my torso vertical.

The Med-tech shoved me down again. "You're not ready to leave."

"I'm breathing, I'm not bleeding."

"There may be a residue of the poison in your bloodstream. I administered an antidote, but it will take some time to complete its cycle."

"I can't sit here," I stated. "I'm not finished with my investigation."

"And what is that investigation?" Conroy just wouldn't give up.

"You'll have to ask Guildsman Martino. He's the one hired me, and I can't say more than that." I grabbed Conroy's arm to steady myself and got off the bed. "See? I can walk just fine. Thank you, Medico, for your help. My donation will be forthcoming. Where's my jacket? And my carry-bag? I had some food in it, and a book."

I looked around for the jacket. I'd spent a bit of coin on having the reversible lining sewn in, matching the stitching inside and out. And I wanted my munchies and that book.

The Med-tech frowned at me. "Your clothing and other belongings were put aside."

"Give them to me."

She went out and returned with my jacket, now stained with the juices from the greenery I'd fallen on, and the carry-bag. I checked the glass jar of preserve and the ceramic honey-pot. Both intact. The book was still there. The cheese was dented, but edible. Nothing stolen, so robbery wasn't the reason for the attack.

I staggered out of the examining-room into the waiting area with the Med-tech behind me.

"At least take this with you." She shoved a paper packet containing three pellets at me. "In case you you feel pain."

I accepted the packet, sure I would never take the pellets.

"Where's the nearest pedishaw stand?"

"There is a public pedishaw stand at the carrier station, but…"

I made it as far as the door to the shrine. I grabbed for the doorjamb. Someone took my arm and led me to a waiting skimmer.

"Eye Drach. You're alive." Sara Atterson greeted me.

"Sorry to call you out for nothing, Captain Atterson."
I held on to the skimmer with one hand and the carry-bag
with the other. "I suppose the Garden Sector Guardhouse
told you there was a body waiting for your attentions. Too
bad I'm still among the breathing."

"I'm not all that sorry," Atterson said. "Life would be
boring without you in it. What did you do to deserve all this
attention?"

"I wish I knew. My best guess? Someone doesn't want
me looking into Audra Martino's demise. And no, I don't
know who or why. But I am going to find out."

"Her death has been ruled an accident," Atterson reminded me.

"So you say. Eduardo thinks differently. So do I." I took
another step.

"For what it's worth, I do, too. So, Eye Drach, I am going to allow you to continue your investigation. Get in the
skimmer. You should be in your rooms, with your plant, not
running around loose where people can find you."

"Take me to my office," I said. Just this once, I'd accept
a ride in a skimmer.

vii

I clung to the side of the skimmer as it hovered over the Central
Plaza and cut over to Clothier's Alley, where it landed in front
of Jake and Holly's Boutique. Atterson helped me out, propped
me up against the door of the boutique, and the skimmer took
off.

The shop was buzzing with customers getting their outfits for the spate of social events leading up to the Grand Winterfest Celebration in the Central Plaza. Parties, soirees,
dances—all required different attire, graduated in complex-
ity of design and elaboration of accessories. Gowns, trou
sets, long coats and hats, and especially scarves for the outdoor events.

I didn't bother with the showroom entrance, just went
around to the back alley to my own inconspicuous door. It

was unlocked, but no one was in the office, not even Zeta. Everything looked intact, but I checked the desk to make sure nothing had been disturbed.

Then I yelled for Zeta.

The young female hustled through the door from Holly's office, her pink tunic rumpled, her face red with exertion.

"I can't be long," she explained. "I have to get back to work. They're going bongo-bongo in there! Everyone's trying to out-do everyone else, and I'm supposed to be helping the try-ons."

"Anyone come for me?" I looked over the desk. No notes, no messages.

"Only one, but she left," Zeta said.

"Female?" Not unusual. Most of my clients are female. Usually asking me to track down errant spouses or runaway offspring. "Did she leave a name?"

"She just looked in the door, saw it was me, and said she'd be back when Independent Eye Drach was available."

"She asked for me by name?"

"She didn't ask. She knew I wasn't you."

Interesting. I don't make a point of being known. Most people pass me on the street without a glance, unless they look the other way. Short, dumpy females in outmoded skirts or trou sets aren't worth looking at in Lorr.

"When was this?"

"Right after you left. You missed her by minutes."

"Did you tell her where I was?"

"I didn't know, did I?" she whined. "I told her you'd be available as soon as you got back from Garden."

"What did she look like?"

Zeta shrugged. "Like a deb. New trou set, bright green, very flashy. Not one of Holly's designs, more like Guernreich. And a green headwrap. That's the newest thing, these headwraps. Fancy scarves with bits and ends sticking out here and there."

"I don't mean her clothes, I mean her face, her hair!" Was this girl really so stupid, or was she putting it on to avoid actual work?

"I didn't notice. I mean, is it important?"

"First rule of Eyeing," I scolded her. "Everything is important. Everything matters. Think, girl!" I was really angry, to call her 'girl' Not polite, it wasn't her fault, I never told her it was her job as my drone to take names. "Can't you remember anything about this female? Young or old? She spoke...Did she sound like an Admin deb, or did she twang like Flatlands? Hair? Skin? Anything different, anything stand out?"

Zeta squinched her face in the effort to recall the fleeting client. "She had that fancy headwrap, so I don't know about her hair, and her skin was ordinary, not totally dark or pale, just...ordinary. And she sounded like everyone in Lorr, not high-toned Admin or low Flatlands, just..."

I finished it for her. "Ordinary."

She'd taken a good deal of care not to stand out, except for that green trou suit and elaborate headwrap. This female sounded like a professional, maybe one of Fee M'Farr's Assassins.

I'd have to have a word with the Master Assassin. Since I did a small service for him, he and I had been...not friends, but at least not enemies. If someone had put out a contract on me, he'd certainly have let me know. And if there was someone edging in on his territory, he'd definitely *want* to know.

"Is that all? Clothier Holly is really busy, and she's my official employer." Zeta edged toward the door.

"One more thing. When you go home to Flatlands tonight, find out what you can about Eduard Martino. Who he is, what's his family, and especially, how he got from Flatlands to Garden."

"Is it important?"

"It might be. And next time someone comes for me, get the name and particulars."

Zeta bolted out of the room, leaving me to ponder this latest development.

This mysterious female knew I wasn't in the office. She knew I'd be in Garden after Zeta told her, but not when. She'd gone to some trouble to be unrecognizable. All she'd have to do is change her outer attire…just like me. Another Independent Eye in Lorr? Not that I mind a little competition, but it would be good to know who and what this person was, and why I was being targeted.

A lot of mights, ifs, maybes. I'd have to think some more.

I rubbed my neck. The injection site hurt. The poison may have been diluted, but I was still woozy enough to take a pedishaw back to Fletcher's instead of walking. I'd have some food, take care of Ficus, and have a look at my new book.

viii

It took a while for me to find a vacant public pedishaw, but I snagged one and rode back to Entertainment Row in moderate comfort. My neck still stung, my knees were shaky, and I wasn't any longer too sure I wanted anything Fletcher was concocting. I could make do with the cheese if I picked up something at the bake-shop next to Fletcher's.

We tooled down the Grand Boulevard towards the river. The Winterfest crowds were out in force, making the pedishaw driver shift back and forth to avoid hitting a walker or getting hit by a two-wheel. I considered stopping by the Urbine Gallery, then thought better of it. I wasn't up to dealing with a bunch of smarties, not until I'd had a chance to think things through.

The crowd thinned slightly at the entrance to the Flatlands Bridge, then filled out again as workers headed towards their row houses in Flatlands while revelers came across to Lorr, where they could find entertainment in the form of drama, comedy, music or gambling. The male and female licensed sex workers were out in force, trolling for as much business as they could find before the winter storms set in, driving potential customers indoors.

I didn't see Randi and Kira. I supposed they'd got a spot on the stage at Central Plaza with Moggy and the rest of the buskers. I hoped they'd do well and earn their fare south, for Kira's sake.

I got off the pedishaw at the entrance to Foodie Alley. The two orators' stands were empty. I didn't see any of the Prophet's hangers-on, but the big fair-haired male and the two other youngsters who had assisted Jox stood by the nearest food-stand, snacking on fried fish-bits and clet.

I slung my bag over my shoulder and staggered past the fish-stand to the bake-shop on the left of my door. Fletcher's Food Shoppe was on the right. I could smell the exotic spices from the Pangkoti food shop across from Fletcher's. The light was on in the rooms above the Pangkoti place; that meant licensees were hard at work upstairs.

I looked over the selection at the patisserie, bought a round of bread and added it to the other items in the carry-bag. I decided to have something warm before I tackled the stairs to my digs.

I skipped the roast beast at Fletcher's, settled for fish soup with cracked grain. Then, I picked up the pail of water Fletcher kept waiting for me by the outside faucet and took it upstairs for Ficus and my morning ablutions.

I stashed the cheese, preserves, honey and bread in the cold-box under the window and lit the alcohol lamp on the table that served for a desk. The blue flame flickered in the draft from the window. I wondered if maybe it might be worth the expense to buy one of those new lamps from South Coast. Then I thought better of it. I'd be buying fuel for the thing forever, and the only one selling it would be the Vikk-shops. By the time I finished paying for it, I'd owe them more than the lamp was worth.

I brewed up a cup of chai on the alcohol burner on top of the cold-box, settled Ficus on the table, and took out the book I'd bought at the Scribes' table. I don't know how much Ficus understands of human speech. It reacts with rustles of leaves and changes of color, but for all I know it's because of variations in the vibrations of sound or exhalations of breath. According to the boffins, some plants on New Earth have evolved a kind of sentience.

For what it's worth, I treat Ficus like a pet. I'm not sure whether the felines or canines brought with the ships from Old Earth understand human speech, either, but their keepers insist that they do.

In any case, Ficus is something living that requires my care and attention, and I give it willingly. And it rewards me with pheromones that keep me one step ahead of people who wish me harm. It's a good trade-off.

I sat down at the table with the book.

"I just got this," I told Ficus. "It's supposed to be about my father." I started to read aloud, starting with the first page.

"*The Voyages of Captain Drogo Drach, Master Seaman and leader of the Drach Expedition, written by Rachel Craston*." Then I noted the small print under the title. "*Edited and revised by L. Segretti.*"

This was the famous instructor, the one who'd picked Audra to be his special pupil. Why she'd rejected the post and gone clear across Lorr to study something completely different with someone else was a line of inquiry I hadn't had time to pursue. I made a mental note to get on that first thing next day.

Across from the title page was a color picture of Drogo Drach in his seaman's garb. It was weird, looking at an image of the one who'd engendered me. He didn't look much like me, except for the green eyes and golden-brown skin tone. My facial structure was closer to Regina Polaris's. Height and weight? Maybe Drogo, maybe Regina, maybe one of their forebears.

Human genome was a gamble on Old Earth, and no one on New Earth really knows how or why it works. The Big Black Box keeps track of where the genetic lines go, to make sure no one line gets too inbred; but that's as much as anyone can do without the special equipment that got left on the ships after the final landing, when the fuel ran out and the shuttles were stranded.

I tried to remember Drogo Drach. I'd only seen him three times, and all of them so briefly I barely recall what he looked like. The third time, I must have been about ten years old. That's the best memory I have of him.

He'd come to our quarters in the Admin Compound at the request of Regina Polaris. She'd decided it was time for him to see his offspring, so I was presented to him when he came to get permission to leave Lorr on that last expedition. He took me to the Waterfront, showed me the newly-built ship. Fresh from the shipyards in Norland, fit to brave the tides and currents, and cross the world ocean to the Archipelagos, to circumnavigate New Earth for the first time since the Second Ship discharged the last settlers and crashed into Silver Moon. For all we know, the wreckage is still up there. No one has left New Earth in three hundred years, not since the Final Landing, to find out.

My father and I walked all the way to the end of the pier. He gazed out over the Estuary and talked about the oceans of New Earth, and the lands on the other side of the world, and how much he wanted to see them. He patted my head and told me the next time he came, he'd take me with him.

Before he could say more, we saw Regina Polaris at the other end of the pier, waiting with my Mothers' Guild attendants, and that was that.

The next day Drogo Drach sailed out of Lorr with a crew of thirty sailors, plus boffins and traders. None of them ever came back to Lorr...until Jox Custo showed up.

I put memories aside and went on to the next page, where Rachel listed her credentials. Born in Norland, studied at the Advanced Academy of Lorr, specialized in the biology of marine life. She gushed over her meeting with Captain Drach.

"'His skin was dark, of a pale brown. His beard was fair, as was his hair. What struck me most were his eyes, of a piercing green.'" I read to Ficus. "Well, that explains my coloring. Regina's very fair, so I get less of the dark skin, but the eyes? That's Drogo Drach."

Rachel was obviously impressed. Ficus not so much. I read on.

"'I was flattered to have been selected to accompany Drogo Drach on his voyage of discovery, despite my youth and inexperience. It would give me an opportunity to explore regions of New Earth charted by the original Founders but never reached since then.' And I'll bet you a copper bit to a gold piece she was delighted to get closer to Captain Drach," I added to Ficus.

Then, I remembered what Jox had told me about her preferences. Maybe she'd changed her mind once she got on board. I'd have to read the rest to find out.

I skipped most of the stuff about the various sea creatures encountered during the trip through the Drogo Strait, named for the person who got through it two hundred years ago to settle the South Coast.

Then, according to Rachel, Captain Drach decided to make Port Chicago his base for the winter season, when the currents, the tides, and the winds would keep all vessels in port.

"'With the spring equinox came a reversal of the winds and tides,'" I read to Ficus. "So, they headed across the Middle Sea. Except..." I frowned at the next few pages that detailed their miseries. "They got stymied anyway."

Ficus rustled its leaves, bending one of its twigs toward me, as if to ask "How?"

"They got caught up in a northbound current that took them up the coast, towards the ice fields. They ran into bad windstorms, lost at least one crewman when the ship heeled over, nearly sank. She's full of praise for Captain Drach's seamanship."

I flipped past a lot of guff about the fish and sea-reptiles they encountered, illustrated with drawings of weird creatures—a head on top of a long neck, a long-billed fish-like critter with lots of teeth. I could see the beginnings of Audra's distinctive style in the heavy outlines and curves of the monsters.

"Aha, Ficus. Here's where it gets better. 'We reached landfall on the thirtieth day of our journey. We had crossed the Middle Sea. Alas, we were doomed to disappointment. The shore was so pounded by the waves that all we saw was a stretch of sand that piled into dunes topped with scrubby bushes and coarse grasses. Some of the bushes bore berries, but when our Medico tested them, he announced they were laced with alkaloids that rendered them inedible to our human systems.

"There were large reptiles that ate those berries, and one of the crewmen decided to kill one to eat. However, the alkaloids remained in the flesh of the reptile, with dire consequences for the crewman who ate it, even after it had been cooked.' Looks like the plants on the Western Shore are even more aggressive than the ones on the Southern Continent, and those are bad enough. Your cousins don't like being eaten, Ficus."

Ficus's leaves turned green in agreement.

I took a swig of chai and tipped a little into Ficus's pot as a treat.

"Here we go again. 'I noted which of the fruits and seeds the animals favored, on the assumption that the plants would mitigate their poison so the animals would eat them and distribute the seeds. This proved to be true, and we were able to make a paste of the ground seeds of the grasses and the ripe berries, mixed with the flesh of the fish we caught in the shallows.

"'Most curiously, some cephalopods emerged during high tide, and these we also caught and ate.'"

There was a drawing of one of them, labeled *kraken*. Not quite Audra's polished style yet, but I could see where she was going with it. Heavier lines, more curves and curlicues.

"'We continued southward, searching for a break in the dunes. Eventually, they gave way to rocky limestone cliffs, even less hospitable to landing. However, Captain Drach spotted an inlet with a small sandy beach, where we pulled in to refurbish and repair the hull of the ship.

"'We found long grasses with shoots we could boil and eat without ill effects, and supplemented this meager diet with fish and crustaceans found in the tidal pools. A small freshwater spring proved to be drinkable after the water was boiled to negate the effects of malevolent microorganisms. We also boiled the leaves from shrubs to brew for tea, which had a relaxing effect on the crew.

"'While the crew scraped and patched the hull, Captain Drach climbed the cliffs with First Mate Jox Custo, leaving the second mate, Abel, and his assistant Ismail to supervise the repairs. I was given the assignment of cataloging all animals nearby. I was astonished to see reptiles covered with feathers, which preyed on the smaller reptiles.

"'The Captain and Jox returned with the skins of some of the feathered reptiles, which resembled the fowls brought in the Second Ship from Old Earth. They also brought mineral samples, which my colleagues thought might have some value once they were properly analyzed in Port Chicago.'"

I was interrupted by noises from the street outside my window. I poked my head out to see what was going on.

A couple of Mechs had emerged from the door to the upper rooms over the Pangkoti food-shop, followed by the licensees who used the rooms for their clients. Some of the food-shops on Foodie Alley keep the upper floors for private parties, but others rent their upper rooms to the licensees who don't qualify for the better pleasure palaces. The licensees have a place to do their business, the landlords get some extra coin, and the customers get their pleasure in relative comfort. Everyone is happy.

The Mechs certainly were! They tumbled out the door singing loudly:

> Outbound and down, loaded up and truckin'
> We're gonna do what they say can't be done.
> We've got a long ways to go and a lifetime to
> get there,
> Find us a brand-new Earth, and another sun.

Another window opened across the street, and a female leaned out.

"Give it a rest! Some of us want to do business here!" She pulled in her head and slammed the window shut.

The Mechs made obscene gestures towards the window and moved on.

"Just jacked-up Mechs," I told Ficus. I closed my window, took another sip of chai, gave some to Ficus, and read on.

"'We wintered in that cove, but there were disputes Captain Drach could not settle. Some of the crewmen became so bitter at the lack of progress they questioned Captain Drach's leadership. They staged a mutiny, tried to launch the beached ship, but only succeeded in wrecking her on the rocky shore. There was a brief fight. Many drowned, others became disoriented and ran into the interior of the Western Shore. We did not hear from them again, and assumed they had been eaten by the larger predators.'"

Ficus's leaves paled in terror.

"Don't worry, Ficus. Rachel got back. Otherwise. how could she have written this book?" I soothed the plant.

The next chapter explained how Drogo Drach got off the Western Shore.

"'Luckily, one of the small boats used to carry materials to and from the shore was still under repair. Not all the crew had defected. Jox Custo and his immediate underlings helped Captain Drach modify the rowing boat, fitting it out with a mast made from the long tough grasses, similar to what was known on Old Earth as bamboo, and a sail made from whatever fabric we could patch together from the discarded clothes of the deceased mutineers. We stocked water from the spring in the hollow tubes of bamboo reeds, and launched, trusting in Captain Drach's seamanship to get us back home.'"

Ficus rustled again.

"Well, obviously, she made it back," I assured it. "But Captain Drach didn't. At least, that's what Jox said." I flipped some more pages. "We're coming to the end…Aha! Here it is. 'Our crew consisted of Barba, a female boffin like myself loyal to Captain Drach, Jox Custo, Abel and Ismail, two seamen who had also remained loyal to Captain Drach, and myself. We set out at the early hour, when the tide ran strong, hoping to get away before the others could follow.

"'Captain Drach steered carefully, following the current that had carried us southward to find its source. It pulled us eastward, with the winds. We found large patches of sea plants, food for fish that were, in turn, eaten by large sea reptiles.

"'It was one of these creatures that attacked our small boat, rocking it from side to side. Captain Drach attempted to kill the creature, but fell overboard. Another creature attacked him, and he died before my eyes.'"

I stopped reading for a moment. There it was…my father was gone. I'd never really known him, but I grieved.

I picked up the book again, to see how she got back to Port Chicago.

"'After Captain Drach's death, Seaman Custo took over, steering with the current until the boat was deposited on the shore. There we were found, more dead than alive, by a squad of Contramonters who had come to collect seaweed. They took us back to their village, fed us, and brought us back to health.'"

Ficus's leaves turned green with relief.

"And that seems to be the end of the story," I said, leafing through the last few pages. "She and Jox made their way back to Port Chicago. She managed to save Captain Drach's logbook, but the rest of her papers were gone. No real proof of any of her story except for what Jox swore to, on the bones of the Founders."

There was a lot more to the book than that, of course. I'd skipped over the sections devoted to descriptions of exotic plants and gigantic animals. Rachel couldn't decide if they were reptiles with feathers or birds with teeth. Whatever they were, they were fierce and attacked anything that moved, on the theory that if it wasn't a plant it was food.

There were also sections devoted to speculations about minerals found in the interior, and whether or not it was feasible to send another, larger expedition to establish a permanent outpost on the Western Shore. I skipped over that guff, too.

I checked the information page again. In the Central Plaza, Jox had been yelling about the Lorr edition being changed.

Changed from what? This prose was like lead. Whoever wrote this could have made the exploits of Founder Mad Fergus MacFarlaine sound like the latest numbers from the fiscal service surveys.

The illustrations were interesting, but Audra Martino wasn't exactly a known commodity. L. Segretti's name might be known in Academic circles, but it meant nothing to me or, presumably, anyone else who wasn't a boffin. I assumed he was the one responsible for the text.

South Coast lingo is not acceptable in Academic circles, and this book had been printed by the Advanced Academy.

Maybe Jox's version was in South Coast lingo, a lot livelier, and maybe spicier, with more about Captain Drach and this Barba person. Not for a serious Academic treatise, not at all nice! But not something Jox would get upset about its being revised.

Then, I started speculating. What if Drogo Drach's expedition into the Western Shore interior had found more than weird animals and poisonous plants? Rachel said he'd brought back mineral samples as well as fauna and flora. What if he'd found that miraculous stuff we'd all heard about but no one could get at—petroleum?

It was one of the things the Founders had searched for, as stated in their records stored in the Big Black Box. It was supposed to be a superfuel and a lot more, made from the bodies of zillions of tiny plants and animals long gone, buried in the planet's interior for untold ages. Old Earth had depended on it for almost everything. Its depletion triggered wars. The results of its consumption had led to catastrophic conditions that had spurred the building of the Ships.

It was petroleum-based fuels that had enabled the two Ships to leave Old Earth's gravity well, and it was lack of it kept us humans here, planet-bound. The Founders had scanned for it, and declared there were signs of deposits; but they were unreachable, locked away in the planet's mantle underground or under the oceans.

Had Drogo Drach found a source of petroleum? Was that why South Coast was being so secretive about the fuel for their new lamps?

If petroleum had been found on the Western Shore, across the Middle Sea, it would be a game-changer, for sure. South Coast was already pushing the Admin for more and more autonomy. As it was, most of the heavy industry on New Earth was located on the South Coast, away from Lorr, fueled by coal from Contramont mines. If South Coast got petroleum, Admin would have a real problem.

Luckily, it wasn't mine.

I put the book carefully on the bottom shelf of the clothes-press in the sleeping-room. I wasn't sure how this volume fitted in with what had happened to Audra, but it was the last thing she'd done before moving to Artist's Sector. A chat with this Segretti character was indicated.

It was late, I was tired and achy. The analgesic from the shrine in Garden had worn off. I grimaced and swallowed one of the meds, just to ease the ache behind my eyes. I got out of my day clothes, pulled on a sleep-shirt, told Ficus good night, and fell into bed.

ix

I woke up suddenly to the sound of thumping downstairs. It took a minute for my mind to process the source of the sound. I looked out the bedroom window that gave onto the yard in back of Fletcher's, shared with the backs of the lodging-houses in the space between Artists' and Entertainment Sectors. I'd crossed that area with Basher and Velda not too long ago, dragging a reluctant Vikk heiress and a dying singer with us. It was dark and empty now.

I stumbled to the front room and peeked out that window. The electrics on the street were dimmed, but I could just make out someone huddled near the narrow door to the stairs that led up to my digs.

"Death and destruction, what's going on?" I muttered.

It took three tries with the snapper before I could light my alcohol lamp to get enough light to see what I was doing. I hauled the trou I'd worn the day before over my sleep-shirt, threw the jacket over my shoulders, shoved my feet into a pair of shoes, picked up the small bludgeon I keep by the door, and stumbled down the stairs.

"Fool Mechs, getting boozed up on a working day, waking people up…" I muttered as I made my way down to the street. "Why don't you go home, and let a body get some sleep?" I groused, opening the door.

A male body fell into the tiny vestibule at the foot of the stairs. I stepped back, then edged around him and poked my head out.

The street was deserted, not even a lizard or feral feline lurking in a corner. All the food-shops were shuttered, including Fletcher's. The upper-floor windows were dark—the sex workers had gone back to their private lodgings. No clients waited for them on the street.

I turned back to the male on my doorstep, knelt beside him, and turned him over.

"Jox?" I gasped. "Jox, what happened to you?"

I checked for blood. No wounds I could see, no bruises. He hadn't shown signs of sickness when I spoke with him earlier that day...no, it would have been yesterday by now.

"Poison? Have you ingested something, someone stick you with something...?"

He lifted his head and tried to speak, but only managed a rasping gargle. "Raaa...Maaaa...."

"Drach?" I repeated. "I'm here, Jox. Pola Drach, I'm here."

His back arched in a spasm of pain, his mouth working to form words that never were voiced. He fumbled under his jacket, found something, and shoved it into my hands. Then he gasped his last breath.

I was stunned. I've seen more bodies than most in Lorr, but I've never seen anything like this! My mind raced. What to do?

My first impulse was to run back upstairs and leave the presence of the Dead. I'd been drilled often enough—once the breath has left the body, it is a mere husk, a shell that should be reduced to its component molecules as quickly as possible.

The other impulse was to wash my hands immediately. But to do that I'd have to go up and down the stairs to the faucet in the yard. I couldn't leave Jox lying there, half-in, half-out of the door. I knew I shouldn't move him, either, not until the Guards had a look at him.

I still had whatever it was he'd given me in my hands. I recognized the red-backed mag he'd been handing out. Presumably, the original of the book I had upstairs. The South Coast copy of the *Voyages of Drogo Drach*. Jox had died trying to get this to me.

Why? What was different about this copy from the one I had, the one authorized by the Advanced Academy? And why was it different enough to kill for?

I stepped over the body and into the street. First, I looked towards Entertainment Row, hoping to see a stray licensee going back to their digs after a night's work. Not a chance —even sex workers have to take a break once in a while.

Then, I checked the other direction, where the bulk of the Grocer's Guildhall and adjoining food market blocked the end of Foodie Alley. There were a few lights visible, even at that late hour...or maybe it was early, depending on how you looked at it.

People would be bringing supplies in from the small farms upstream from Lorr. Root-veg and leafy greens, fowls and rabbits for protein, goat milk and other dairy products, to be checked for mold and insects by the Dark Ones before being offered in bulk at the food market. The Grocer's Guild would keep a close eye on the produce as the food vendors made their choices. Some of the merch would go to the food-shops, some to small stands here and there along the Waterfront and Fishmarket. Some would be packed into pedicarts, to be vended in Garden and up and down Striver's and Arrivers' Hills.

Unfortunately for me, all the action was on the side of Grocer's Guildhall facing the river, not the back end that blocked Foodie Alley.

Early as it was, I hoped there might be someone on the way to open one of the clet-stands. I thought I saw something headed my way. I shouted, "Anyone there? I need help!" and waved madly to get their attention.

A two-wheel wobbled out of the mist, pedaled by a stout male in farmer's denim trou, a goatskin jacket, and a fuzzy cap, a pair of fowls squawking in a basket tied to the handlebars.

"What's the trouble" He took one look at what was lying in the doorway and started to pedal away as fast as he could. No one wants to be in the presence of the Dead.

"Get the Guards!" I yelled after him. And then, I waited.

It was a long, cold wait. I sat on the stairs and tried to make out the lettering in the red-backed mag. It wasn't easy, trying to read by the dim light from the electrics at the two ends of Foodie Alley. The paper was coarse, the print was the fuzzy type used in South Coast. There were rough drawings, not the elegant cuts Audra Martino had done. The text was South Coast lingo, a mash of Lorran and Pangkoti, spelled as it sounded in Lorran letters, not Pangkoti ideograms. However, it was a lot shorter than the hardback upstairs, less guff about sea critters.

I'd have to do a more detailed search, one copy next to the other, to see why Jox was so outraged about the changes. Was that what cost him his life? Or was there something else going on?

I set the mag aside when I heard the hum of a skimmer overhead. The sun was just reddening the sky over the river when the Guards lit down, followed by another skimmer with the Dark Ones red-and-white sigil.

Captain Sara Atterson emerged from the first skimmer, not a hair out of place, making me look even more disheveled than I felt in my mismatched jacket and trou over the sleepshirt.

"Eye Drach! Can't you stay out of trouble long enough for me to get some rest?"

121

"How's business, Captain Atterson?" I asked politely. "And it's not my fault. Seaman Jox Custo has expired on my doorstep. What would you have me do, leave him here for the lizards and felines?"

"Interesting life you lead, Drach." Atterson nodded toward the body as Dark One Kelvin and his crew dealt with it. "Care to tell me about it?

"Give me a minute to change into something more fitting." I didn't wait for permission, but bolted up the stairs to my digs. I dropped the mag on the table next to Ficus, dipped my hands into the pail of water I'd brought up for my morning splash, then traded the brown jacket for a blue one with matching trou, and a clean shirt. It wasn't pretty, but at least I felt ready to face what was waiting downstairs.

What was waiting was Fletcher. He was not happy to see the Guards skimmer, even less to see the Dark Ones and why they were there.

"Who...? What...? Is this one of your people, Pola?"

"Not a client," I told him. "Someone my father knew, a long time ago."

"A...thing...in my food-shop..." Fletcher sputtered. "No one will come in if they see this..."

"The Dark Ones will take it away," I soothed him. "And no one has to know."

"But...how?"

"Killed," I said. "Poison, I think. Not infectious."

"He wasn't killed here." Dark Kelvin announced, as if that made the situation any better.

"He died here." Atterson was blunt to the point of obscenity. "Why?"

"The cause of his demise is yet to be determined," Kelvin said. "As to the reason he chose this spot to depart this life, I cannot say."

They turned their gaze on me. I shrugged. "I don't know why he came here. I was asleep upstairs."

"You know who he was?"" Atterson stated.

"I just told you. His name was Jox Custo. He was a seaman, sailed with Drogo Drach's expedition from South Coast to the Western Shore years ago. Been working in South Coast ever since. Came back to Lorr with his tales and a mission to clean up the ocean. He's been orating on Entertainment Row. That's all I know about him."

Atterson frowned at me. "Orating?"

"Preaching about the oceans, and how we're all destroying them, the way Old Earth was destroyed. He gave away pamphlets and mags. I have a few upstairs. I can get them, if you like."

Atterson thought that over. "Sounds like a scam artist to me."

"He wasn't asking for coin, just attention. If you're looking for a swindler, check out the character across the way from him, the one who calls himself the Prophet of Doom. He's telling the crowd about a bunch of rodents coming from Out There to destroy our planet, and how they can all escape destruction if they join him in some private enclave in the mountains somewhere. And he's taking coin to finance the escape."

Atterson smirked. "I'll leave the Prophet to Fee M'Farr and his Fatsos. What else can you tell me about your friend Custo?"

"Nothing. I had a meal with him two days ago. He told me what happened to Drogo Drach."

"And…?"

"And that was all. Except yesterday I saw him again in the Central Plaza, near the South Coast kiosk. I didn't say much more than 'How's business?' before he took off, chasing someone."

"I don't suppose you know who?"

"Whoever it was, they were behind me," I said. "Sorry. I was busy buying a book."

"Gone literary, Drach?"

I shrugged. "It was about Drogo Drach. I thought it might have something to do with his disappearance."

"And did it?"

"The writer said he'd been eaten by a sea reptile. So did Jox, so I guess that answers that question."

"No chance this could be related to what happened earlier today...no, yesterday...in Garden?" she amended.

"I don't see how. As far as I know, no one knew I'd be there, except maybe the office drone at Jake and Holly's." Who'd told a mysterious female I was going to Garden, but that was for Atterson to find out, if she pursued the matter. Which she probably wouldn't."

"I had a word with the medico who treated you at the shrine in Garden," Atterson said. "She thought the poison came from South Coast. Any ideas why someone from South Coast wants you gone?"

"I've never been to South Coast, have no connections there."

"What about that lad you got exiled? Gorgeous Gyorgi Delrey? Wasn't he exiled to Port Chicago after that little incident involving the Contramont lad?"

I thought that over, then dismissed it. "He doesn't have the clout his big brother has, and there's no profit in petty vengeance."

"Don't be too sure," Atterson warned me. "The Delreys have a long arm and a longer memory. Gorgeous Gyorgi may not have clout, but Vernor and Selva aren't finished in Lorr, not yet." She nodded towards the Dark Ones skimmer, which was taking off with the remains of Jox Custo. "Keep out of this, Drach. Let my people handle it. It's what we're paid for."

I shook my head. "I can't do that, Captain Atterson. Much as I would like to, I can't. Jox came to this door because he was in trouble, thought I could help him. Maybe I can, maybe I can't, but I have to try."

"You didn't take his coin?"

"I didn't have to. He sailed with my father, that's coin enough. You do what you're paid to do, Captain, and I'll do what I must."

"Try not to get killed doing it. I've got too much paperwork as it is." Atterson mounted the skimmer, and off she went.

I went back upstairs to think things through.

I hadn't taken coin. I didn't really owe Jox anything. But he *had* come to my door, and he *had* tried to tell me something. I didn't know what.

I only knew I had to find out what—and who—had killed Jox...and whether it had anything to do with the murder of Audra Martino.

PROPHETS AND LOSSES

THE STREET WAS COMING TO LIFE. THE VARIOUS FOODIES were starting their preparations for the day. The bakers next door had stoked their ovens. The food purveyors and cooks at the food shops were taking down the shutters. The clet-brewers and kiosk vendors had made their way from the market to their stands along Entertainment Way and beyond to fire up their urns and start brewing their odoriferous liquids.

No one so much as glanced at Fletcher's doorway.

Fletcher and his partner had begun morning chores, fetching water from the outside faucet, stoking the burner with bundles of dried reeds, grinding the clet beans that would be filtered into the urn.

"Just boiled grains and chai," I ordered. Chai and mush weren't the tastiest, but they'd soothe my tum and fill my calorie needs for a few hours.

Fletcher scowled at me. "I don't know why I let you stay here. All you do is bring trouble."

I smiled blandly back. "You won't get another tenant as easy as me. Sure,, you can rent the rooms by the hour, but I'm steady, just me and Ficus. And I come up with the coin every month, unlike someone who may or may not have it on hand when it's due."

Fletcher grunted his disapproval of Ficus. "Sensation plants are dangerous."

"Only to the ones who overuse them," I said. "And I don't."

Not now, when Ficus is still recovering from being uprooted and torn apart. It's doing nicely, but I don't want to strain it.

"Chai!" announced Fletcher's partner, a rotund male called Mazeroni, setting the mug and a bowl in front of me. "Mush." He added a small dish of honey, and went back to the cooking area.

I grabbed the chai, took a cautious sip, added honey to the mush and ingested it. The honey added both taste and calories, and I needed them.

I also needed information. And cleansing. I could get both at the Entertainment Baths.

Once I'd finished the mush, I popped upstairs to care for Ficus. I gave it water, bonemeal and clet, checked its leaves for mites, set it in its favorite spot in the window, and assured it I'd be back by nightfall. I briefly debated whether to take Jox's mag with me but decided to leave it where it was. No one knew I had it…yet. Just to be on the safe side, I stashed it in the cold-box, where I was sure no one would look for it.

That done, I headed for the bathhouse run by the Entertainment Guild. As an Independent, I'm supposed to pay a small fee to use the facilities, but I usually got in on goodwill and my association with Basher Bob.

I dropped my jacket and trou at the cleaning station to be refreshed, took one of the wrappers provided by the managers, did a quick sluice in the shower-bath to get the grime off, and made my way to the warm pool for a good soak. My neck still itched from the dart, my shoulders were stiff from the fall, and I needed to catch up on interrupted sleep.

The pool was nearly empty, just one old female sitting in the shallow end soaking her bones. No one else in the pool meant no gossip to overhear. I was on my own.

I considered my options while I soaked. Entertainment Row and Artist's Sector are Basher's territory. He's the one the licensees and buskers go to when they have a problem, just as the shopkeepers and office drones come to me, and the higher-ups go to The Brain. I didn't like to intrude on his territory.

However, he already knew about my interest in Audra Martino, and Jox Custo's death was personal. I'm as well-known on Entertainment Row as Basher, and we've helped each other out from time to time. I wouldn't be stepping on his toes if I asked a few questions. I might even get answers he wouldn't.

The aches were soothed, the bod was cleansed. I let the warm water wash over me for a bit, then climbed out, dried off, donned the wrapper again, and ambled over to the hairdressing station. Maybe I'd find some of my answers there.

My favorite hairdresser, Angie, was at his stand, with a female draped in a sheet seated in front of him.

"How's business, Angie," I greeted him.

"I'm busy." That he was, dabbing liquid on strands of hair, then twisting each strand around a piece of paper, pinning the result to his customer's scalp. When it was finished, it would look spectacular, if not exactly natural.

I studied his customer's features more closely. "Marta, isn't it? From the Urbine studio? What a coincidence, finding you here! I thought you'd be on your way home for Winterfest."

"My choice of baths is no concern of yours. And my home is Lorr, also no concern of yours." She closed her eyes, clearly dismissing me. I didn't take the hint, but sat down on the chair next to Angie's station.

"That's a really interesting color." So it was. Not quite purple, not exactly red, nothing anyone was born with, but definitely striking. The kind of hair you remember…but not the face under it.

"I don't see that it's any business of yours what shade my hair is."

My, my, wasn't she defensive about coloring her hair. I thought I saw a few gray strands under Angie's fingers.

He glanced at me, then went back to his work. "This is the very newest color," he told me, carefully wrapping paper around another strand. "A new preparation from Hinterland, distilled from mountain plants. It's called henna. You should let me lighten yours, Pola. You are far too beige."

"I like being beige," I said. "You know, Marta, I'm glad I found you here. I need some more information about Audra Martino."

Marta jerked away from Angie's hands. Angie yanked her back into place.

"What is there to say? She fell into the river chasing… who knows what?"

"That's just it," I said. "Her father wants to know what she was chasing. You were her roomie. Did she ever tell you what was on her mind?"

Marta winced, maybe because of Angie's probing fingers, maybe because recalling Audra was painful. "She didn't belong there. She wasn't an artist, she was a boffin. Even her pictures were more science than art. She reproduced what her eyes saw. She had no imagination."

"What about the one in the gallery? It isn't an exact replica of anything I've ever seen."

"Well…maybe not that one. But her other work? Exactly what was there, nothing more. Accurate, but no soul." Marta dismissed her rival's work with a wave, then tucked her hands under the protective sheet.

"I didn't see any of your drawings at the gallery." Implying that Audra's work was more deserving of notice than hers.

She didn't rise to the bait. "I'm going into three dimensions. Sculpture. Not drawing, not painting."

"Was that your work I saw at the studio? The clay model?"

She nodded, and Angie twitched her back into place.

"Interesting. I thought Urbine deals in painting, drawing, décor. I didn't see any sculpture pieces in the gallery."

"Sculpture has its place in architecture," Marta insisted. "Construction Guild and Craftsman's Guild cooperate in exterior decoration. And I don't see what my advancement has to do with Audra's demise. She was nothing to Urbine, nothing at all!" Her voice rose to a screech.

I tried another tactic. "I heard there's to be a Service of Consolation for Audra. I suppose you're going?"

"You may suppose what you like. Guildmaster Urbine may attend. He was taken in by that innocent air of hers. There is no need for me to be there."

"Oh?" I let that dangle.

"Not that it matters to me. Guildmaster Urbine's fancies are no concern of mine."

"He fancied her?" Implying physical contact.

"He said he was impressed with her talent. Not that she had any, besides being an accurate recorder of what was in front of her. She was good at that." Marta closed her eyes, clearly wishing I would go.

I persisted, while Angie continued dabbing and winding.

"You didn't keep an eye on her? I thought you're in charge of new apprentices."

"We weren't friends. We were thrown together by the rules of the Guild. Some of the senior Guildsmen are sticklers for Second Ship propriety, that males and females do not room together unless they are formally bonded. We were upstairs, Chezan was down."

"No other apprentices?"

"Guildmaster Urbine is very particular. He has many commissions and doesn't take many apprentices. He fulfills his commissions himself, does not leave it to apprentices as some do."

"When you ask for Urbine, you get Urbine?" I hinted.

"Of course. Guildmaster Urbine fulfills all commissions with his own hand. His apprentices are there to observe his techniques. Then Audra showed up. I didn't know her before she arrived, and I didn't pay much attention to her while she was there. She would have left of her own accord soon enough. Life in Artist's is not for the weaklings raised in the comfort of Garden."

Marta shut her mouth and her eyes, signaling the end of the conversation. Angie was intent on his work, carefully mixing henna with whatever else he concocted, and dabbing it on strands of hair. My nose twitched at the tangy aroma of the stuff. I only hoped he'd rinse it off before Marta left his stand. The Dark Ones might have something to say about a product that left the user smelling like a stagnant pool.

There was nothing more to be gotten out of either of them. I left Angie to his work, retrieved my clothes and small bludgeon from the cleaners.

So, where to, and with what end in mind? If, as I suspected, what happened to Audra was somehow connected to what happened to Jox, I might as well combine the two investigations. That meant either the Waterfront, or the Advanced Academy. I wanted to track down those youngsters who staffed Jox's stand on Entertainment Row, and the best place to do it was the Waterfront. Like it or not, though, I'd have to talk to L. Segretti, and find out just what had made Audra change her mind about being an Academic.

I opted for the Waterfront, being closer. I had to notify the Seaman's Guild about Jox, anyway, assuming the City Guards hadn't already done so. I had to find that lad Hannes and the rest of them. I wanted to talk to Jox's old seafaring pals.

I chewed over what I knew as I plodded back to my digs via Entertainment Row. Why kill the old male? Did he know something about Drogo Drach's last voyage that was so important he had to be silenced? Or was this just another "accidental ingestion of pharmaceuticals," something for the Dark Ones to be worried about but not deliberate?

A fine point, to be argued later. Right now, my mission was to find out exactly who had it in for Jox Custo, and what, if anything, it had to do with Audra Martino's demise.

And what did either of them have to do with putting a poisoned dart into me?

ii

I strolled along Entertainment Row, which was relatively free of people. At that hour, most of the going-to-work traffic had eased off, and the going-to-the-show crowd wouldn't start for several hours. Buskers and sex workers were sleeping off the previous night's efforts. The only people around were having mid-morning clet at the stands between the casinos and the theater. The sun was shining, the wind had died down. A perfect day in Lorr.

I stopped at the entrance to Foodie Alley. The two speakers' stands were set up, but only one was occupied. The acolytes of the Prophet of Doom were trying to hand out their pamphlets to passers-by, but most of them were casino workers heading to and from their posts. None was interested in rodents coming at us from Outer Space.

Jox's stand was empty, not even his second Hannes in sight. I wondered if the lad even knew Jox had perished. I'd have to track him down, if only to tell him where Jox was. I hoped the Seaman's Guild had been notified by now. I didn't relish a trek across Flatlands to the Guildhall on the the Flatlands Piers.

There was a flurry of activity at the Prophet's stand. The acolytes lined up to greet their master, who arrived in a pedishaw emblazoned with the three gold circles of the Delrey clan.

Interesting, but not totally unexpected. Someone must be financing this character, and the Delreys had several lodges in the Mineral Mountains. Selva was stuck in one, Vernor lurked in another. There was also the rumor the youngest Delrey, Gorgeous Gyorgi, was the result of Old Gregor's union with a Hinterland temptress. As for Old Gregor, no one had heard or seen him for years, but that didn't mean he was actually gone.

Conclusion? The Prophet must be financed by the Delreys, one way or another. He certainly had the good looks and confident air fancied by Selva Delrey, and his followers looked like the sort of beauties that surrounded Old Gregor. Vernor's taste ran to joyboys, not popsies, so I counted him out of this particular scam.

The Prophet descended from his perch. He looked even better by daylight than under the electrics. Tall, light-brown skin color almost a match to me, but with dark hair and eyes, long straight nose, thin-lipped mouth. He wore a long robe over tight trou and undershirt. Good bod, what I could see of it. I understood why females might want to get closer to the Prophet, no matter what he was preaching.

The Prophet greeted his followers with aplomb, passing a hand over each female's cheek. He looked around, assessed the lack of crowd, then focused on me.

"Pola Drach, Independent Eye." He made it sound like a command, beckoning me towards him.

"That's me." No use denying it, but I wasn't going to move at his orders, either. "And who are you? Besides the Prophet of Doom? Any connection to Old Gregor Delrey? You're using his pedishaw."

"I have many friends," the Prophet intoned. "They know I speak the truth. There are beings in the Cosmos, creatures that hate humans. They are coming to destroy us!"

"They haven't found us yet, and there's no way to tell whether they ever will," I countered. "And if they do, we can't do anything about it, so why worry?"

"We can hide from them, in the mountains," the Prophet declared. "Only a few silvers will earn you a place far from their probes."

"Really? Is Selva so hard up for coin she has to beg for it in the street?"

"Do you refer to Master Banker Delrey? She is one of our most fervent followers, but even she cannot provide for all who wish to avoid destruction."

I'd hit a nerve there. He was mortally offended at the very thought he wasn't properly financed.

"And what about the old male who spoke on the other side of the street? Did he take away from your profits, Prophet?"

"An Unbeliever." the Prophet sniffed. "I did not know him."

"Are you sure? His name was Jox Custo, he sailed with Drogo Drach."

"His name means nothing to me."

Not quite true…I could smell a slight change in his body odor that indicated a lie, but what was he lying about? And why?

"In that case, I have nothing more to say to you, Prophet. Have a successful day." I turned away.

He moved in on me, cutting me off. "But I have more to say to you, Pola Drach. You are pursuing a course that will destroy you. You must go no further."

"I'm going where the truth leads me." I stepped back, only to be trapped against the pedishaw.

I don't like to be that close to any male, particularly one with that intense glitter in his eye. He was close enough for me to feel his breath, smell his personal odor. I tried to edge away, but he was there, looming over me.

"You are in great danger, Pola Drach. You have angered those who should not be angered. Be very careful who you speak to. There are matters afoot that should not be meddled with!"

His voice boomed harshly. I'd heard it before, on the road to the Urbine studio. Now I knew who'd accosted me

—and maybe who'd doped my drink at Smokey Joe's. But why?

I didn't have time to find out right then. Another thing I'd have to look at later.

I favored him with a bland smile, sidling around the pedishaw, trying to get into Foodie Alley.

"Sorry, Prophet, but that's my job. Meddling in things people don't want known. Right now, I want to know more about Audra Martino and Jox Custo. Are you sure you don't remember her? She was taken out of the river two days ago. Passed by here two days before that."

I fished the picture out of my pocket. He glanced at it.

"She may have passed by, but I do not recall anything else. There are many who listen to the words of the Prophet. You should do so, too."

His voice was syrupy, his eyes fixed on mine, Once more he tried to block my passage, once more I tried to get around him. I opened my jacket, ready to use the bludgeon if I had to.

Out of the corner of my eye I could see someone large moving behind the pedishaw. Someone in black leathers. One of the Flatland Force, going off duty?

"Oyo! Eye Drach! Is this fella giving you any grief?"

I never thought I'd be grateful to Brutus for turning up, but he broke whatever spell the Prophet was trying to cast. One look at the big Pangkoti in Flatlands Force black, and the Prophet backed away.

"No trouble, Force Brutus," I assured both of them. Nodding towards the Prophet, I told him, "You've been very informative. Tell Selva I said 'How's business'."

I had the Prophet figured out. He must be one of the many males Selva Delrey had picked up on her way through life. She had a taste for exotic types, artists like Rafe Urbine or pirates like Ishka Kunine. She used them, had her fill, and dropped them before they got tired of her. This Prophet might well be one of them, but I still wasn't sure if he was using her or she was using him.

And why drag me into it? Was this personal or professional? No time now, but later…

I smiled sweetly at the Prophet, and took another look at Jox's old stand. No one there, not even a Guardsman.

"Eye Drach." Brutus was at my elbow. "I got a message for you from Master Assassin Fee M'Farr."

That got my attention. Usually it's me who goes to him with information. The last time he came to me, it was a private matter he wanted me to clear up.

"What does the Master Assassin want with me?"

"He's got some information you gotta hear. And he told me to tell you, if I saw you, that he'll be waiting at your office."

"You can tell Master Assassin M'Farr I'll be in my office before noon."

Interesting. The one time he came to me, he made sure he wasn't seen. Something big must be going down. Maybe he had a lead on who was trying to put me out. Whatever it was, it would have to keep. I had other fish to haul in this morning.

Brutus headed back to the Grand Boulevard, and I ducked into Foodie Alley. Fletcher's Food Shop was half-full; word hadn't got out about the evil that had occurred, no harm done. I ran up the stairs, gave Ficus an extra spritz and a dollop of dried clet. It tried to give me a little pheromone jolt.

"Save your strength and grow leaves," I told it while I placed it carefully in the best spot, out of the draft, in the sunlight. Not easy to calculate, with the day so short and the wind picking up.

I picked up the book I'd bought at the Scribe's Guild kiosk and stuffed it into the llama-hair carry-bag I'd bought at the Norland kiosk. I thought briefly about bringing the South Coast copy with me, but decided to leave it in the cold-box.

"I'll be back by nightfall," I promised Ficus. I only hoped that was true.

I went through my agenda for the day as I proceeded back to Entertainment Row. Waterfront, Office, Advanced Academy…I'd be all over Lorr. I decided to splurge on a pedishaw for the day to save myself shoe leather. Like the Mech's song, I had a long way to go and not much time to get there.

I checked the pedishaw rank in front of the Opera House. I was in luck. Daredevil Aziz, my favorite driver, was available. He'd got me out of a bad situation once and was probably the most efficient driver in Lorr.

"I'll want you for the full day," I told him. He grinned, we settled on a price, and off we went.

"Seaman's Hostel, behind the Fishmarket," I ordered.

I didn't care if someone overheard me. I doubted anyone could keep up with Daredevil Aziz when he really put his legs to work. He'd got me through at least one mad dash through Lorr. Now I let him wheel along while I plotted my next moves in this crazy game of feline-and-lizard.

My plans were simple—chat up whoever I could find at the Seaman's Hostel, then get to the office and check messages. From there, find out all I could about Audra Martino and the kraken at the Advanced Academy, complain about censorship at the Scribe's Guild, and deal with Master Assassin Fee M'Farr. Not necessarily in that order.

Of course, things didn't quite work out as I planned. They never do.

iii

Entertainment Row ends at the Fishmarket Bridge where the Waterfront begins. The fishing fleet was in, riding the morning tide. Fishmarket was in full cry, with buyers and sellers yelling at the top of their voices in Lorran, Pangkoti, and variants of both.

Aziz managed his pedishaw with skill, skirting the stands with their loads of flopping fish and avoiding collisions with living beings on two or four feet. He dodged handcarts with aplomb, waving at his Pangkoti compatriots, exchanging greetings and shouting warnings at anyone who got in his way.

"Turn here," I ordered when we got to the alley at the end wall of the Fishmarket.

The Seaman's main Guildhouse had been moved to Flatlands when the big docks were built to accommodate the large steam-driven freighters from South Coast and Pangkot. They kept the old Guildhouse as an annex and hostel for the sailors who still docked at the Waterfront.

It was tucked into the alley behind the Fishmarket, a relatively small cinderblock structure built in the previous century but still serviceable. Nothing so grand as the Guildhouses on the Central Plaza, it served its function, the best that could be said for any building in Lorr.

Aziz pulled up in front of the old building. A clet-stand was set up against the back wall of the Fishmarket, with a bench to accommodate customers; a female of middling age sat with her urn to serve anyone who ventured past. A trio of oldsters relaxed on the bench, leaning against the back wall of the Fishmarket.

One was large and fair, one was short and brownish, and one was long and lean with very dark skin. They wore Seamen's canvas jacket and trou, and their odor nearly overwhelmed the aroma of the Fishmarket on the other side of the wall. Clearly, none of them had availed themselves of the services of the Fishmarket Baths for some time.

"Wait here." I slid out of the pedishaw seat while Aziz obediently remained on the saddle. I strolled up to the bench and greeted the oldsters. "Oyo! How's business, Elders. May I have a few minutes of your time?"

"We got nothin' but time." The large fair seaman grinned at me.

"I got this book, it's supposed to be about Captain Drogo Drach, but there's a fella on Entertainment Row says it's a fake. Do any of you know Jox Custo? He's yelling on about how the Scribes' book is wrong, he's got the real skinny about Captain Drach. He's even got the South Coast book to prove it. So, which is the right one, his book or the Scribes'?"

"How d'ya mean?"

"It's about Captain Drach. The Scribes' book says he was taken by some huge creature from the Middle Sea. Is that true?"

The darkskin nodded. "Jox is in port. Ask him yourself. But do I believe a sea monster ate Captain Drach? Not deathly likely!"

"More likely he got muzzy," the largest male chortled. "Fell in the drink and couldn't find his way out."

"Nah. A jealous male potted him!" the smaller darkskin sniggered.

"But the reptile story is the one in this book." I fished out the item from my carry-bag. "See? It says right here…"

The lanky one spat. "What do them scribes know? They wasn't there. Jox said that book's a fake, and he was there, so he should know."

"When was this? When did he find out about the book? When did you see Jox last?"

"That's a lot of questions." The tallest of the trio looked me over. "Who's asking?"

"Pola Drach, Independent Eye."

"Drach?" The short one picked up on it. "The Captain's get?"

I nodded. No point in denying it.

"And you're Eyeing? For who?" The middle seaman scowled at me. "I got no time for Admin, and I know the Seaman's Guild Eyes. You ain't one of 'em, and you ain't Guards, neither."

"I'm Independent, not connected with Admin or any of the Guilds. I sometimes work with Basher Bob."

The trio muttered together. Then, the middle sailor said, "We know Basher. If he says you're a righter, then you are."

"So, what can you tell me about Jox? When did he get into Lorr, and what has he been doing since he got here?"

The short one took up the tale. "Jox came in about a week ago, got a bed and a meal, went out again. When he come back, he was in a state. Insisted he had to see folks at the Advanced Academy. Don't suppose they'd have anything to do with the likes of him."

"Someone did," the oldest said. "He went out yesterday, said he'd found someone who believed in him. Didn't come in last night, though. Don't know where he went."

"I have bad news. He fetched up on my doorstep this morning. The Dark Ones have him now."

The three oldsters reacted with shudders, gasps, and moans.

"I told him he was playing a dangerous game," the big one said. "I'm Jim Hawkeye. You can ask anyone on the Waterfront, they'll tell you I know what I'm talking about. You don't last as long as I have without you sail careful, watch the currents, get out the way of the sea critters."

"Including the kraken?" I guessed.

"Don't know nothing about kraken," Jim said, but his eyes shifted away, sure sign he was lying.

"What about Jox?" I turned to the other two. "Who are you, and how well did you know Jox?"

"Never sailed with him, didn't know him. They call me Billy Bones." That was the one in the middle, the tall skinny one. I could see how he got the nickname.

The scrawny oldster on the end of the bench scratched his scruffy chin. "I'm Izzy Hanson. I come from Norland a good while ago, sailed with Captain Drach when he first come to Lorr." He grinned, revealing toothless gums. "I was there when the Admin female, Regina Polaris, came aboard to check out the ship for cargo tolls. You could tell they was drawn, first time they laid eyes on each other."

And I am the result, I thought. "What happened to Jox when he came back to Lorr? I saw him on Entertainment Row, pushing some kind of Conservationist program at his stand, yelling about cleaning the oceans of waste, saving the great reptiles."

"Waste of time," Jim scoffed. "He said he was going to Admin with his findings, once he'd checked in at the Guild-hall to verify his standing as a Master Seaman, collected his badge and sigil. Said he'd lost them in some storm on the Western Shore. Told a whopping good tale about it!"

The other two nodded and chortled to each other.

"Jox told a good tale," Billy agreed. "But when he tried to get to the Advanced Academy folk, they'd have nothing to do with a Seaman, not even an officer. Nothing below a captain would rate with them. I tried to tell Jox, but he insisted on chasing down the one who writ the book."

"First Mate usually counts for something," I put in.

"Not with those grand folk." Billy snorted. "He was right furied about that. Said he'd take his message direct to those who were most affected. That's when he set up shop on Entertainment Row with his youngsters."

"I heard him," I agreed. "Where are the youngsters he had with him? Are they housed here, at the Seaman's Hostel?"

"They come with him from South Coast," Billy volunteered.

"Not registered with Lorr," Jim added. "They lodge somewhere else. Maybe Fishmarket, maybe at one of the places in Flatlands. Jox let them go their own way, so long as they stood up with him at that stand of his."

"Any idea which lodging?" I didn't fancy a long slog across Flatlands to the main piers where the heavy-duty freighters from Pangkot and South Coast docked.

Billy thought a bit. "There's a South Coast lodging just across the bridge in Flatlands. I think they might be there."

Another thing to chase down, but not immediately. I'd give Atterson a little time to do my work for me, let Hannes and the rest of them know Jox had met his end.

"It's dry work, answering all these questions," Jim hinted.

I got the message. "Thank you for your information, Elders." I handed each of them a coin. "This for clet, or brew if that's your choice. And be ready to answer some more questions," I added. "It's likely Captain Atterson of the Guards' Special Squad will be around. Tell her what you told me."

"One thing…" Jim said. "It may be nothing, but there was some female sniffing around yesterday, looking for Jox."

"A female? Description?"

"Not old, not too young. Couldn't say what she looked like, but she wore something green and glittery, and had one of them new headwraps with bits and ends sticking out. Not what you'd expect to come to see an old Seaman, for sure."

Interesting. I pulled out the picture of Audra. "Was this the female?"

Jim glanced at it, then looked harder. "Not the one asking for Jox, but could be I saw her, maybe last week? Can't be sure, time sort of drifts when you're beached."

"She had an interest in the kraken," I ventured.

The three oldsters exchanged knowing looks.

"We don't talk about kraken," Jim stated.

"It's bad luck," Billy added.

"They don't like it," the third sailor said.

"How do you know?" I wondered.

"Blue-water Seamen know. The kraken stay away from us, we stay away from them. Let them go, they're fine. Catch them? They're wary, they'll fight. Don't mess with them. Don't ask, don't tell, that's the way it goes."

And that was all I was going to get out of this trio.

I returned to where the pedishaw stood parked and got back in.

"Take The Avenue to Clothiers' Alley," I ordered Aziz.

I wanted to chew over what I'd learned.

The Avenue is the heart of Business Sector, a strip of four- and five-story buildings that line the broad street between Entertainment Row and Central Plaza, leading into The Boulevard. Shops and galleries fill the ground floors of the buildings, offices are upstairs. Not the most fashionable of either, but the Avenue is where those Lorrans who aren't quite up to the Boulevard do their buying and selling. The inevitable clet-stands and food-carts provide sustenance for shoppers and office drones.

This is where the real business of Lorr is conducted, under the eyes of the Guilds. Everything is organized in Lorr, everyone knows what they're supposed to be doing.

Of course, there are always people who want more than they've got, and that's why we have the Regs, and the Guards to enforce them. And there are people who don't fit into the neat slots of the Guilds, which explains Independents like me.

It was getting on for noon. The Avenue is crowded at that hour, two- and three-wheels, public and private pedishaws, and pedestrians filling the road and sidewalks. Messengers carrying packages, office drones hustling to meetings, shoppers comparing prices in this or that boutique. Aziz managed not to hit anyone, or let anyone hit us, while I thought over what I'd learned.

My eye was caught by the black-lacquered pedishaw parked in front of Jake and Holly's boutique. The last time Fee M'-Farr had consulted me, he'd done it incog, making sure no one knew he'd been there. He'd been spotted anyway, but he had been trying not to be.

This time he might as well have announced his presence with a brass band and full complement of buskers. Jake and Holly would not be pleased.

Aziz stopped his pedishaw and helped me down.

"Take a clet break," I told him. "I have a meeting."

"Long?" Aziz jerked his head at the Fatso pedishaw.

"Not very, I hope. Stay nearby, I've got a few more errands before nightfall."

143

I went around to the back alley, one of the many unnamed and unnumbered access points where the Dark Ones pick up discarded items, carefully separated into containers for edible and inedible scraps. Nothing gets wasted in Lorr.

The door to my office stood open. I grimaced. Someone showing off lockpicking skill, but better than having the door bashed in.

Fee M'Farr was sitting in the uncomfortable chair, across from Zeta, who jumped up from the comfy chair behind my desk as soon as she saw me.

"I couldn't stop him," she blurted before I could say anything.

"Master Assassin M'Farr goes where he wants to go," I said, taking my rightful place behind the desk, ousting Zeta to the corner. "No fault of yours. How's business, Master Assassin?"

He rubbed his nose in a fit of embarrassment. "Eye Drach, I heard what happened to you yesterday. I wanted you to know, not one of mine."

"I didn't think so," I told him. "Not your style. Dropping something in my drink, sticking a needle in my neck? I didn't think you were going in for poison. That's sneaky, and your people aren't sneaky. A knife in the gut or a bludgeon on the noggin, that's your way."

"Not anymore. I've been trying to keep things quiet," he said. "Go by the Regs, I tell my people. Show your badge and sigil, let people know what to expect. The shoppers know about Thieves, and if someone's stupid enough to be taken in by Swindlers, it's their own fault for being greedy."

"What about that character on Entertainment Row, the one that calls himself the Prophet of Doom. Is he one of yours?"

"He's not in the Guild,.He claims he's covered under the Regs for Religious Liberty. I'm keeping an eye on him, though." He shifted uneasily in the chair. "And this business of attacking you...I got the word out. Drach is one of ours, hands off! I don't like it when someone takes a contract outside the Guild."

I rubbed my neck, which was starting to itch again. I wasn't too happy about being associated with the Fatsos. I *am* supposed to be Independent.

I changed the subject. "Could this be connected to those pink pellets being handed around the Waterfront and Fishmarket like sweeties? The Dark Ones boffins know about them, they've posted warnings about them. Any word from Fishmarket about where they come from?"

M'Farr's frown deepened into a scowl. "One of those street lizard youngsters had his head blown out from taking one. Word I got was, he took it from someone he was chumming with at the Green Dragon. I've got my people keeping an eye on the Waterfront, especially anything coming from Pangkot."

"I have a source who says the stuff is nothing like what comes out of Pangkot. More likely South Coast, or maybe Hinterland."

M'Farr slammed his fist on my desk. "Deathly excrement! I don't care a deathly futter what the South Coast Junta pulls in their own territory, but I told them keep out of mine!"

"This may not be South Coast," I said. "This Prophet's got a Hinterland tang to his voice. More than that, he's using a pedishaw with the Delrey sigil. There may be a connection with the Delrey clan—they've got lodges in Hinterland. And he as good as told me he's being financed by one of the Delreys."

"Hinterland don't interest me." M'Farr waved the scattered settlements in the Mineral Mountain aside. "There isn't enough coin to make it worth my while to move in, and they are too busy fighting each other to bother about Lorr.

"But the South Coast Junta can keep their deathly hands off Lorr!" M'Farr was definitely peeved. "If one of their Assassins is in Lorr, I'll find them and take care of them. I owe you, Drach, and I'll pay this debt."

145

He marched out, leaving me wondering whether I really wanted Fatso protection.

v

I sat quietly, trying to absorb all I'd heard and seen in the last hour. Of one thing I was certain—both Audra Martino and Jox Custo were connected to that book *The Voyage of Drogo Drach*.

I slid the book out of the carry-bag and took another look at the inside front page. Nothing unusual, other than the citation for the illustrator. The little I'd read of the South Coast version during my wait on the stairs didn't seem too different, other than the illustrations. I would have to sit down and compare the text of the two more carefully, but not now. I had work to do.

I slipped through Holly's private office to the try-on booth where I kept a private stash of jackets and scarves. I picked out a particular jacket—drab gray-green on the outside lined with a gaudy green-and-yellow check that would give anyone pause, cut in a style fashionable three years ago. I turned the jacket inside out, added a long red scarf to the ensemble, slung the carry-bag with the book over my shoulder, and headed out the door.

Holly had other ideas. She grabbed my free arm before I could leave.

"You can't go out looking like that! Use the back door!"

"Afraid I'll turn the customers away?"

"Bad enough you had Fee M'Farr's pedishaw outside," Holly groused. "At least I can say he was buying something for his latest popsy. But if you go out of the shop in that outfit, I'll be ruined! And what is that?" She pointed to the bag.

"It's a carry-all from Norland. They're selling them at their kiosk on the Central Plaza."

Holly eyed it with distaste. "It doesn't go with that jacket."

"It's not supposed to."

"Does anyone else sell them?"

146

"Not that I know"

"An exclusive?"

"Like I said…" I was itching to get going. "I suppose they'd do a deal for whatever's left after Winterfest."

I left Holly contemplating her next financial coup, called Aziz away from his pals at the clet-stand, and ordered, "Academy Way".

vii

While Aziz threaded his way back in that direction, I wound the scarf around my head and tied it at the nape of my neck, letting the ends dangle down my back. I mentally rehearsed my next encounter while Aziz turned onto Academy Way, the main road through Industrial Sector.

A hundred years ago this was where manufactories turned refined ore from Hinterland into everything from two-wheels to eating utensils. The factory owners built rows of small houses for the Mechs, slightly larger ones for the Techs to oversee the production lines.

Then there arose objections from the boffins at the Advanced Academy at the other end of the road. The factories were sending smoke into the atmosphere, the odors were distracting, the detritus from the factories was causing illness. And the Mechs and Techs were rowdy, annoying the students and instructors.

One by one, the factories closed, their buildings taken over by Dark Ones or appropriated by boffins from the Academy. Now the factories lay across the river in Flatlands, or down the coast in Pangkot; and the rows of houses are occupied by Techs and boffins associated either with the Temple of Healing or the Advanced Academy.

The Scribes took over one of the Tech houses for their Guildhouse instead of building one for themselves. It's not as if Scribes need a big place, not like Entertainment, which has to put on a show, or Merchants, which has a whole battery of office drones keeping records of who's selling and buying, and for how much. Most of the Master Scribes do their work from home, and since a lot of the Scribes don't earn their living writing, they have a reciprocal agreement with the Academy and Admin to allow double memberships with whatever other Guild they may depend on for coin.

Most of what goes on at the Guildhouse is handled by office drones, setting rates for mag and book writing and fending off any complaints against what's been printed in the mags. Merchant's Guild handles the actual sales, giving a cut to the printers, who give a cut to the scribes who wrote what gets printed in the mags. By that time, there's not much left, which explains why Scribes have double incomes.

"Stop here," I ordered as Aziz passed the Scribes' Guildhouse. He found a place on the street between the two-wheel racks.

I slid out of the seat. "Wait for me. I won't be long." At least, I hoped I wouldn't. You never could tell with Guilds. There was always someone who had to bar the door against anyone who didn't come up to their standards, whatever those were.

Aziz sighed deeply. There was no clet-stand in sight. No place for him to sit except on the saddle of the pedishaw. He folded his arms and prepared to wait.

I straightened my jacket and marched into the Scribes' Guildhouse as a truculent fish-vendor, ready to do battle. The door opened into a dark hallway lit by a single shaded electric lamp in the ceiling. A sleek male sat behind a table barring further entrance. He regarded me with raised eyebrows.

"May I be of service?" His tone implied the service should come from me, not him.

"You sure can!" I fished the book out of my bag and shook it at him. "I want to report a fraud!" I yelled in my most raucous Waterfront accent.

"Indeed?" The male sniffed. You'd think he smelled fishy remains on my jacket.

"You bet! I got this-here book at the kiosk in Central Plaza. It's supposed to be about Captain Drogo Drach, the great explorer, and it's supposed to be true."

"And…?"

"There's bits missing. That's my complaint. When I sell a carp, I say it's a carp, it ain't a stingray or a shark. This is supposed to be about Captain Drogo Drach, and he was a one for the females—they still talk about him on the Waterfront. There's a few bits in this, but not all of it. And there's a fella in Entertainment Row, he's giving out different copies. This one cost me two days' sales, and if it ain't what it says it is, it's a fraud!"

The Scribe favored me with a condescending smile.

"Friend, you should read the small print." He pointed to the notice on the reverse of the title page. "This edition has been revised, for use in the City of Lorr. The original text was written in South Coast, and was submitted to the Scribe's Guild for vetting and editing."

"Editing, you say?" I echoed. "You mean it ain't what I paid fer!"

"That is not the concern of the Scribe's Guild. If you are unhappy with your purchase, you should take it up with the ones who sold it to you, or the Merchant's Guild. Be well, Friend." It was an obvious dismissal.

"What about the one who writ it?"

"For that, you would have to go to the Advanced Academy."

"And see who?"

"The name is on the title page." He flipped the book open and pointed to the small print—*L. Segretti*. "Be well, and have a profitable day."

I backed off, like any fish-vendor would when faced with a Guild superior. Something was off, I could sense it. The Scribe wasn't just sniffy; he was really unhappy that first text had surfaced.

I stuffed the book into my bag and stomped away, the very picture of an outraged Waterfronter. However, I didn't leave immediately. I hovered in the shadows of the doorway, turning my jacket inside out, switching the garish lining for the drab exterior. I tucked the head-wrap inside the collar so only a sliver showed.

I heard the ting-click of the comm. I'd assumed the Scribe's Guild would have one, most Guildhouses did, but I didn't think there would be instant communications at the front desk. That was reserved for the Guildmasters, in the upper tiers.

The Scribe didn't bother to keep his voice low. Thanks to Ficus, my auditory receptors could take in every word.

"There's been a complaint…some Waterfront female… the Drogo Drach book…Of course not! I sent her away to the Advanced Academy…I don't think so. She won't get far there… Segretti? He knows nothing. But I thought you should be informed. If the Posts got wind of this…Yes, of course, if she comes back…Yes, I understand."

Interesting. I'd obviously stirred up something, but what?

"Strangers' Hostel," I told Aziz. I hoped my connection there would shed some light on what was getting murkier by the minute. Someone didn't want the truth about Drogo Drach's last voyage to reach Lorr, but why? And what did it have to do with Audra Martino? Maybe I'd find more answers with Audra's particular friend at the Advanced Academy.

vii

My main connection with students at the Advanced Academy is the Norland female Britta, who claims kinship with me through Drogo Drach. I hoped I'd catch her at the hostel before she left for her stint at the Norland kiosk in the Central Plaza.

I had to wonder why she'd decided to stay in Lorr for Winterfest. They take it seriously in Norland, a lot of revelry before the ice sets in for the long dark cold winter. There's a lot of jack, a lot of food, a lot of music and dancing, and a lot of miscellaneous futtering. Most Norland infants are born in the autumn because of all the fun and games at Winterfest.

I found Britta Drach going out just as I arrived. "Oyo! Student Drach!" I hailed her from the pedishaw. "How's business?"

She looked around, then recognized me. "Eye Drach?"

"It's me. Have you a moment to spare? I have a few questions to ask."

"I am on my way to meet with my instructor." Britta edged away from the pedishaw. "What do you want of me?"

"Step up, sit with me for a moment. I need a little information about one of your former classmates. And maybe about one of the instructors."

She eyed the vehicle dubiously, assessing its capacity and Aziz's physique.

"There's room for two," I assured her. "And Aziz is stronger than he looks."

Britta looked up and down the street. No one else was in sight. She hoisted herself into the pedishaw, which groaned under her heft. She wedged herself next to me.

"Which classmate and which instructor?"

"Audra Martino." I watched her carefully for reactions. "And Boffin Segretti."

"Instructor Segretti is my mentor. He is an expert in the field of cephalopod development, which is my field of study."

"As in kraken?"

"They are not supposed to exist," Britta stated. "According to the instructors at the Advanced Academy, who rely on the information from the Founders' initial surveys, there are no other sentient beings on New Earth, only us humans. All others are mere animals, relying on instinct rather than intellect for survival."

"But you don't believe it."

"There are stories, sailors' tales, of having been attacked by one kraken, only to be saved by another. These are generally considered fables, stories told for amusement. No one in Lorr believes them,"

"But you do?"

Britta shrugged. "I cannot say whether or not I believe the sailors. Instructor Segretti has initiated certain experiments on the creatures found in the waters around Lorr. I am assisting him in these experiments. It is interesting work"

"I heard he asked Audra Martino first."

"Audra had other plans."

"She moved across town to Artists' and took to sketching," I said. "And wound up in the river a week ago."

Britta drew her breath in sharply, stung by my brutal assessment.

"With no good explanation of why she went in," I added. "Nor how she got out. I found her on the bank, above the high water mark."

"Why do you tell me this? I barely knew Audra."

"Now, that's an interesting turn of phrase," I said. "I saw the sketch she made of you. *Bare* is the word for it. So, I have to assume you knew each other well."

Britta hesitated. "I cannot deny it. We shared several classes, we collaborated on projects for Instructor Segretti's. We were...friends, of a sort." She choked, barely concealing her emotion.

"That wasn't quite all." I lowered my voice and slid into the Norland dialect. "Audra's sketch was quite detailed. You have a small mole on the right breast, near the..."

"Yes, we were...intimate." Britta finally admitted. "She was looking for companionship. I was lonely, away from home at Winterfest last year. We found each other."

"But?" I heard the hesitation in her voice.

"She was more interested in my tales than in my person. And perhaps she was frightened by extreme emotions. After Winterfest, our meetings grew less frequent."

I caught the drift. "Perhaps you wanted more than she was prepared to give. You know she was raised in the Conservationist philosophy. Same-sex unions are unprofitable, since they do not result in offspring."

"That is so." Britta sighed. "And perhaps I was too… urgent. I felt something more for Audra than she did for me, and it may have upset her."

"Did you feel animosity towards Audra? For rejecting your…friendship? Or, perhaps, for grabbing Instructor Segretti's attention?"

She turned to face me. "Never! We continued to work together in class. She just…" She bit her lip and looked away. "There was a coolness, yes. But I did not resent her expertise in providing Instructor Segretti with illustrations for his book. She had a gift, I did not. If you are implying that I would harm her? No, I would not."

"Someone did."

"It was not I," Britta stated firmly. "I did not see Audra after the certification ceremonies."

"You didn't go to the gathering afterwards? At her parents' home in Garden?"

"I was not asked," Britta said stiffly. "Although, I heard that she moved to Artist's to pursue an apprenticeship with Guildmaster Urbine."

"Didn't she send you an invitation to the gallery opening?"

"She did not." Britta shifted in her seat.

"I thought you might have gone anyway, if only to see what she was doing."

Britta tried to slide out of the pedishaw. "I did not. And now, if you do not mind, I will be late for my meeting with Instructor Segretti."

"Aziz can take us up there. Aziz, we can go ahead now."

As the pedishaw lurched forward, Britta blanched. "Will he be all right? We are not a light load." Meaning she outweighed me by several kilos.

"Like I said, he's stronger than he looks. Tell me more about Audra. Did she make other friends?"

"She did not make friends easily." Britta said. "I think I was the only one she was close to. She never invited me to her home. I never met her family. I think she found her parents…intimidating. Our relationship was brief, if intense."

More on her part than Audra's. That made sense. The males in Norland are away for most of the year, so the females turn to each other for friendship, companionship… sometimes intimacy. If Britta initiated something, and Audra was attracted, she might have been caught between desire and dread. Now I understood part of why she wanted to get away from Garden, and the Advanced Academy.

I changed my approach to something less personal. "Was Audra a good student? How did she stack up in classes?"

"She was diligent," Britta said carefully. "She produced her essays on time. We collaborated with Instructor Segretti on some experiments with captured cephalopods found in the Estuary. She produced excellent drawings of them."

"I saw some of them in her sketchbook. What about these?" I scrabbled around, found my carry-bag, and took out *The Voyage of Captain Drago Drach*. "Quite an assignment for someone who's just a student."

"That was Instructor Segretti's idea," Britta said. "He had seen the original drawings when he was handed the copy of the book printed in Port Chicago, and thought they could be improved. He asked all of us, including myself, to submit our own illustrations based on the original images taken by the First Ship survey for review, and selected Audra's as the most accurate. I could not disagree. Her work was outstanding."

No jealousy there, just admission someone else's work was better than hers.

"So, he handed her the job, and gave her a full credit line in the book. Not bad for someone who didn't even bother with an apprenticeship in the Craftsman's Guild."

"That was his decision. Not something for me to question."

I thought that over. "Is that why she decided to change course and move to the Artist's Sector to study art instead of sticking with the Academy?"

"I don't know why she did that. As I said, our…involvement…cooled after last year's Winterfest. By the time she got her certificate, we were no longer meeting each other outside of classes." Britta hedged. "As I said, she was fascinated by the Norland tales of the kraken of the North Seas. Not the short-lived specimens here in Lorr, or the ones found near Pangkot. These kraken are quite different,"

"How?" I wouldn't let it go.

"According to the legends, they can grow to great size, they were here before we came, and will be here when we leave."

"But cephalopods are supposed to be short-lived," I reminded her. "They hatch, feed and grow, then mate, lay eggs, and they die. No time to pass knowledge to the next generation. At least, that's what they teach in Secondary biology class. Am I wrong?"

"That is true for most cephalopod species," Britta corrected me. "But there are tales of great kraken fortresses under the oceans, in deep caverns, where the most ancient beings live. They are the true kraken. The others are just creatures that, as you say, live a year or two at the most. The ones in the deep seas are the dangerous ones. We Norlanders do not interfere with them as long as they do not interfere with us. We take from the oceans only what we need and leave the rest for them."

"That works for Norland, but what about Pangkot and South Coast? They send out their ships to fish, they've got the large steam-driven transports hauling cargo. Jox Custo was raving about how those ships disturb the kraken, discard all kinds of garbage, take too many fish at a time."

"They are greedy." Britta declared. "They will find out the price of their greed. The kraken are waiting, there will be a reckoning."

And it wouldn't be pleasant, either. I was beginning to get a sense of what the kraken were. The more I learned, the more I was certain the best I could do for whatever had helped me when I was tied up under the bridge would be to stay away from it, and keep anyone else away, too.

We had reached the end of Academy Way. The Great Hall loomed over us. Not one of the old factories, but a purpose-built edifice of grand proportions.

Aziz stopped, and Britta looked around. "I have no more to say. Instructor Segretti will be upset if I am late to our meeting."

"I'll come with you," I decided. "I want to meet the great Instructor Segretti."

Britt eased out of the pedishaw, which rocked alarmingly under her weight. I slid out the other side.

"Aziz, you can wait for me at the carrier-station at the end of Academy Way. There's a kiosk there, you can have clet and something to eat. And if there are other pedishaw drivers, ask if any of them took up an old sailor, either to the Advanced Academy or going back to the Waterfront."

"Aha!" Aziz followed my reasoning. "Is this the same old male you ask about at the Seaman's Guild? He would need transport, yes? I will ask and find out. I am a worthy person, to assist Independent Eye Drach!"

He pedaled off on his mission. I turned to Britta.

"Introduce me to Instructor Segretti. I have a few questions for him."

"About Audra?

"And kraken. And an old sailor called Jox Custo."

"The one who has a stand on Entertainment Row? I have heard him speak. I do not think Instructor Segretti knows him."

156

"Maybe, maybe not. But Jox Custo tried to see some-one at the Advanced Academy, and the only one I can think of who had anything Jox wanted was this Segretti charac-ter."

Britta gave me a look that said *It's your funeral!* and led me to one of the smaller buildings nestled next to the Great Hall. A sign in Lorran and Pangkoti letters declared it was the Natural Science Building.

The place where people go to find answers to questions raised by the peculiar flora and fauna of New Earth. And where I hoped to find a few answers of my own.

viii

The Natural Science Building was smaller than the Great Hall, larger than the Stranger's Hostel, dating from the same era as both. It perched on the very edge of the cliff, with a paved path lead-ing from the elaborate front door to a more modest side en-trance. A flight of stairs provided access to the beach below.

I stood for a moment, hoping I didn't have to go down those stairs. I do not have a head for heights; and the last time I went down that cliff to the mud flats of the Estuary, I had a very bad encounter. This time I'd have Britta with me, but I still didn't fancy it.

As it turned out, I didn't have to use the stairs. A tall, stringy male at least a generation older than me clambered over the rim of the cliff. He was followed by several young males and females, all in heavy denim jackets and trou, all carrying metal buckets with water that sloshed over the rims.

Britta hailed them. "Instructor Segretti! Forgive my tar-diness. I was detained by…"

The pack leader cut her short. "You are late, Britta. No excuses! The tide does not wait!"

"It was unavoidable," Britta explained. "This person has some questions for you, Instructor."

I answered his unspoken inquiry "Independent Eye Pola Drach." No point in putting on an act with this character.

"Drach?" He stopped in mid-stride. "Related to Captain Drogo Drach?"

"Yes, but…"

"If this is about that ridiculous book, I refuse to comment. I was asked to revise the South Coast lingo text for Lorran readers. I was not asked to verify the findings of the South Coast author. I may have added a few words of explanation here and there, but I did not alter the meaning of the text, no matter what that ridiculous old man said. I did what was required and was adequately compensated. I have no further comments."

He brushed past me, his students trailing after him, pails sloshing.

I trotted alongside him. "I do have some questions about the book, but that's not why I'm here. If I may have a moment of your time, I would like to consult you on another matter entirely. Audra Martino."

That stopped him. "Audra? I heard what happened to her. Dreadful, dreadful! An accident, surely."

"I've been hired to look into the specifics. Her parent does not accept the findings of the Administration."

Segretti frowned. "I do not see how I can add to their findings. I offered her a position as my assistant. She preferred not to accept my offer."

"Of apprenticeship?"

"The Academy does not offer apprenticeships. We are not a Guild. She would have been one of my chief assistants, with the opportunity to advance in the Academy to Instructor status." He snarled. "She decided otherwise. I have not seen her since she left the Advanced Academy. If you will excuse me, I must get these specimens into their new homes before they expire."

He marched forward again. I hustled along next to him, fending off his eager followers. "But why did she refuse your offer of internship? After she'd spent all that time earning certification, why go off in a totally different direction?"

Segretti stopped in mid-stride. "She did not confide in me. Now, if you please, Eye Drach, I have work to do."

He beckoned to his students. They followed him, and I tagged along behind them up two flights of stairs to a large room filled with tanks of water. In them, small fish darted through lumps of rocks that pulsated with tiny, tentacled beings. Electric lights hummed over each tank. Some tanks had tubes sending air bubbles through the water, others were still.

Between the lights and the aerators, this one room must be using more electric in a day than was allotted to Fishmarket in a year. Whatever Segretti was doing here, Admin must have thought it worth the effort, and the Academy was willing to pay for it.

He led the group to the largest tank. The students tipped their pails in, letting small creatures with multiple arms loose into it. Some sank to the sand at the bottom, some wriggled free and swam around their new habitat.

Segretti peered into the tank, watching his latest captives explore their new home.

"Thank you, class. We are finished for now. You may turn your reports in to my office. Instruction will resume after Winterfest. Have a joyous holiday."

The students accepted their leader's dismissal, two males happily, one female unhappily. Britta shot a despairing look at me. Segretti's eyes remained firmly fixed on the tank.

"Instructor Segretti…"

"Are you still here?" If he thought he'd get rid of me by running up to his workspace, he'd have to think again.

"I still have questions," I said. "Instructor Segretti, according to her parents you were Audra Martino's primary mentor at the Advanced Academy. What is your opinion of her?"

He turned from the tank to face me. "Audra Martino was one of my best students. I was impressed with her dedication to the study of sea creatures, but unfortunately, she went somewhat…overboard, if I may use the phrase." He smiled indulgently. "I make it clear to all my students that the pursuit of science must be free of emotional ties. She became… attached…to some of the specimens we were studying. She said they were suffering from being confined in these tanks, that they should be set free to rejoin the others of their kind."

"One of her classmates told me she was interested in the kraken—"

"There are no kraken." Segretti stated firmly. "That is a mistaken notion. There are merely cephalopods of various species. The use of the term 'kraken' smacks of Old Earth folklore, which has no place in scientific research."

"Really? According to what I heard, there are creatures in the deep oceans that have been dubbed 'kraken' by the Norlanders. And in the original South Coast edition of the book, there are several descriptions of critters that sound a lot like those kraken."

Segretti frowned. "How did you obtain an original manuscript?"

"Audra Martino's parents let me examine her copy. She decorated it with some interesting drawings. Not like the ones that wound up in the Lorran copy, the official copy. And the seaman, Jox Custo, has been distributing the South Coast version on Entertainment Row from his lecture-stand. How'd you come to get it?"

"The original book was submitted to the Advanced Academy of Lorr by a boffin at the Advanced Academy of Port Chicago," Segretti admitted, after what seemed like an internal struggle. "Of course, the Academy passed it on to the Scribe's Guild, to be certain it was up to Lorran standards of literary merit.

"It was then given to me because I am an expert on ocean life. In addition, I met Captain Drach once, many years ago, during his last stay in Lorr, when I was quite young. He encouraged me to continue my studies past Secondary instead of joining my family fishing fleet."

That answered one question. I'd wondered why, of all people, the Scribe's Guild would have entrusted such a sensational book to this particular boffin for vetting. It also explained the book's leaden prose. No one would care to read much of it after the first chapter. Academics aren't known for lively text, whether in Lorr or anywhere else, and this character sounded worse than most.

"So, the Guild decided you'd be the best one to check out the book and rewrite it to their specs," I summed up. "I've seen both versions. I haven't had the chance to examine either of them closely, but I could see the illustrations were done by different hands. The Lorran book was done by Audra Martino, Why pick her? Wasn't someone in the Craftsman's Guild competent to do the work?"

Segretti nodded. "There may well have been, but they did not have Audra's expertise in depicting ocean creatures. I knew she would be accurate. She was also immediately available. The Academy wanted to put the book out in time for this year's Winterfest sales."

"You even gave her a credit for the illustrations," I pointed out. "Was Audra going to get paid for her work?"

"That was out of my hands. I submitted the revised manuscript with her illustrations. It was accepted by the Scribe's Guild and the Advanced Academy's publications department, and that was the end of my responsibility in the matter."

"And the material about the kraken…?" I hinted.

"The kraken do not exist," Segretti repeated huffily. "They are the stuff of sailors' tales, legends, and lies. I could not let a book marketed as a true history contain such nonsense. I eliminated any such references."

"Did Audra Martino consider the kraken nonsense?"

Segretti took a deep breath, and sighed. "Audra was a dedicated student of ocean life, but she was obsessed by the tales of the kraken. She was convinced there are intelligent lifeforms in the deepest oceans, and that they, and not we humans, were the true inhabitants of New Earth."

"Any idea where she got these notions?"

"Who can tell?" Segretti shrugged. "Young females get strange ideas. It was a sore point with her. In fact, it was one of the last discussions we had before she left my class. She objected to some of my experiments, told me they were hurting the specimens in the tank."

"What sort of experiments?" There are Regs about cruelty to nonsentient beings.

"I tried various stimuli on different specimens, to observe their reactions to such things as changes in the chemical composition of the water in the tank, changes in diet, and so on. I used an electric prod on some of them."

"And she objected to that?"

"She seemed to think the specimens felt pain."

"Why would she think that?"

"She pointed out their skin color would change, and that they would attempt to get away from the probe when it was put into the water."

"And you didn't think so?"

"I pointed out that without nerves or a brain, no creature can feel pain, or anything else. She insisted they did. I told her point-blank, if she persisted in this obsession she would do better as an artist than as a boffin."

"And she took you up on it. Didn't that upset you?"

"There are other students who are eager to work with me."

"Like Britta Drach."

Segretti smiled smugly. "A most attentive young female. She has a knack for finding good specimens and caring for them. She will go far in the Academy. With my backing, of course."

I looked around at the bubbling tanks. "You're certain these things don't feel pain?"

"The shelled creatures are mere lumps of protoplasm encased in limestone. They respond to light, they respond to a touch, but one can hardly call that pain. They have no brains, no nervous system. Neither do the cephalopods. There are no advanced creatures in the oceans. If there were, the First Ship surveys would have found them before they even landed," Segretti stated. "They found the large ocean-going reptiles well enough, even the ones that dived to great depths."

"And you'd be the one to know," I muttered. "You're the expert."

"I am," he said. Not proudly, just a statement of fact.

"But you were challenged," I reminded him.

"There was that seaman who tried to see me," he admitted.

"Jox Custo."

"Is that his name? He followed me when I was on my way home after classes and accosted me in the Central Plaza. I told him the same thing. There are no kraken. There is no intelligent species on New Earth other than humans."

"When was this?"

"Yesterday. He came roaring into the Advanced Academy some days ago, demanding to be heard about the wretched state of the oceans around South Coast. Of course, he was turned away, but he persisted. Yesterday, he waited outside the Great Hall until I left for the day, and followed me to the Central Plaza."

All this time he had been walking around, peering into one tank or another.

"So, it was you he was yelling at," I said, following him from one to the next.

"He was very upset about the book being sold at the Scribe's Guild table. Went into a rant about how I had distorted the words of his friend in South Coast. He demanded I issue a retraction, that the book be revised a second time, and re-published with the corrections. I told him point-blank that was impossible. The book was finished and would not be revised yet again."

"What about his claim that the kraken are being killed and the oceans being polluted?"

Segretti grimaced. "He thought I should help him in his efforts. Not my concern! I am a scientist. I study the life in the sea. It is as it is, I do not change it, or challenge the authorities who are responsible for the well-being of the creatures in it. I told this Custo I was not interested in his crusade, and that he should take his complaints to Administration."

"He tried to get a hearing," I said. "He tried to get Admin to listen to him. They didn't, and he took to the streets. He was handing out copies of the South Coast version of the book on Entertainment Row."

Segretti looked as if he'd swallowed a sundew pod. "What? He wouldn't...He didn't! I'll have the Guild on him!"

"Not a problem anymore. Jox Custo is...gone."

"What!" Segretti really was stunned at that news. "Why? How?"

"That's what I'm trying to find out."

Segretti turned pale, then purple with rage. "You cannot think that I...I!...had anything to do with that! I am respected in my field, what I wrote is true, and this Jox Custo was deluded. As for Audra Martino, I have no idea why she would jump into the river. She was quite animated at the..."

"Urbine Gallery showing? I thought you weren't there."

"I may have dropped in, to see how she had progressed. I didn't stay long, and I didn't speak to her. She was surrounded by well-wishers, empty-headed young persons. There was a great deal of chatter, nonsense most of it. Her drawing had attracted much attention."

"So I've heard." I thought it over, then said, "Instructor Segretti, about those illustrations...How was Audra able to depict the sea reptiles so accurately? The drawings in the South Coast mag were bare outlines, and Jox Custo's complaint was that the great reptiles have been harried to extinction."

Segretti admitted, "I was able to provide some of the images taken by the Founders' surveys. Audra was fascinated by them. Not one of them showed any cephalopod larger than the ones in the waters near the Lorr coast."

"From all I've heard, Audra was not a fanciful person. So, why would she come to the conclusion your experiments were causing the specimens pain?"

"From observing changes in the specimens she said were connected to the stimuli. Until she put forward this thesis, I had always considered her quite detached. It is why I offered her the position in the first place. She had the makings of a first-rate scientist."

"You were not...um, involved personally?"

Segretti went from panic to distaste. "That is a ridiculous accusation. I have been comfortably espoused for many years to a fellow scientist, as anyone connected with the Academy can tell you. I regarded Audra Martino as a promising student, nothing more. That is all, Eye Drach."

He turned back to his tanks. It was a definite dismissal.

"Thank you for your time and information, Instructor Segretti. Have a profitable day."

I left him standing there, amid the tanks of sea critters. I hadn't learned much, but I had some sense of where Audra and Jox met, and it all had to do with kraken...which Segretti insisted didn't exist.

ix

I still had a few questions I wanted answered before I went back to the office. I took a minute to switch to my fish-vendor persona. Then, I strode into the Great Hall exuding righteous wrath.

The Great Hall of the Advanced Academy had started as a simple cinderblock structure, meant to house the Big Black Box. Over the centuries, it had been added to, surviving floods, fires, windstorms, and the Merchants' War. It rose now to five stories, plus the two towers that held the comm equipment and the wind-turbines that powered it. The Big Black Box lurked somewhere underground in the Admin compound, attended by the boffins, Techs, and Mechs who kept the ancient information source humming; the Academy had access through the comm links.

The interior of the Great Hall is dominated by the central staircase leading up to the second floor landing, from which the Principal can address the entire Academy personnel on solemn occasions. Overhead, a skylight let in what rays of sunlight penetrated the clouds driving in from the south. A more discreet staircase led to the upper floors where students and instructors met to discuss the deeper meanings of the Old Earth writings. Boffins had their working laboratories in other buildings; the Great Hall was supposed to be devoted to Pure Learning.

I joined a group of students entering and looked around, getting my bearings. It had been a long time since I'd entered those doors as a student—a lifetime ago.

Several persons were setting up Winterfest decorations. A small conifer in a tub of soil stood beside the notice-post next to the grand staircase. Two females and a male draped strings of colored beads around it, symbolizing the stars. Others organized the other ornaments—glass baubles, shining metal twisted spikes, folded paper items, all sparkling like hoarfrost.

"Oyo," I hailed them. "Who's in charge here?"

One of the females looked me over, assessing my status from my garb and accent. I clearly didn't rate very high in her estimation.

"What brings you here?" she countered.

I reached into my carry-bag. "This here book. I went to the Scribes, and they told me to come here. It's wrong, and I want to know how come it's being sold when it's not what it's supposed to be."

"That is not our concern," the female told me. "If you have a complaint, you must make it to the proper authority."

"I tol' ya I done that. I been to the Scribes, and they sent me here."

The female drone grimaced, maybe at the (nonexistent) aroma of fish.

"Try the offices on the fourth floor." The other female smiled at me as if to indicate she, at least, was ready to be helpful. "Feldman edits the boffins." She pointed to the stairs. "It's the Academy Press office."

I trudged onward, up stairs and down a corridor that led to another flight of stairs. At the top of yet a third flight I found a door marked *Academy Press*.

I tapped on the door, which opened at my touch. Inside was a single desk covered with papers. Behind the desk, a female of my own age, her jacket and trou similar in style to the reverse side of mine. but her jacket was faded blue, her scarf was pink, and her hair was dark brown.

"Oyo. How's business?" .

She looked up from the pile of papers. "Who are you, and how did you get here?"

"I'm Independent Eye Pola Drach, and I'm here to find out more about this." I produced *The Voyages of Captain Drogo Drach* from my bag and laid it on the desk.

The female flipped through it and put it down again. "Oh, this one. Sure, I edited it, but don't come to me with any more complaints about the contents. I'm not responsible for what people write. All I do is check for grammar and spelling errors. Style isn't my job, either, so if you don't like how it's written, take it up with the one who wrote it."

I raised my eyebrows. "Is this not the Academy Press office?"

"Yes," she said, "but—"

"And are you not the one who prepares the books for publication?"

"I'm just the line editor, not the copy editor," she protested. "What's the problem? I went over that book twice. If there are typos, that's on the printer, not me. Like I told the old geezer yesterday, you don't like it, take it up with Segretti, not me."

"What geezer...?" I started, but Feldman was well and truly steamed.

"Look, Drach, or whoever you are, I get paid to check the text, and wretched pay it is, too. I do my job. You can tell the Scribes I did what I was contracted to do, and that was it. That's what I told the oldster, and that's what I'm telling you. And that's all I have to say about it!"

She bent over her desk. This interview was also over.

x

I left the Great Hall and looked around for my transport. I spotted Aziz and his pedishaw at the carrier station on the corner of Academy Way and Garden Way.

I needed a break, some time to gather my thoughts and, incidentally, have something to eat. My insides were reminding me it had been a long time since I'd ingested the mush.

Aziz sat at a small table next to the kiosk with one of the other pedishaw drivers, a small but sturdy male in typical Desert Folk garb—baggy trou, loose jacket, and multicolored headwrap.

"This is Davik," Aziz introduced him. "He is one of the drivers assigned to this station by the Transport Guild. He has information about the old seaman."

"Jox?" I looked over the assortment of edibles on the counter in front of the kiosk. There wasn't much, just a twist of paper with salted nut-and-seed mix and some honeycake. I ordered the honeycake and chai, and joined Aziz and his friend while the old male in charge of the kiosk brought the hot beverage and cold cake to the table.

"If you say so," Davik said, with a strong Desert accent. "He did not give his name. I only remembered him because he was very old, white hair and not properly shaved, white hair on cheeks."

"You asked the old males at the Seaman's Guild about this male Jox Custo," Aziz reminded me. "I think, if he was not used to Lorr, and he is old, and he may not walk well, he

168

would need a pedishaw, yes? So, I asked, and here is the one who took him from the Central Plaza to where he met someone." Aziz beamed triumphantly.

"Good work," I said, between sips of indifferent chai and bites of stale honeycake. "So, Driver Davik, what can you tell me about Seaman Jox Custo? When did you pick him up, and where did he go?"

Davik glanced at Aziz for reassurance. "I was going back to the Transport Guild—I had finished my time at the carrier station and was not supposed to pick up any more fares. But the old male looked tired, and I thought this would be a Good Deed to be reckoned by the Nameless One in my final hours, so I let him on. He asked where he could find a certain place where he was to meet someone, a tavern called the Lizard's Claw. He said it was on Artists' Way, near the Flatlands Bridge."

I nearly choked on my chai. This was unexpected! "Are you sure it was the Lizards' Claw?"

"Oh, yes, because I looked at the sign. I had to help the old male out of the pedishaw, he was not well. There was a female waiting for him, and she helped me get him down from the seat."

"Waiting for *him*, or just anyone?"

Davik got my drift. "Oh, not a licensed female, not at all. Covered up, green jacket and trou, wrap on head. She stood in front of the tavern looking this way and that, so I think, waiting for someone. When she see him, she wave her hand."

"And what did they do then?"

"I do not know. I had to get back to the transport station to put in my travel log and get my pay." Davik looked to Aziz again for assurance. "I did not know what would happen to the old male. I later learned that he was taken away…" He stopped. "May the Nameless One have mercy upon him." He made the Desert Folk sign of blessing.

I considered this development. The female in the green suit seemed to pop up everywhere. Another Eye in Lorr? Or an Assassin, on her own, not sanctioned by the Fatsos? I couldn't recall anyone like that on Garden Way, but I hadn't been looking for an attacker. More fool me! I'd have to be more careful.

"I thank you for your time, Driver Davik." I left some coppers for his clet. "Driver Aziz, I think we'll be going now. Through Central Plaza to Artist's Sector."

The carrier approached, slowly bumbling along, wheels rumbling over the brick paving. Davik stood beside his pedishaw, ready to grab the next person needing a ride to Industrial or Garden. Aziz helped me up to the seat of his vehicle, and we were off again.

The sun was dipping towards the westward horizon, sending shadows across the Central Plaza. Office drones leaving work, students freed from classes, visitors and tourists looking to spend some time before heading for food shops—all drawn to the kiosks, looking for Winterfest bargains and exotic gifts for friends and family—filled the open space to the point where Aziz could barely move without striking someone.

He slowed to a crawl, giving the pedestrians right of way, while I scanned the crowd, looking for a green suit.

The Entertainment Guild had set up sound-enhancement gizmos so the buskers' music could be heard across the plaza. Moggy, Randi and Kira led the crowd in a general singalong, reminding people of the First Ship and its intrepid crew of Mechs, Techs, Admin and boffins, all searching for the one planet that would replace Old Earth.

I hummed along.

> Earth that was, Earth that was,
> Though we live so far away,
> Earth that was, Earth that was,
> We remember you today.

Everyone within earshot sang loudly, waving their arms upward to remind us where we came from.

The song ended with a wail of regret. I blinked a sudden tear from my eyes.

Aziz wobbled along, trying to find a way through the crowd.

"I might as well walk," I decided.

I slid the bag with the book under the back seat. "Take this bag directly back to my office. Give it to the big young female from the workroom, tell her to put it somewhere safe."

I handed Aziz one more silver and watched him veer away into one of the alleys that led back to The Avenue.

I was on my own, on foot, in the crowd, surrounded by sensations of all sorts. Sounds of chatter and laughter and bargaining, in accents ranging from the singsong of Pangkot to the harsh gutturals of Norland. Scents of exotic spices from the Pangkoti kiosk, and frying fish, and clet, always clet, with added herbs and spices for the season.

I caught a whiff of something that wasn't clet or fish, something strange and yet familiar. I'd smelled that tang before. I couldn't remember when, but it must have been recently. Someone was behind me, pressing against my back.

I shifted to one side, trying to see who it was. I could hear the creak of the approaching carrier. The people around me pushed me aside to make room for the line of cars, filled with riders, slowly making its way down the brick-paved road that circled the Central Plaza. The smoke from the coal-oil engine made my eyes water.

The whoop-whoop of the carrier's whistle alerted the crowd. People pushed on every side to get out of the way. I elbowed my way to the front of the crowd to see what was coming.

The Transporteer at the wheel of the carrier tooted the whistle again. I felt a hand on my back between my shoulder-blades. I twisted to see who it was just as a shove sent me into the path of the carrier.

My leg twisted under me as I kicked back, trying to gain my feet. I fell hard onto the paved road, but managed to wriggle away from the oncoming cars, then rolled across the road, dodging feet. The people hopped out of my way, stumbling over each other in a wild sprawl of shoes, boots, and sandals. Someone went down, then another. With yells, screams, oaths, and curses, it was like one of the wildest scenes in a farce.

I managed to roll out from under someone who had been imbibing spiced clet, judging from their breath. The rough bricks rasped my hands and tore my trou as I wound up in a patch of prickle-weed that had been used by passing lizards and felines as an elimination place.

People screamed. The heavy carrier screeched to a halt. I gasped for breath, scrambling away from the prickles, trying see who had pushed me. Whoever it was had faded into the crowd. All I had to go on was that weird, tangy scent.

Someone hauled me to my feet. I staggered into the arms of the one person I did not want to meet in my disheveled condition.

"Can't stay out of trouble, Drach?" Sara Atterson stood before me, immaculate in her uniform, not a hair out of place.

"Would you believe me if I said I was pushed?"

"I might. We'll see what the Chief has to say. Hop in. You're wanted in Admin." She shoved me toward the official skimmer.

I hesitated. "Couldn't it wait? I'm not looking my best."

"The Chief said bring you in. Now!"

No help for it, then. I mounted the skimmer and wondered what I had done to bring Commander Regina Polaris down upon me. Whatever it was, it couldn't be good.

xi

The skimmer zipped over the heads of the crowd in the Central Plaza. I thought we'd stop at the Guardhouse, but no, we went straight on to Admin Hill—the outermost and highest remnant of what the boffins assured us was a thoroughly extinct volcano.

We put down in the plaza in front of the entrance to the natural cavern where the Founders had set up their first campsite. Now, twenty generations on, it was the nerve-center of New Earth, where the Administrators kept what was left of Humanity from destroying each other and the planet they lived on.

Of course, each Settlement insisted on its own customs, with the usual conflicts of interest; but those were what Admin was for. Someone had to be the final arbiter of what was and was not acceptable.

And deep in the bowels of the cave lurked the Big Black Box, the final arbiter and repository of all knowledge left to us from Old Earth, tended by the people who kept it working.

Atterson marched me through the entrance with a minimum of ceremony, just a curt nod to the Guard and the brief announcement "The Chief wants to see this one, right now."

I felt the hill pressing in on me, smelled the rank odor of too many bodies in too small a space. No one else seemed to notice. Probably used to it.

You'd think the Chief of Security for an entire planet would give herself the luxury of a suite in the upper reaches of Admin Hill, with a window overlooking the City of Lorr. Not Regina Polaris. Her lair was deep in the old cave, a cubicle only a little larger than the others along the corridor. No placard on the door, nothing to distinguish this room from any others. That wasn't the Polaris way. She knew who and what she was, and where she came from.

She was the direct descendant of Aurelio Polaris, Captain of the First Ship, Founder of New Earth, and was the last of a long line of Administrators. She didn't have to knock anyone over the head with the trappings of power. She'd had it since she was born.

It was the great barrier between us, because she wanted to pass this power on to me, and I would not accept it.

Atterson knocked at the door.

"Come." The voice was sharp, clear. She knew who was there.

The room behind the door was plain to the point of boredom. White walls broken only by small screens with flickering lights and constantly changing messages. A desk with two comm receivers and a transmitter. A chair behind the desk, none in front of it. Nothing personal, no tokens that anyone actually occupied the room. Totally functional. That was Regina Polaris.

I felt an all-too familiar clenching in my stomach. The last time I'd faced her it had been in my own digs, on my own turf. Now, I was in her territory, and I didn't know why.

She stood to greet me, saluted Atterson. The captain returned the salute and stepped back, ready to leave.

"Captain Atterson, please remain. I don't want to have to repeat this information."

Allright, this was going to be official, not family. I was horribly aware of my scruffy appearance. My jacket was grimy, there was a rip in the knee of my trou. I had tried to put my hair into a twist at the back of my neck, but I had no clips; and I was sure there was a smudge of dirt on my face.

I pasted a bland smile on my face and regarded my mother with what I hoped she would consider was civility. Atterson looked from the Security Chief to me and stepped farther away from us. She glanced at me, uncertain how to react.

She knew I was Regina Polaris's child; everyone in our class in the Guards did, even though I had changed my name. I shrugged slightly, trying to convey that I understood her feelings, and realized neither of us had much choice in the matter. What Chief of Security Regina Polaris wanted, she would get.

Except where her only offspring was concerned. She could bully me, she could coerce me, but she couldn't control me. She'd tried, but I resisted. It was the sorest point between us.

I broke the silence. "Security Chief Polaris, why am I here? I've done nothing against the regs."

She gave me the narrow-eyed stare that had set me into cold shivers when I was much younger. "Independent Eye Drach, you have been questioning the Scribe's Guild and the Advanced Academy's decision concerning the publication of a certain book."

"*The Voyages of Captain Drogo Drach*? I found some changes from the original text and brought them to the attention of the Scribes' Guild. They sent me to Advanced Academy. I had no idea the matter was of such importance as to involve planetary security."

"The revisions were made at the express orders of Administration Security, for the good of the City of Lorr and the people of New Earth."

"Revisions? You mean Jox was right? You changed Boffin Rachel Craston's text to suit Admin's agenda?"

"The South Coast Advanced Academy allowed certain statements to be published. The Advanced Academy of Lorr disputes them."

"So, you had the book changed. Removing the material about the kraken, for instance?"

"The kraken do not exist."

"They do. I know it, you know it. So do the Norlanders, who have seen them."

"Anecdotal evidence," Polaris snapped. "No one has succeeded in capturing one alive. None of the cephalopods found in coastal waters near Lorr has more than instinctual intelligence. They don't live long enough to pass information from one generation to another."

"There are other ways to determine intelligence."

Polaris would have none of it. "The Founders were certain there was no other intelligent species on this planet when they landed. They searched carefully. As for the kraken, they show no signs of sapience. They don't use tools, or construct lasting edifices, all signs of advanced intelligence as the boffins define it."

175

"According to the Norlanders they communicate with each other through color and gesture," I countered. "And they might not build things because they may not need to. Just because the Founders didn't find something doesn't mean it's not there. It took a while for the boffins to figure out about the vampire vines and sensation plants, too." I quoted a popular ditty: "'You won't recognize a predator if it looks like a tree.'"

Polaris made an impatient noise. "Tcha! This gets us nowhere."

"You didn't send Captain Atterson after me to lecture me about books or kraken. Why am I here, Chief Polaris?"

"You are pursuing a line of questioning regarding the death of an aspiring artist, one Audra Martino." She bit out the words as if they cost her major coin.

"I am, but I don't see how that concerns the Administration. Captain Atterson hired me to find out where she was, because she didn't come home when she was supposed to. I found her, but too late. I left the investigation in Captain Atterson's hands. All according to the Regs."

"The Administration decided the young female met with a fatal accident." Polaris said. "Do you question those findings?"

"I do. Not just me, either. I've had a word with the Dark One who examined the body, and he agrees with me. And so does the young female's parent who hired me, as per Regs, to go deeper. I found some factors previously not considered when the case was deemed closed."

Polaris glared at me. I was supposed to be intimidated. I maintained my bland expression.

"The case is closed. You are not to pursue it further."

"I can't do that."

Polaris' glare deepened into a scowl. "Are you defying a direct order from the Administration?"

I ignored the tightness in my innards. "I've signed a contract and taken coin. According to Regs, I have to fulfill the terms of the contract. Are you telling me to ignore the most basic of the Regulations of Lorr? 'A contract, once signed, must be fulfilled to the total satisfaction of all parties.'" I cited the Regulations of Lorr, the sacred document all Lorrans revere, the rules by which we live, as laid down by the Founders when they arrived on New Earth and set up the City of Lorr.

"There is no evidence of any other factor in the demise of Audra Martino."

"There are marks on her arms and legs that are not accounted for," I pointed out. "And there is evidence she was forcibly thrown into the river, and something got her out. It's all in the medical report from Dark Kelvin."

"I read the report from Dark Kelvin. What, exactly, are you suggesting?"

"I think there was something in the water that saw what happened and tried to help. A creature that some call a kraken."

"Impossible. Cephalopods inhabit oceans or brackish waters, not fresh streams."

"The river is a tidal estuary and I had an encounter with such a creature recently. So, why not admit they exist, and let it go at that?"

"Because if we did, there would be mass panic," Polaris confessed. "There would be hunts to remove them. Just as happened with the walking trees when the Founders realized what they were. We and they do not communicate, but we know of each others' presence on this world.

"As with the trees, so with the kraken. We have made a *modus vivendi*, a way of living with them. They rule the oceans, we have the land. They cannot come out of the sea, we cannot explore underwater. It worked well enough…until now. Apparently, there are some of them who are not pleased with the situation, and are taking steps to confront those who are destroying their space."

"The South Coast junta is exploring aggressively," I said, thinking it through. "They sent Drogo Drach across the Middle Sea, and they sent Jox Custo to the South Continent. They're grabbing every resource they can find, exploiting every angle, building factories and using Contramont coal to fuel them. They're tipping the balance. That's what old Jox Custo was trying to do, warn Admin. It may be why he was killed."

"South Coast junta is worse than the Pangkot autocracy," Polaris snarled. "Exploiters, all of them! They have no idea what they're doing!"

"Short-term gains, no long-term plans," I agreed. "Audra Martino was fascinated by the kraken. She may have got involved with Jox Custo and his followers. I don't know whether or not her involvement had anything to do with her demise.

"Look, if the kraken are involved, I'll try to keep it private, but I can't stop now. Someone's trying to kill me. I must be getting close to the truth."

Polaris sighed. "You will not stop looking into this matter? In the face of a direct order from the Administration?"

"I can't," I repeated. "I've taken coin and signed the contract."

"As stubborn as your other parent. He insisted on pursuing his dreams, too."

"And look where it led him," I finished for her.

"To a spectacular end." Polaris allowed herself a brief grin, then turned back to me. "Isveta...Pola...why do you do this? Why can't you do what is expected of you?"

Because doing what is expected leads to trouble, I wanted to say. *Because if people know what you will do, they use that knowledge to destroy you.* But I didn't say that aloud. Instead, I changed the subject.

"One more thing, Chief Polaris. Regarding certain pink pellets that have appeared on the Waterfront and Entertainment Row."

"That is none of your business."

"It is when one is slipped into something I drink. I think they might come from Port Chicago. Jox told me he'd brought a squad of boffins on his ship to explore the biota of the South Continent. It's possible there's some connection."

"Your suggestion is noted, Eye Drach. Captain Atterson!"

Atterson sprang to attention.

"Remove Independent Eye Drach. Let her go about her business. If she insists on endangering herself again, you are not responsible."

"Yes, Chief."

That was all? Nothing more about Drogo Drach and his unfortunate demise? Nothing about Jox Custo? Nothing about the Prophet of Doom?

Not from Chief of Security Regina Polaris.

Still, I had a lot to think about as I followed Atterson back through the corridors to the plaza and breathed the fresh air of Lorr.

xii

So, there we were, Captain Sara Atterson of the Lorr City Guards and me, Pola Drach, Independent Eye. Two females with a shared history, with a lot to say, who didn't want to say it. Ahead of us, the lights of Lorr began blinking on one by one. The wind off the estuary had picked up, bringing the tangy smells of fish and brine and cooking oil.

Atterson turned to me. "You're not quitting, are you." A statement, not a question.

"I can't. Your relations deserve answers. So do you. And so does Audra."

"I've had my answer. Audra went into the water, came out, died of hypothermia before someone could find her. End of story."

"Not for me. I don't think Audra went into the river un-aided. Someone stuck a poisoned pin into her and pushed her in. Something else rescued her, dragged her out of the water, but she was too tired and cold to cry out. Even if she had, who would have heard her?" My voice hardened. "That just doesn't sit right with me, Captain. I'm going to find out who did this, and when I do, that someone will pay, one way or another."

"Chief Polaris just ordered you not to."

"I'm not in the Guards, I'm Independent. Security Chief Polaris has no direct jurisdiction over me."

Atterson frowned. "I'm under her orders.I can take you into custody for disobeying Regulations."

"Except I haven't disobeyed anything...not yet," I said.

She gave it another try. "Why? Why do you do it?"

"Do what?"

"Poke, pry, insist on finding out what happened, no matter who it hurts. Why do you have to keep at it? You're not in the Guards, you don't have a Guild to back you. You insist on being Independent. Why?"

"It's just something I have to do," I said. "Maybe it's what drove Drogo Drach to make that last voyage of discovery. Maybe it's what keeps Regina Polaris at her desk in that hole in the mountain."

I tried another explanation. "I once heard a tale of Old Earth. There was a ruler, he'd come into the position unexpectedly, and no one thought much of him. He had a sign on his desk, 'The Buck Stops Here,' meaning he'd take full responsibility for what he did. As it happened, he had to confront many obstacles, meet challenges he wasn't prepared for. He was sorely criticized for what he did, but in the end he was respected for his decisions.

"I don't know if I'm descended from that ruler, but I understand how he felt. I can't let things pass. I have to make things right. Not for everyone, all the time, just for one person at one time. I only wish I'd been able to get to Audra sooner. I'm truly sorry for your loss, Captain. I can see how much Audra meant to you."

Atterson stared out into the gathering dusk. "I didn't know her that well. I was in the Guards, and after the Merchant's War, the Guards were…"

"Not where you wanted to be," I finished for her. "They lost, the Merchants won."

"True. But it's the Guards that keep the peace in Lorr, not the Merchants. I wanted to do something to make things right, and the Guards seemed to be the way to do it."

I nodded. I understood how she felt. I'd done the same when I got back to Lorr after my stay in Norland. Atterson and I had been kindred spirits, fifteen years ago.

Then, I reported something I'd seen, which I thought was treason but turned out to be a lovers' tryst. Embarrassing for two males at the time, but not against Regs. One of the males insisted on my dismissal. I left the Guards, took up Eyeing.

Atterson had been more discreet.

"Was that after Audra?" I asked.

She sighed "You've probably figured it out already, if you've seen my sister."

"Audra was yours. Eduardo was the father, she had his coloring. Was it consensual?"

"Yes…and no. One of those Hinterland things, to diversify the genetics."

"I didn't know you were Hinterland. No accent."

"I've worked hard to blank it out. Mam was an overseer in the mines. Geri's father was one of the boffins in charge of the assay office at the mine, Lem Atterson was one of the other overseers. Mam didn't keep either of them around very long."

That's Hinterland for you. Lots of futtering, not much permanence. People moving on, in the name of genetic diversity or just plain restlessness.

"Eduardo came to the mine with the Construction Guild team to investigate the safety of the mine after an accident that killed several, including Mam. He and Geri hooked up. Geri saw a way to get us out of Hinterland, Both of us went with Eduardo to Flatlands. He took both of us, slept with both of us. Geri didn't conceive, I did. I had the child, they raised it. I went into the Guards, Geri stayed with Eduardo, organized Garden Sector while he rose in Construction Guild."

It must have cost her a lot to tell me this.

"You kept your distance," I said. "If it helps, I found out one reason why Audra moved across town. There was a friendship that went sour. She might have been trying to escape someone's unwanted attentions."

"A thwarted lover?"

"Maybe. Trouble is, there's no proof. And you know the Regs...no proof, no case." I shivered in the wind. "I'd better be on my way. It's a long walk back to Clothier's Alley."

"I can take you as far as the Guardhouse," Atterson offered. "I have paperwork to finish before my shift ends."

I winced at the thought of yet another skimmer ride, but bowed to the inevitable.

"I'll take that ride, Captain, but I'm not done yet. There's something else going on here besides kraken. It's those pink pellets that have me worried, not creepy-crawlies in the river. Maybe Audra stumbled onto something she shouldn't have."

"We're looking into that. If Audra saw or heard something, she may not have understood what she saw," Atterson said.

I nodded. "It's happened before."

We mounted the skimmer and sat silently for the few minutes it took to fly back to the Central Guardhouse. When we landed, I turned to Atterson.

"What are you going to do about Jox?"

"The Dark Ones are still working on him. Do you think he got one of those pink pills into him?"

"It's possible. According to my sources, he met someone in the Artist's Sector before he turned up at my door."

Atterson's eyes narrowed. "Who?"

"No idea. I only found out about it right before I got shoved under the carrier."

"Someone really doesn't like you, Drach. You should take better care of yourself."

"I'll try," I promised. "But I won't stop looking for answers. Audra Martino and Jox Custo deserve that much. What I *can* tell you is that Audra spoke with Jox the night she was killed. He claimed he didn't recall what she said, but it might have been overheard by someone. And if that was so, the two demises might be tied to the same person."

"That's a very big 'if,'" Atterson said. She looked over the plaza toward the Boulevard. "It's nearly moon-up. Get back to your plant, Drach, and let the Guards take charge."

"One more thing," I said. "It seems to me every time I try to go to the Artists' Sector to have another look at Rafe Urbine's studio, I get put off. Someone tries to kill me, someone tries to give me another job. Maybe there's something there someone doesn't want me to see."

"Maybe you should stay away from Rafe Urbine," Atterson warned. "He's got Upper Tier connections."

"Like Selva Delrey? I thought that was over. And Selva's stuck in a lodge somewhere in the Mineral Mountains."

"The Delreys cast long shadows. You've ruffled their feathers too many times. I've heard a few whispers, Drach. Take this as friendly advice. Go home, have a meal, and get some rest. You've earned it."

I looked around and saw Aziz waiting in the shadow of a clet-stand. He pedaled to meet me.

"I see you pushed under carrier and skimmer take you away. So, I stay here until you come back."

"You didn't go to my office? The carry-bag is still with you?" I reached under the seat. The carry-bag with the book was still there.

"I've got a ride," I told Atterson. "And I'll consider what you've said. But remember, Captain, the buck stops here.

And I won't stop until I get the answers I need to finish the investigation."

WAYS AND MEANS

*WHAT I SHOULD HAVE DONE WAS TAKE ATTERSON'S AD-*vice, go back to my digs and let the whole thing go. What I did was have Aziz take me to Clothiers Alley.

I sent him to the nearest clet-stand where he could get me a meat-pie and spiced hot chai, plus something for himself, to fill the tum until I could get a more substantial meal at Fletcher's. Then, I went back to my office, sat at my desk, and considered what I had learned in the last thirty hours.

None of it seemed to make sense.

Audra had grown up in the safety of Garden, coddled by loving parents, schooled in proper behavior. She'd gone through Secondary and Advanced Academy with the intention of continuing as a boffin, studying sea creatures. Then, suddenly, she decided to move away from the life she knew. She changed careers, started a whole new course of study, moved into a communal lodging with people she'd never met before. Why?

Was she running away from a friendship that had gotten too intense? Was she trying to escape family tensions? Or was she running towards something she couldn't find in the constricted society of Garden?

I took the picture of Audra Martino out of my jacket pocket and stared at it. Edard might have preferred to paint blobby flowers, but he could capture a likeness when he chose to. Audra stared out at me from the page, an intensely intelligent young female with a beaky nose, arched eyebrows, thin mouth. I could see the resemblance to Sara Atterson in that stare, and she had her father's coloring. But who was she, really?

And what, if anything, did she have to do with Jox Custo? Or was it just a coincidence that they'd passed a few days apart?

Aziz arrived with the pie and the chai. As he set the food in front of me, he glanced at the picture. "Aha! I have seen this one!"

"On Entertainment Row?" I took a bite of the pie, followed by a sip of chai. Not bad, for street food.

"On the Waterfront. She came with some of the people from the Advanced Academy to speak with the fishers. They were collecting information about the catch—what fish were spawning, and how big was their haul."

"Checking on overfishing?" It sounded like something an officious boffin might come up with.

"Who knows? They were there, and they did not get correct answers, because no one wants to let the Admin people know how large the catch is for fear of having to pay a larger toll for it."

Of course. Everyone wanted to beat the taxman!

"What makes you remember this one?" I tapped the picture.

"She is interesting to look at," Aziz said, with a grin. "And she kept asking about whether any of the fishers sees the kraken."

"And had they?"

"That I do not know. I only saw the Academy students from the pedishaw ranks. But I saw her later, on Entertainment Row, not with the Academy people. Then, I heard a young female had been found under the Waterfront Bridge. That was she?"

I nodded. "I'm trying to find out what happened to her. When did you last see her on the Waterfront?"

Aziz screwed up his face. "With the Academy students? Oooh...last spring, I think. Before we made our great run. And on Entertainment Row, that was maybe after our great run? Two, three weeks?

"It is not that I looked for her," he added hurriedly. "But once or twice, I saw her with two others. A male, very thin, short, in Pangkoti dress, and a female, taller, her hair very red, I do not think a natural color."

Chezan and Marta. That made sense; they'd done the tavern rounds on Entertainment Row together. And from what Marta'd said, Audra had tagged along, whether or not she'd been invited.

"Do you want me to wait?' Aziz broke into my musing. "Because it is nearly dark, and there is much to do before Winterfest for us who follow the Nameless One. We have a festival, we light lights to fight the Darkness and beckon the Nameless One to bless us for the coming year."

"I've got one more stop before I'm done for the day," I decided. "Did you get something to eat?"."

Aziz grinned. "I have had clet. I will wait." He took up a position just outside the door, keeping a careful eye on his pedishaw.

I munched my pie, sipped chai, and pondered what I'd learned. Then, I slipped through the connecting door to Holly's office.

As always, the tiny room was cluttered with papers and scraps of cloth. Drawings of Jake's designs were pinned to the wall, invoices and bills stacked on Holly's desk. In the middle of it, Zeta and Holly were bickering about something that was missing.

I interrupted their spat. "Holly, Zeta. What can you tell me about the Martinos?"

Holly glared at me. "The Martino clan doesn't patronize Lorr clothiers. They get their duds from some no-name

187

in Flatlands." Which meant they didn't put coin into her pouch, so she didn't know or care about them.

Zeta was more informative. "I did what you said—I asked my mam about the Martinos. She does not like them much. She tells me to go to my Auntie Cococha, so I did, and she told me all about them."

"Mam Cococha is the worst gossip in the Clothier's Guild," Holly put in. "She's the one the upper Flatlanders go to for their duds." Instead of Jake and Holly, left unsaid.

"True," Zeta admitted. "But she knows everyone in Flatlands. She says the Martinos are mostly in Construction. Techs —and First Ship Techs, at that. They mostly live in and around their personal compound on the seacoast, except for the one who married up and moved to Garden." Zeta sniffed "Too good for his cousins, that one! Got an Academic spouse, and won't have anything to do with the Techs anymore."

"That's Eduardo," I told her. "What about the others?"

"Started as builders, but now they're suppliers," Zeta explained. "There's a Martino brickyard, and they've got connections to Norland for timber, and Hinterland for stone. They've got connections to Transport Guild, too, for carrying the supplies to and from Lorr to building sites."

"Trampling on Merchants' Guild toes?" I guessed.

"More connections." Zeta smirked. "Eduardo Martino could be a Guildmaster, if he pushed it. Instead, he got into the Frauds office. Mam says he made a name for himself ferreting out bad construction in the Hinterland mines, nailing some Construction Guild biggies who'd been using bad materials to shore up the shafts. Mam said it made Eduardo a marked man in Flatlands, turning in his own Guildsmen."

"No wonder he moved out of Flatland," I commented. "It must be tough, being responsible for exposing your own Guild's wrongdoing."

Zeta nodded. "Mam says you mustn't turn on your own. But there was an accident, people were...hurt. And then Ed-

188

uardo Martino showed up with not one, but two Hinterland brides! That's another thing got Mam in a twiz. She gave me an earful about how Eduardo Martino took two sisters out of Hinterland and tried to set them up in Flatlands."

"Double union?" Holly's eyebrows went up. "That's Hinterland for you! It never works."

"According to Mam, one was out to here." Zeta gestured around her middle. "Mam was about my age then, and she said it was a real scandal, that a Martino should go to Hinterland for a mate and come back with two of them."

"One at least stuck with Eduardo," I mused. "The other?"

"Mam wouldn't say. But Eduardo got the house in Garden soon after the baby arrived. Got in on the ground floor, so to speak!" Zeta sniggered.

"That building scheme in Garden was part of the deal they worked out with Admin to settle the Merchant's War with the Guilds," I reminded her. "Get the small farmers off the land, build houses, sell them to Guild uppers who wanted out of Flatlands and weren't ready for Striver's Hill."

"I suppose." Zeta had no interest in ancient history. "My people stayed in Flatlands."

I did some rough calculations. "That was over twenty years ago. Eduardo must have been a rising star in the Construction Guild to have rated a house back then."

"They were going cheap," Holly said. "No one wanted to live that far away from Striver's Hill back then. But things change. Now Striver's Hill is too crowded, and I hear Garden is getting very pricey." So spoke the one who kept her fingers on the pulse of fashionable Lorr.

"More houses going up," I said. "Reaching towards the Pangkot border. And up the hill, too. I saw a Vikk-shop on Garden Way. Maybe an outlet for Cococha clothes?"

"Not my people," Holly declared. "I don't need those customers."

I changed the subject. "Have you heard anything new about Rafe Urbine?"

Holly was more willing to gossip about fashionable Lorrans than review ancient Flatlands gossip. "Only that he's spending more time running his gallery than he is painting walls. And that the gallery is becoming known as the place to find the most unique works of décor on New Earth.

"What Urbine doesn't create himself, he gets from his so-called apprentices. Or else he imports it from wherever. Pangkot, Hinterland, even South Coast, you name it. He's making coin like no one else in Artist's Sector. He can even afford one of Jake's outfits for the follower he calls his Muse."

"I thought he didn't have anyone special in his life."

Holly shrugged. "Not for Post Six, but she's been around, lurking behind him, ever since he came out from under Selva Delrey's shadow. Jake's seen her, and he's intrigued, trying to find the right material, the right color for her. Not easy, considering her coloring. Pale skin, red hair…"

"Henna-dyed?" Marta must be moving up in the world to rate one of Jake's personal creations.

"He didn't specify the shade," she said. "But Jake's been trying to come up with something that won't be as garish as what she wore the last time he saw her."

"When was that?"

Holly closed her eyes briefly. "Jake went to that gallery opening about a week ago. Just before…" Her voice trailed away as she realized what she'd said.

"Audra Martino disappeared," I finished. "Why didn't you tell me he'd been there?"

'You didn't ask. And you can ask him now yourself. Jake!" She yelled toward the upper floor. "Come down! Pola has a question for you."

Jake stomped down the back stairs, tall and spare in a pink smock and trou, hair standing on end. "Not now! I've got orders for four original gowns for the Winterfest All-Guild Ball, and the Pangkoti fabric is not here yet!"

"If what you're talking about is patterned silk, it's still on display in the Pangkoti kiosk on the Central Plaza," I told him. "What can you tell me about the Urbine Gallery opening?"

"Is that what this is about? You tear me from important work to ask about something that happened two weeks ago?"

"A young female was thrown into the river that night. She was at that opening party. You might have seen or heard something that led to it."

Jake ran a hand through his hair, disturbing it even more. "I wasn't there long, just long enough to check out whether our designs or Guernreich's dominated. It was jammed with all sorts of people, most of them chattering about Art, and how unusual the paintings were."

"Did you notice anyone in particular? Like...her?" I showed him the drawing of Audra.

He glanced at it, then looked closer. "Oh, her. Very striking face, had the good sense not to distract from it. Wore a plain gown, no trou, very simple, classic line. But good fabric, some kind of linen, I think. Not one of ours. Not Guernreich's, either. Is that the one...?"

"Audra Martino. She was the one who did the odd drawing of the riverbank, with the swirly water."

Jake nodded slowly. "I do remember that one. Very interesting use of heavy black lines, to draw the observer in. And the suggestion of something under the water. I wondered if I could get that effect in some kind of embroidered trim..." He stopped. "There *was* one thing...Something someone said..."

"Jake!" A yell from upstairs. "Merchant Hanna is here for her fitting!"

"Business calls," Jake said. "I'll try to remember..."

"Get the gown done," Holly ordered. "Merchants' Guild comes first, Pola can wait."

"I'll have to," I said.

Nothing to do about it. Business always comes first in Lorr.

I locked up for the night, and summoned Aziz. One more stop, and I could relax.

Or so I thought!

ii

It was dark when Aziz and I hit the Grand Boulevard. The electrics had come on, and the storefronts glittered. The Upper Tier had had its turn at showing off. Now it was the office drones who filled the street with two-wheels, three-wheels and hired pedishaws. Aziz steered carefully around pedestrians and wheelers. I was in no great hurry. I only hoped I'd find my quarry at Urbine's gallery.

I hopped out of the pedishaw just in time to see Urbine enter his domain.

"Oyo!" I called out. "Guildmaster Urbine?"

He stopped in midstride.

"Yes?" He looked me over. "You're that Independent Eye, Pola Drach. You pretended to be a prospective patron. Then, you went to my studio and asked questions about Audra Martino."

No mites on him!

"I found her," I said.

"A sad accident, I was told."

"Perhaps not. There are some questions about her sad end still pending. Her parents aren't satisfied with the Guards' report."

He frowned. "I thought that was settled. A great pity, too. She was a unique talent." He continued into the gallery.

"Is that all you have to say?" I followed him inside...

"What else is there?" He turned to face me, visibly annoyed. "She was here, and now she is gone. I did not know her well. She was with my studio for two or three months, no more. I saw her when I visited the studio, and only then. I had no contact with her outside of the studio. I told that to the investigating Guard—what was her name? Atterson.

192

I have nothing to add to that statement. Go about your business, Eye Drach." He turned his back on me and headed towards the rear of the gallery.

I persisted. "I thought she came to you for instruction. Isn't that what your studio's for?"

Once again, he faced me. "I do not run a school for beginners, Eye Drach. My studio is a place where those who are almost ready for Craftsmen's Guild membership may complete their work requirements in expectation of attaining full membership. They are not Secondary-school apprentices learning their craft, as set out by the Guild regulations. I accept only those who have already shown they are proficient in their skills. I cannot waste time with mere beginners."

"According to that Pangkoti, Chezan, you were supposed to be giving some kind of instruction. He was very put out that you weren't in the studio doing it."

"I make sure the work they do is up to Guild standards," Urbine huffed. "Each week, I set a particular subject for each of them to depict, in any way they choose. A portrait, a landscape, a collection of objects. I then check the result for accuracy and use of technique. The interpretation of the theme is up to the individual. That is what makes the true artist!"

I looked around the gallery at Edard's blobby flowers and Chezan's weird fuzzy squares and triangles. "Those pictures don't look finished."

"So you might think. But the true artist captures the essence of the subject, not necessarily the exact likeness. An impression, one might say, not a specific delineation." He had forgotten to be annoyed in his enthusiasm. "Each of the artists in my gallery has a unique vision, something new and exciting, not the same boring theme over and over. That is what draws the Upper Tier of Lorr to the Urbine Gallery, and that, Eye Drach, cannot be duplicated."

By this time we had reached the back wall, where Audra's drawing had been moved into a better position under one of the electrics.

"What about this?" I indicated her riverbank scene. "That looks pretty real to me, except for the water. That's weird, as if there's something lurking under it, or maybe it's just the way the ripples swirl."

Urbine looked smug. "That is the point, Eye Drach. Your eyes may be fooled by the lines into thinking there is something there when, in fact, there is not."

"Or maybe she's recording exactly what she saw," I countered. "I've seen the drawings she made for the book about Captain Drogo Drach. Is that why you were willing to take her into your studio? Did that make her enough of a professional without an official Craftsmans' apprenticeship? Or did her father's influence get her into your exclusive studio?"

Urbine let out an exasperated sigh. "True, I was aware of Audra's previous work for the Advanced Academy. And yes, I have had previous dealings with her father, Eduardo Martino, through his work with the Construction Guild. We met at several sites where he was checking the quality of the materials used and the progress of the decorations."

"Sites such as Selva Delrey's little hideaway in the Mineral Mountains?"

"Banker Delrey took an interest in my designs. She was known as a patron of the Arts. A pity she has retired from the social scene."

"So, you did know Audra before she came to the studio?"

I'd caught Urbine in an open lie, and he backwheeled.

"I did *not* know her," he emphasized. "When Martino brought Audra's work to my attention, I told him I was ready to look at her sketchbook with an open mind. He invited me to a gathering at his house to celebrate her certification from the Advanced Academy, and she showed me her drawings.

"I found them impressive for one who had not been specifically trained in drawing. She was a surprisingly accurate draftsperson. I told her I thought she should continue to draw, to improve her technique, that her work had definite commercial possibilities."

"And Audra took the bait?"

"Audra was interested in improving her craft. I pointed out that, in the interests of convenience, she might wish to take residence in the studio rather than ride her two-wheel across the city. She was willing to do so...one might even say eager. Her parent agreed, and was willing to provide some financial aid."

"In other words, Eduardo paid the tuition fee."

Urbine drew breath sharply. "I do not charge for tuition! I repeat, I do not instruct. Instruction is the province of the Academics. Martino paid for Audra's room, board, and materials. Paper, ink, styli, paints, brushes—they cost, Eye Drach."

"What about the others in your studio? Are there any other apprentices besides Edard, Chezan, and Marta? What brings them here ? Are they competent artists? Ready for admission into the Craftsman's Guild?"

"There are no others. Edard is quite competent at his craft. He was admitted to the Craftsman's Guild as a Journeyman, at the lowest ranking, last year. He has submitted several paintings to the Guild as examples of his technique, besides the one on exhibit here in the gallery." He indicated the blobby flowers.

"What about Chezan?" I asked. "Do you approve of his technique? Does he show promise of expertise?"

"Chezan has a unique vision," Urbine declared. "And you might not think it, considering his rough demeanor and appearance, but his family is considered Upper Tier in Pangkot. They have connections to the Dark Ones' pharmaceutical operations here in Lorr."

Meaning there was plenty of coin in the family, and a lot of it could be funneled off to keep the Urbine Studio and Gallery afloat.

"And Marta?"

"Marta is a competent artist, but she also makes herself useful in other ways," Urbine said slowly. "She assists in the gallery, organizes sales of works in the Flatlands Street Markets. She manages the lodgings, monitors the kitchen."

"I thought the cook did that. She made it clear she was in charge of the catering."

"Marta oversees the expenditures of the studio, which includes food and drink. She purchases the materials, the foodstuffs, that sort of thing. She has the final say on who lives in, and who must find lodgings elsewhere."

"Including Audra?" I reminded him. "Marta wasn't too pleased about having to share sleeping quarters with her."

"As to that, I could not say. I do not live in the studio. I have my own quarters on the Artist's Sector side of Striver's Hill."

That said a lot about Rafe Urbine's place in Lorr. The sunny side, the side that got the afternoon light, was the fashionable side. The shady side was the "wrong side", the border with Artists' Sector. North light was supposed to be good for making pictures, but the rooms would be cold and damp from the winds off the Mineral Mountains.

"How long has Marta been with your studio? She's getting on, isn't she? A little old to continue as an apprentice?"

"Marta and I met during my stay in Hinterland.".

"That was at Selva Delrey's lodge? Wasn't she the one who brought you to the attention of the Lorr Admin uppers?"

Urbine turned huffy again. "Banker Delrey was good enough to exhibit some of my work, and to introduce me to some prospective patrons, but I have had no dealings with the Delrey clan for at least three years. Do not try to link me with their misdeeds."

All of which had come to nothing because of my intervention…which did not get onto the newsposts. But that's a story for another time.

"Marta is from Hinterlands?" Interesting, as was the Delrey connection. "When does she apply for full Guild membership?"

"'She can do it at her discretion. She hasn't done it yet, as far as I know."

"At your pleasure?" I added a salacious wink.

"Exactly what are you implying? I have never considered her anything but a devoted follower—a Muse, if you will. I am not responsible for her thoughts or actions, especially not towards those females who choose to find me... attractive."

Which gets you off the fishhook if Marta's jealousy gets out of hand, I thought. Aloud, I said, "Just to satisfy my curiosity, Guildmaster, where were you this afternoon, say between high noon and the third bell after?"

Urbine reacted with a grimace. "It is no business of yours, Eye Drach. But to satisfy your curiosity, I was consulting the Construction, Entertainment, and Grocer's Guildmasters about the All-Guild Winterfest Ball. I am in charge of the decorations, and there is a great deal to be done before festivities."

"And they will all vouch for your being there all afternoon?"

"I'd just returned from the meeting when you accosted me," Urbine said testily. "And I am done with this questioning. I have no more to say about Audra Martino and her unfortunate demise."

He moved on to contemplate another drawing. There was no mistaking that beaky nose, the arched eyebrows.

"That's Audra."

"A preliminary sketch only. A commission from Eduardo Martino. I suppose I should destroy it."

"Don't destroy it," I told him. "Show it, or hide it, but don't destroy it. If nothing else, it will remind people that Audra Martino existed."

I left him there, contemplating the portrait, and found Aziz waiting anxiously, the remains of a bun in his hand.

"May we go now? I wish to make my final accounting to Transport before puja."

"Foodie Alley," I ordered.

I had a lot to think about, and I needed a few peaceful hours to do it in.

I didn't get them.

iii

The crowd was thick at the Flatland Bridge as Aziz turned the pedishaw onto Entertainment Row. Construction had been busy putting up the Winterfest decorations.

Electrics had been strung from rooftop to rooftop to rooftop, linking them in a chain of twinkling lights. The two theaters had each added a conifer on either side of their entrances, also decorated with lights and cheap tinsel. The casinos, not to be outdone, had added tinkling music to the clang of the wheels and shouts of the winners and losers within.

Even the Green Dragon had gotten into the action, its iconic critter sporting a tasseled cap and long scarf, holding a bag of Winterfest gifties.

Aziz took his time winding around other pedishaws, exchanging greetings with his fellow drivers. He and I were both looking forward to the end of a long and eventful working day.

It was about to get even longer and more eventful.

Trouble was brewing at the intersection of Entertainment Row and Foodie Alley. The Prophet of Doom was still at it, but he wasn't alone. Jox Custo's followers hadn't taken his demise easily. They were back, angry and vocal, and they had their own ideas as to why their leader wasn't with them.

"You killed him!" That was the youngster Hannes. Jox's Second, a stalwart young male in seaman's garb, red bandanna around his neck, knitted cap on his head.

One of the females clustering around the Prophet retorted, "He was old, he was sick, he would have gone anyway."

"He was alive, now he's not!"

"Not our concern!"

Two big males in black lizardhide leathers shoved through the crowd.

"You! The one who calls himself the Prophet!" Brutus, my erstwhile guardian, yelled at the male in the middle of the pack of females. "You're in violation of the rulings of the Honorable Guild of Forgers, Assassins, Thieves and Swindlers!" He emphasized the last word. "Master Assassin Fee M'Farr wants his cut! Or get back to Hinterland and take the coin off the miners and woodchoppers!"

This brought a knowing laugh from half the crowd, an angry growl from the other half.

I spotted Basher Bob on the edge of the crowd, Velda at his side, and edged towards them.

"What's going on?"

"Fee M'Farr's had enough of this character evading him, calling his grift a 'religion' and so exempt from paying any toll, fee, or tax. This Prophet's not connected with any of the gods of Pangkot, he's not listed with the Academy as being a Philosopher, and he's got no business stirring people up with reptile-poo about rodents coming down from Outer Space to annihilate us on New Earth."

"So?"

Velda didn't like the Prophet any more than Basher did.

"So, if he's not any of those, and he's taking coin, he's a Swindler, selling bad merch. He's got to pay up, like anyone else, and join the Fatso Guild. Or get out of Lorr, and take his nutterlings with him."

"What about the other lot? Doesn't M'Farr have something to say to them? Aren't they taking coin for those mags?"

"They're giving them away," Basher pointed out. "They don't take coin, they don't promise anything. Nothing for M'Farr to worry about. Let the Merchants' Guild sort them out."

I tried to assess the situation. All I wanted to do was get around the crowd, get to Fletcher's for a meal, get upstairs to take care of Ficus and nurse my assorted bruises. Instead, I was stuck behind an angry mob getting angrier by the minute.

The Prophet mounted his stand and waved his hands skyward. "Unbelievers! They are coming for you all!"

"Go peddle your stale fish to the miners!" someone at the back of the crowd hooted.

"You defy Buda-Ganesha!" That from one of the Pangkoti Fatsos.

"Buda-Ganesha will be useless!" the Prophet insisted.

"Mata Deva will destroy the rodents!" Another Pangkoti believer.

"Kali Mara will devour them!" I'd heard the name before, but I didn't remember when. The latest Pangkoti import? There are so many deities in Pangkot, I lose track.

"The Nameless One is above all others." Aziz joined in the chorus. "No rodent can withstand the might of the Nameless one!"

Nothing like a good religious dispute to get the Pangkotis riled. All of them converged on the Prophet, joined by the Fatsos who didn't care one way or another about the gods of Pangkot, but weren't about to lose the coin due them from the Prophet's collection-box.

I tried to get out of the scrum using one elbow while I fumbled to unhook my small bludgeon, but the crowd pressed in on me. Someone let loose a heavy object in the direction of the Prophet. The crowd surged forward.

The Fatsos were surrounded by angry, shouting, people. The Prophet's acolytes yowled for help. I was shoved this way and that while toes got trampled, elbows jammed into ribs, and everyone yelled epithets, prayers, and curses.

I felt something poke my back. I was getting really tired of being a target for whoever had it in for me. I shoved backwards with my right elbow and got the bludgeon out with my left hand. I stepped back onto someones' foot. Then someone yelped, struck out, and hit someone else.

That did it! The mob turned into a fight, bludgeons and sticks and fists. I only hoped no one pulled a blade.

Brutus and his buddies managed to whack their way to the front of the crowd, where they could hold off the mob until the Guards got there to take charge of the mess.

I smelled something strong and tangy. Henna? I'd smelled that before, when I'd been shoved under the carrier.

I turned to see who had poked me, thrusting the bludgeon forward to catch whoever it was. I connected with someone who yelled something about Mata Deva. Not the one who smelled of henna dye, someone else. My attacker seemed to have melted into the press of people converging on the Prophet's stand.

I had to bash my way to the edge of the crowd. I wound up on the wrong side of Foodie Alley, across from Fletcher's with a surging mass of shouting, struggling humanity between me and my destination.

I wriggled into the nearest doorway, a patisserie that specialized in Norland breads and nutcakes. From this niche of safety, I could scan the crowd, looking for telltale red hair.

It was hard to pick out one person in that mob, with the lanterns throwing weird shadows across the road and the yelling mixed into one roar. I scanned the crowd again, but I didn't see any telltale mop of red hair. I did catch sight of Chezan working his way through the mass to freedom.

At this point, the City Guards arrived, four of them. They waded into the scrum using batons and bludgeons right and left, aided by Fatsos. I stayed where I was, well out of the way, and let the various sides battle it out.

Chezan sidled along the edge of the crowd. I reached out, grabbed him by the jacket, and yelled, "Let's get out of here!"

He turned to see who'd nabbed him. I got a firmer grip on his arm, and pulled him down Foodie Alley away from the fight.

"You look as if you could use a meal," I told him once I could be heard over the shouting. "And here we are, where we can get one."

Chezan pulled his arm away and straightened his jacket and headwrap. "If you're buying, I will eat with you." He glared at me. "But I don't know anything about how Audra died, so don't ask me."

"I wasn't planning to," I assured him. "I want to know how she lived. And that, Friend Chezan, you do know. What's your fancy?"

"Here." He stepped into the Pangkoti food shop across Foodie Alley from Fletcher's. "If I must talk to you, at least let it be over something worth eating."

iv

I followed him into the food shop. I don't usually indulge in Pangkoti fare—the exotic spices play havoc with my tongue and my tum. But just this once, I decided to take a chance. I'd already subjected the bod to mayhem during the day, so a little more wouldn't do much more damage. And once the ruckus died down, I could cross the street and find refuge in my own digs.

The place was filled with chattering diners, not only Pangkoti but a few daring souls willing to try something that wasn't the standard fried fish or roast beast served at most tables in Lorr. Chezan took a seat without being asked, clearly a long-time patron. He beckoned to a harried-looking server.

"You pay in advance," the server demanded. "Or no food."

"What's on the menu?" I asked, sniffing the aromas emanating from the pots on the stove visible from our table.

The server reeled off a list of incomprehensible items.

"What's in them?" I wasn't about to ingest something totally inedible.

Chezan came to my rescue. "Mostly fowl. And there's rice wine."

"Chai for me." I wasn't about to go muzzy on some kind of exotic jack, and Pangkoti chai is considered the best on New Earth. "Easy on the spices."

Chezan relayed this to the server. I produced coin, which opened the server's eyes and gave him incentive to get us the food and drink.

"Now," I said, after Chezan had his bottle of rice wine and I had my pot of chai, and both of us were refreshed. "Tell me about your life, Friend Chezan. Why did you decide to come here? Why choose Urbine's studio?"

"I came to Lorr because that is where everyone comes. Lorr is the center, Lorr is the marketplace, Lorr is where things happen. Pangkot is boring." Chezan snorted his opinion of Pangkoti society. "Pangkot art is boring. Same images, same techniques. Ink on paper, images of the gods or the Autocrat or the legends of the past. I wanted—needed—something more."

"So, you came to Lorr." If there's ever a place that welcomes the new and different, it's Lorr. Fashion is everything, and Fashion is always changing. "What did your family think of that?"

Chezan took another swig of wine. "I am a fourth son, no use to anyone, or so my parents say. I could go my own way. All I had to do was make a few contacts, pass on a few messages, and I'd get a stipend and freedom. A good deal all around."

Sure it was, for whoever was pulling his strings in Pangkot.

"Why choose the Urbine Studio "

"Why not? Urbine has the Guild connections, both Craftsman and Construction. He has the gallery, to promote the work he produces. He's got the technique, when he wants to use it. He promotes his apprentices into the Guild, gets them noticed. By the Upper Tier."

"But you're not satisfied with his mode of instruction?"

"What instruction?" Chezan snorted. "The first year I was there, he'd come in twice a week, look over the work, make suggestions. Now, he spends all his time at the gallery.

Once a week he comes in to give an assignment. Edard does the rest."

"What sort of assignments?"

"The usual. An assortment of objects. A plant in a pot. A portrait of one of the other students. The scenery outside the studio. Once we had a female come to sit what we call 'for the figure', so that we can learn anatomy. Another time it was a male. Also unclad." Chezan snickered into his rice wine. "Audra had a fit over that! I don't think she'd ever seen a male undressed before."

"Ah, Audra." I wondered when he'd get around to her. "What was she like?"

Chezan waved one of his eating-sticks dismissively. "Audra? I don't know what she was like before she came to the studio. She was only there for a few months, so I can't tell you anything about her home life, if that's what you're after. At the studio, she was all business, serious about learning the craft. Followed Edard's suggestions, completed the assignments."

"What about after the lessons? She lived at the studio, you must have had meals with her. Marta said she tried to come with you when you went to Entertainment Row, and you mentioned something about her accompanying you to puja...was she interested in religion?"

"Not religion. She just followed me and Marta to see where we went. " Chezan looked away, then back at me. "She followed us to the river, to the puja for Kali Mara."

"The newest arrival from Pangkot? Which one is it? I get confused, all these deities."

"Kali Mara manifested herself to sailors when they sailed from Pangkot to settle South Coast. Some of them invoke her name in storms."

Not that it helps much. Between the two moons pulling the tides around and the odd currents, the oceans of New Earth are treacherous. Sailing them is always dangerous, even for puffers.

I put Kali Mara aside for the moment and went on with my questioning. "So, there are two males, plus Urbine, at the studio. Where does Marta fit in?"

"Marta manages things." He took a last swig from his bottle and looked around for the server.

"And how did Audra get on with Marta? Friendly? Stand-offish?"

"She tried to be friendly, but Marta would have none of it. Guildmaster Urbine paid Audra more attention than he ever did Marta."

"Oh?" I let that hang in the air.

"Hovering around her when he deigned to show up for instruction, praising her work, putting it into his gallery. I don't think Audra understood what he was doing. Marta did, though. Not happy about it, either."

He beckoned for more rice wine and leaned forward. I got a whiff of it as he whispered, "I tell you one thing strange about Audra. She was good at what she did. She could take a likeness. She listened to instruction, tried to follow what Edard said about line and shading. What came out was accurate, but...

"No soul," he decided. "Just what was there. Might as well be one of those diagrams in the manuals handed to Techs at the manufactory to show what the finished product should look like. Or the ones in the mags to show customers what they are getting. Plain, unadorned, an exact replica of what she saw. Nothing of herself in it.

"All very well, if you want that sort of thing, but not..." He struggled for words. "Original. Something more than anyone else could do."

"Not like your work," I said. "What did Guildmaster Urbine think of your interpretation of his assignments?"

Chezan grinned. "He liked them! Said they were different, a new way of seeing. He put one up front in the gallery. People have commented on it. I even got some notices on Post Four."

"I saw the notice. The art critics didn't like your paint-ings."

"What do critics know?" Chezan waved the critics away with his eating-sticks.

"What about their opinion of Audra's work? The river scene?"

"That was something odd. We were given the assign-ment of 'a landscape in a dream,' and Audra couldn't do it."

"What do you mean, couldn't do it?"

"We were told to imagine something, and she said she couldn't do something that wasn't there. I imagined a scene in the Mineral Mountains that I'd once heard of but never seen, and threw in one of the djinn from the old fairy tales. Marta came up with a fantastical house with many odd win-dows and roofs. Even Edard painted a sky with stars in strange cloud formations, weird color combinations.

"But Audra couldn't depict anything beyond what her eyes saw. No imagination, I suppose. She couldn't draw it if she never saw it." He chortled happily at his own wit as he slurped up what was left of the sauces on the plates.

"Then how did she manage those illustrations of weird sea creatures in the book?" I wondered.

"Probably copied from the images taken by the First Ship surveys. They took their time before making landfall, study-ing the planet. The images are still available in the data stored in the Big Black Box. And there are bones of creatures that wash up on the shores. They are at the Advanced Academy for study, if anyone really cares about them." Implying he didn't, by the twist of his mouth.

"What about that weird drawing, the one of the river? Was that what she came up with for the dreamscape?"

"That assignment was supposed to be 'the view from the riverbank'," Chezan said. "But now you bring it up, it *was* strange. She couldn't imagine a dream, but she must have imag-ined whatever she drew in the water. Because it couldn't have been there, could it? Unless…"

"Unless?" I prompted him.

"She might have seen Kali Mara, the Goddess of the River. Some of the Fishmarket river-runners swear they've seen her."

"The ones who steer the barges around the Estuary?" Mostly Pangkoti refugees who row small boats here and there, picking up passengers or small packages, carrying messages up and down the river. Doing on the water what the pedishaw drivers do on land. No one bothers them, even though they aren't in the Seaman's Guild.

They keep to themselves, live in makeshift shacks around the estuary on either side of the river. Some of their youngsters become street lizards, young thieves, grabbing what they can from the Fishmarket vendors. A lot of those, as I mentioned, have signed on as Fatso apprentices.

I got back to basics. "What about the night of the gallery opening? Marta mentioned that Audra followed you to Entertainment Row. The Prophet and Jox Custo both saw her. So did some of the buskers. What about you? Did you see her after you left the gallery?"

Chezan's face stiffened. "I didn't ask her to come along. If she followed me, I didn't notice. I met friends at some taverns on Entertainment Row."

"Like the Green Dragon?"

"Perhaps." Chezan shrugged. "I have some particular friends there."

That said a lot about Chezan's choice of companionship, and why Audra held no allure for him. Not my business—he was certainly over puberty, and as long as it's consensual, same-sex intimacy is no one's concern except the two involved.

"Marta was with me for a while, then Edard showed up to put me into a pedishaw. She says she was the one to get me back to the studio, but by then I wasn't thinking much. I woke up the next day with a head beating like a temple drum."

"But you can't say for *sure* she was with you all night?"

"Not for certain, no." Chezan frowned. "I'm not even sure when *I* got back."

"Are you going to continue at the Urbine Studio?"

"Maybe, maybe not. I'll stay there until after Winterfest, but I may decide to strike out on my own. I might even sell a painting or two. Or I may go back to Pangkot and bring the Lorran approach to a new audience. Who can tell what the gods have in store for us?"

With that, he swaggered off, leaving me to pay the bill.

υ

I checked both ends of Foodie Alley for rioters before I crossed to get to my digs. The crowd had been dispersed, either by the Guards or because they got bored and went off to do something more productive.

The Prophet had been removed, whether by the Fatsos or the Guards was anyone's guess. His stand was empty, his acolytes vanished.

Jox's stand was still occupied, but not for long. Hannes was directing the rest of the gang as they packed the mags into square baskets.

"Oyo!" I strode over to the stand. "Hannes? Is that your name?"

He stopped his labors. It was the first time I'd had a good look at him. He was taller than me, but not by much. His skin had been tanned by sun and wind and his hair bleached by the weather, so it was hard to say what their original tones had been.

I tried some quick calculations. It had been twenty years since Drogo Drach had left Lorr. Give five to sail to Port Chicago, mount his expedition, get across the Middle Sea, another to father a child…could Hannes be a brother I didn't know I had?

Then I checked the eyes. Blue, not green. Whoever Hannes' male parent was, it wasn't Drogo Drach.

208

He also looked me over. "You're the one Jox told me about. The Independent Eye, Pola Drach."

"That's me. Jox fetched up on my doorstep yesterday. I was there when he…" I hesitated.

Hannes had no reservations about naming the unnameable. "He died. I know. The Guards… that woman, Atterson…" He choked on his emotion.

I forgave him the vulgarity. South Coast doesn't have Lorr's delicacy about assigning gender.

"Captain Atterson's checking into the circumstances. If there's anything wrong, her people will find out."

"I don't trust them. Jox didn't, either. He warned me about the Administration, said they'd cover up anything that didn't agree with the way they wanted things run."

I couldn't deny it. Admin tends to whitewash things, to keep the peace and keep business moving in Lorr.

"I'm looking into things myself," I assured him. "I've been tracking Jox's movements since he got to Lorr. What about before? Do you have some time to talk to me? We can sit down at Fletcher's, if you need a meal."

Hannes hesitated, then told one of the other youngsters, "I'll be in a space. Pack up the baskets, take them back to the lodgings."

"What then?" one of the South Coast males asked.

Hannes shrugged "Jox would want us to keep on with his mission, but…"

"We'll talk about it at the lodging-house." His friends continued with their chores, while I led him to Fletchers.

"What's your potion? They don't do jack here, but you can have clet, chai, or brew. Roast beast or fish stew." I motioned towards the bowls set out on the counter where Fletcher's partner dished up edibles.

"Chai. And fish stew. Jox told us to stay away from anything that wasn't fish."

I had a mouthful of spices from the Pangkoti cuisine to counteract. I claimed my usual seat and ordered a fruit pastry for me, a bowl of fish soup for Hannes, and chai for both of us.

The server arrived with our food. Hannes dived into the bowl of soup as if he hadn't had a square meal in days. If he'd been eating the usual Flatlands slop, Fletcher's fish soup would be a revelation.

I munched my pastry, fresh from the patisserie next door, and sipped chai. The lingering spices were overcome by the sweetness. The chai was not as good as the Pangkoti blend across the street, but it was better than clet.

I got down to business. "Tell me about Jox. Where did you hook up with him?"

"I have always known Jox," Hannes said slowly. "He lived in lodgings with my mama when he wasn't at sea. He taught me the ways of the water, how to sail a boat, how to survive in a storm. He took me with him as apprentice when he sailed to the Southern Continent. He insisted he was not my parent, but I always thought of him as such. And now..." He swallowed hard, took a pull at the chai to hide his emotional response.

"What brought him back to Lorr?"

Hannes pulled himself together. "He'd been beached after his last voyage, the one where they'd landed on the Southern Continent. When he got back, he was upset about the state of the oceans, and he started to protest. The Junta was not pleased."

I bet they weren't! The South Coast Junta was even more ruthless than the Lorr Guild Council in protecting business. Anything that interrupted the flow of coin was to be put down, even if it meant human lives would be endangered. No Dark Ones to oversee the factories, or prevent adulteration of foodstuffs, no one to speak for the health and safety of the Mechs who did the actual labor. And it didn't matter what damage was done to the land or water, so long as the coin kept flowing into the pockets of the Junta and their supporters.

"But Jox would not be silenced. There was someone who had been with him on the voyage with Drogo Drach. She was at the Advanced Academy at Port Chicago. Jox met with her, persuaded her to publish her notes about the voyage, with the purpose of alerting people to the danger facing them if they did not stop destroying the life in the oceans."

"So, Jox was behind that book. No wonder he was so upset when it got rewritten!"

"*The Voyages of Captain Drogo Drach* was not especially popular in Port Chicago," Hannes observed. "It was put out by the Academic Academy without much fanfare. Drogo Drach was no longer around, and memories are short in Port Chicago, unless the someone in the Junta wants to stir things up against one or another of their enemies.

"But then someone sent a copy to the Advanced Academy in Lorr, and someone else picked up on it, and the word got out that the book was going to be published in a revised version. So, Jox came here to speak to the Administration directly. And you came along?"

"I was with him, yes. We had a paid passage, we did not work the ship. Jox recruited some of the other passengers, young people bound for the Advanced Academy in Lorr."

"And what happened when you got here?"

Hannes swallowed hard. "He went to the Seaman's Guild to renew his membership. He went to the Administration to register as a legitimate lecturer, so he could place his protest before those who would move the Administration to act against the Junta's desecration—his word, not mine—of the oceans. And he went to the Advanced Academy to have it out with the person who had rewritten the books."

"Where were you while he did all this?"

"I was with Kemal and the rest of them, at the South Coast Sailors' lodgings. Across the river, near the bridge."

"Not with Jox?"

"That place is for the Lorr Seamen's Guild." Hannes said. "Most of the puffer's crew stayed in lodgings close to the

Flatlands docks, to be near the ship, but Jox wanted us closer to him, so we got rooms with the fishers on the Flatlands side of the bridge."

I pulled out the drawing of Audra. It was starting to get a little worn around the edges, and the graphite had smudged, but it was still recognizable.

"Ever see her?"

Hannes gazed at the drawing, then handed it back to me. "She came to the stand. She talked to Jox."

"Not to you?"

"No." There was a world of longing in that one syllable. "She wanted to know about kraken. I could have told her... but she didn't ask me."

But you wanted her to, I said silently. "When was this?"

"She came with some people...friends, I think. A man and a woman...that is, male and female. I forget, sometimes, what to say in Lorr. In Port Chicago, it's not so finicky." He smiled, and his whole face lit up. "She was with them, but not one of them. They were loud, making jokes. She was quiet, interested in what Jox was saying. I didn't speak to her then..."

"But later?"

He rubbed his nose. "It was after her friends left. She looked for them, made as if to follow them. I...I followed her. I thought I would catch up with her and tell her what I knew about the kraken."

Aha! Maybe Hannes was the mysterious figure Brutus had seen in the river mist! I waited for him to tell his story, itching to prod him, knowing he had to do it in his own way.

"I looked for her in the small taverns, but didn't see her... and then I thought I saw her on the Waterfront piers with some-one else..."

"Male or female?" I blurted.

"It was starting to get misty, I couldn't tell. About the same height, not broad or tall like a male, but it could have

212

been a small, scrawny male. I could make out legs, so maybe wearing trou, maybe a long coat or jacket."

"Where did they go?"

"They went to the bridge. Together." He stopped. I got a sense of his longing for this mysterious female—not love, but fascination with the unattainable. "I didn't see anything more. The fog got thick, and Jox came after me and took me away."

"Jox followed you?" I tried to get this straight. "You followed Audra, Jox followed you. What then?"

"Jox made me go back to the stand to pick up the books and pack up the rest of the gear. And then I went back to the lodgings, but I did not see the girl...you call her Audra? I did not see her on the bridge. I did not see anyone except the big Flatlands Force fella who made me pay toll."

"And you've been at your lodgings ever since?"

"When I wasn't with Jox. Why?"

"Because, young male, you have escaped Jox's fate. Be very careful what you eat and drink, and don't accept any gifts from strangers."

"Do you think...the other person on the bridge?" It dawned on him. "Jox saw or heard something..."

"Or whoever was on that bridge with Audra thought he did." I finished. "That's what got him killed. Not the foofaraw about the kraken, not the pink pellets. Just someone trying to cover their trail. And I'm beginning to understand just who that someone is. Be very careful, Hannes. I may call on you again."

I headed upstairs to feed and water Ficus and think my way through the tangle of plots and motives. I had two problems to solve—three, if you counted the attacks on me—but I wasn't sure how they all fit.

"It's all wrong," I told Ficus while I spritzed it and spooned extra bonemeal and clet powder into its pot. "The only thing that links Audra to Jox is that she stopped by his stand once,

213

to ask him about the kraken. Someone keeps shunting me away from the Urbine studio, but is it because of Audra or something else? And where do those pink pellets fit in?"

Ficus had no answers for me. I flopped down on my bed and closed my eyes to think it over.

When I opened them, light was streaming into the bedroom window. I was still in the muddy jacket and trou from the day before, and my head was full of wisps of dreams. My tum was roiling, I had a foul taste in my mouth, and I really needed the "place" downstairs in a hurry. I vowed never to eat Pangkoti food again.

Fletcher wouldn't be ready to serve yet, so I boiled a little pot of water for chai over my alcohol stove, fed and watered Ficus, and indulged in the end of the loaf of bread smeared with my recently bought Norland honey. I changed my muddy garb for a smart set of matching jacket and trou of a discrete Norland wool in a neutral light brown, and a neat off-white shirt. Let Angie sneer at beige, it works for me!

I went over my plan for the day as I sipped chai. I had a good idea who was after me; the only point I had to settle was why? Was it a paid hit, or just personal? And what did it have to do with either Jox or Audra?

vi

I thought this over as I joined the rest of the workday crowd on the Grand Boulevard. I checked the newsposts at the corner of the Boulevard and Clothier's Alley. Nothing remarkable, not even a notice about an elderly seaman found departed in Foodie Alley. That was only to be expected. No one wanted to keep people away from the main venue for edibles on Entertainment Row.

I found my office door unlocked. Zeta must have been more than usually officious. I'd have a word with her.

But first there was business to attend to. Eduardo Martino awaited me. He'd settled into the wooden chair opposite my desk.

"Friend Eduardo…" I began.

"I saw what happened on Garden Way," he said. "Horrible! Violence, in Garden!"

"Not what you want in such a nice sector," I agreed. "You didn't happen to notice who stuck me with a dart, did you?"

"Is that what happened? I saw you fall and called the Dark Ones and the Guards."

"And for that, I owe you a life-debt. Your quick actions got me attended to, and the poison—"

"Poison!" He hadn't heard that bit of news.

"Someone stuck me with a poisoned dart or needle," I explained. "If I hadn't been treated as fast as I was, the poison would have had more time to take hold. However, I got the antidote in time, and my would-be killer was foiled."

Martino frowned. "Why would someone want to poison you?"

"I'm not sure. It may be because I am very close to finding out what happened to Audra."

"How close?" Martino leaned forward. "Sara came by last night. She said you had been warned off, by no less than Security Chief Polaris!"

"I'm almost certain it was one of two people, but I cannot accuse either of them without proof. I intend to get it, but I need your help."

"Whatever it takes."

"Not much," I said. "You are planning a Service of Consolation for Audra, once her physical remains have been reduced in the vats?"

Martino gulped back tears and nodded. "Sara brought us the information. The Dark Ones have reduced Audra's chemical residue and re-introduced it to the soil. Geri thought we might hold the service tomorrow afternoon. It takes a bit of time to get things ready, and we'll have to send the cards around to let people know when and where to come."

"Good. Invite Instructor Segretti and his assistant, Britta Drach, to attend."

"Really? They aren't family, but I suppose they should," Martino said slowly. "But will they come? It has been more than a week, and the Founders said mourning should be private, so as not to burden the community with needless ceremony."

"Britta was Audra's closest friend at the Advanced Academy. I think she will attend, even at short notice. You may have to use a little personal persuasion, but make sure Instructor Segretti is there, if only to refute the suggestion he had anything to do with Audra's decision to change from the Academic to the Craftsman's Guild. There are always insinuations of misconduct when a young female attracts the attention of an older male."

Martino nodded.

I went on. "There are a few more people who should receive personal invites. Guildmaster Rafe Urbine, and his student Chezan. And Marta, who acts as Urbine's assistant, but may be more than that."

"That's quite a crowd," Martino objected. "There may not be room for them all in my house. Maybe I should reserve the Central Hall at the Construction Guildhouse, and put in an order for refreshments with the Grocer's Guild."

I ignored the sarcastic edge in his voice. "Too public. Use the Meeting-house in Garden. There are a few others who may be interested in attending. A Pangkoti called Brutus and a South Coaster called Hannes. You don't know them, but they may have been the last to see Audra alive. Brutus is the Flatlands Forcer who saw her on the bridge. So did Hannes. They should be there, to add their voices to Consolation. And make sure Captain Atterson comes. We may need her before the Service is over."

Martino frowned. "Does this mean you'll tell us who destroyed Audra?"

"By the end of the meeting, you'll know."

Martino left, muttering about sending Construction Guild messengers with invites, and arranging for Grocer's Guild to send supplies.

The Brain isn't the only one who can set a trap!

Zeta popped her head into the office, interrupting my gloating.

"Admin messenger's been. There's something for you." She passed me a handful of folded papers, all marked with the Admin sigil.

"Probably a tax notice," I grumbled. Admin messengers circulate around Lorr on a regular schedule, useful for sending personal notices that don't belong on Post Six.

I scanned the messages. One was a reminder to pay my quarterly toll on income. One was a list of official Winterfest doings. And one, an elaborately engraved heavy paper document, was an invite to the Administration Winterfest Gala.

I get one of those every year, courtesy of my relationship with Security Chief Polaris. I never use them.

This year, though, I gave it more thought. What would the Admin tier think if I actually attended, dressed in Jake and Holly's best? What message would it send to the Delrey faction? And who would I bring as an escort?

I didn't really know anyone Admin would consider suitable. Maybe Reg Bonwit...but he was already committed to Julian Hunt, and she never left her house on Arriver's Hill. Basher Bob was also taken. There was Dark Kelvin, but Dark Ones are not welcome anywhere except within their own Order. No one wanted to be around those who dealt with the unmentionable.

And then there was Brutus. I tried to picture Polaris's face if I showed up on the arm of a hulking Pangkoti ex-pirate, now Flatlands Force! But it would give Brutus ideas I'd just as soon he didn't have regarding our relationship.

I tossed the card aside. Admin Galas were boring, just a lot of people trying to one-up each other. I'd have a better time at Smokey Joe's with Basher and Velda and the rest of the gang. And I wouldn't have to rig myself out in an elaborate gown, either.

I wrenched myself out of fantasy and back to fact. Something was nagging at the edges of my mind.

Someone was tailing me, waiting for opportunities to strike. So far they'd missed. I was still alive, thanks to my own reflexes and Eduardo's call to the Guards. What bothered me was, how did this stalker know where to find me? Where did they pick up my trail? And what were they so afraid of that they'd resort to such drastic measures to stop me?

What did Audra know they didn't want me to find out?

And who were "they"? The Delrey clan? Vikks? Or someone I didn't even know?

I had to start over from the beginning. I'd go back to Artist's and take another look at Urbine's studio by daylight.

But first I had to find Brutus and Hannes, and persuade them to attend a Service of Consolation for someone they'd never actually met. Then, I had to deal with whatever came out of it.

I told Zeta, "I'm going out. If someone calls for me, write down their name and affiliation and leave it for me. And from now on, don't open the office until I get there, no matter who's waiting."

"But where are you going?" she whined

"Here and there." I waved vaguely in the direction of the Central Plaza. "I may not be back until tomorrow."

"That's no way to do business!"

"It's the way I do it."

And with that, I headed out, back into the crowded streets of Lorr. I had a plan. I just didn't want Zeta to be able to give away my whereabouts to whoever was waiting for me to make another mistake.

viii

Finding Hannes took some time.

I went back to Foodie Alley to check on the two speakers' stands. Both were gone.

"What happened to the Prophet? And the other bunch, the Friends of the Oceans, or whatever they called themselves?" I asked at the nearest clet-stand.

"Took down by the Guards," the server said. "After the rumpus last night, Admin declared both of them Persona Non Grata, which means Get Out of Lorr. Fatsos claimed the Prophet was an unsanctioned swindler, took him off for questioning. And the others, the South Coasters, they got a warning, cited for Inciting to Riot."

"What about those acolytes, or whatever they were? The ones who follow the Prophet?"

The clet-stand owner shrugged. "Dunno. The Fatsos only took the Prophet, left the rest of them to pick up the pieces and skiddoo."

Skiddoo to where? Maybe Velda would know. She had contacts with most of the females working Entertainment Row. Unfortunately, Velda was a late riser. She wouldn't be at her usual seat in Smokey Joe's until after noon.

I strolled down Entertainment Row to the Flatlands Bridge. Hannes had said he and his friends had lodgings near it on the Flatlands side. I just hoped they hadn't decided to decamp and take the next ship back to Port Chicago.

I also hoped Brutus was at his post on the Flatlands side so I could smack two pteros with one stone.

No luck—just a lonely youngster, barely out of her teens. Probably one of the recently-recruited street lizards.

"Oyo!" I waved at her. "How's business?"

"The usual," she said. "Techs and drones going in to work. Vendors coming out with pedicarts. Everyone pays their tolls. Not like last night."

"Oh?"

"Lots of to-ing and fro-ing. Force Brutus was on duty—to hear him talk, you'd think he stopped the riot all on his lonesome."

"I heard the South Coasters got into it with some scam artist calling himself the Prophet of Doom," I said casually. "I didn't know it carried on all the way to the bridge."

"The Prophet's females chased the South Coast males," the Force deb gloated. "There was a grand to-do. I wish I'd been there! I'd have showed them what I'm made of!"

"Sounds like a good fight," I commented. "How did it end?"

"Oh, the Guards stopped it," my informant said. "They claimed the Force had no jurisdiction on the Lorr side, and the Prophet's females were not included in the Fatso's case against the Prophet, so they were free to go back to their own lodgings. And the South Coasters got away, back to their place, over there." She waved at a two-story building on the Flatland side of the bridge.

"I'm sorry I missed the action," I said. "Have a profitable day."

I was about to leave her when she held out her hand. "Don't forget the toll," she warned.

I dropped a copper bit into her palm and headed into Flatlands.

The bridge let out onto a brick-paved street lined with cinderblock houses facing the river. The riverbank had been reinforced against flooding with more cinderblocks, the standard building material of Lorr once the walking trees had walked.

I looked at the row of identical houses, trying to decide which was the South Coast lodging-house. They all had signs in the front windows—*Rooms for Travelers*. The one in the middle of the row had the South Coast spiny tree painted on the front door.

I mounted the two steps to that one, rapped on the door, and scanned the street for any action.

A lanky dark-skin male in a South Coast caftan and embroidered cap opened the door. He gave me the fish-eye and started to close it again.

"I'm looking for Hannes and the rest of Jox Custo's crew," I explained. "Four lads from South Coast. Not seamen, students."

The South Coaster kept his face blank. "That lot? They said they'd find lodgings at Advanced Academy after Winterfest."

"Hannes isn't a student," I said. "Is he here?"

"Said something about finding a berth back to South Coast." The landlord jerked his chin in the direction of the ocean-side docks.

My heart sank. I'd hoped not to have to haul myself clear across Flatlands

The landlord tried to close the door again. I blocked it with my foot.

"Where is Hannes now?"

"What's going on?" Hannes shoved the landlord aside and glared at me. "Why are you here? I have nothing more to tell you."

I countered with another question. "Why are you leaving? The Dark Ones haven't finished with Jox yet. And the Guards may have a few more questions for you."

"I found a place on the puffer going south tomorrow, I have to sign on with the purser before they leave. They'll take me on as crew. They're South Coast, no Guild papers necessary."

"What about Jox's mission? Are you going to let that go?"

Hannes flushed. "Those others, the ones he found at the South Coast Advanced Academy…The people here will listen to them. They wouldn't listen to Jox, and they surely won't listen to me. I'm a seaman, I want to go back to sea."

"Not before you attend a Service of Consolation for Audra Martino," I told him. "It's tomorrow afternoon, at the Meeting-House on Garden Road. I need you to be there."

"I can't! This is my chance to go home!"

"You must, for Audra's sake. I need you to identify the one who was following her to the bridge."

"But I didn't see who it was!"

"Whoever it was also killed Jox," I reminded him.

Hannes thought it over. "Are you sure?"

"Reasonably sure." I wasn't quite that certain, but there didn't seem to be any other reason for Jox to be a target.

"Meeting-House, Garden Road. Take the carrier around the Central Plaza, it'll let you off at the junction with Academy Way. You'll see the Meeting-House next to the Dark Ones' Shrine."

I took my time going back over the bridge. I stared down at the water, trying to see what Audra had seen. I didn't see anything but murk. If there was anything lurking under there, it was keeping itself well hidden.

I decided it was time to go back to where all this had started. To Audra. And that meant the Urbino studio, and the people connected with it.

ix

I grabbed the nearest passing pedishaw and headed back to the Grand Boulevard. I wanted another look at the drawing in the Urbine Gallery. Nothing had happened to Audra until that was displayed. There must been something in that picture I'd missed the first time I looked at it.

The glowing review seemed to have set off a buying frenzy—the gallery was jumping, in spite of the early hour. I mingled with a well-dressed gang of would-be buyers, all displaying their artistic good taste by acquiring the most fashionable doodads for their abodes.

I noted the gaps in the displays. Edard's blobby flowers had been removed, replaced by a recognizable assortment of fruit in a basket. The stunning portrait was now off to one side, exchanged for a painting of a scene in the Mineral Mountains of craggy peaks against a glowering sky, two tiny figures at the bottom of a gorge, all done in careful detail. All very ordinary, the sort of thing any rising Guildsman would put in their house to show they were Patrons of the Arts.

Audra's riverbank scene had been placed front and center, under a good electric lamp, where it could be viewed by as many as could get to it. A lot of people wanted to get to it. I had to shove a nattily dressed male away to get closer.

On second viewing, the picture was less mysterious. Maybe it was the lighting, maybe it was knowing what it was sup-

222

posed to be, but I wasn't drawn to the swirls in the river as much as the stems of the plants on the bank. Under the stems, I spotted small circles or dots. Seeds? Pods? Where, exactly, was Audra when she drew that scene?

I heard Chezan's mocking voice: *Unless she saw it, she couldn't draw it.*

I had to find that specific place along the river.

The most obvious place to start? The Urbine Studio. It was close to the river, so where Audra was most likely to find that particular stretch of riverbank.

I let the rest of the crowd get a good look at Audra's masterpiece, and took the carrier to Artist's Way; then walked past the taverns and shops to the River Road crossing.

At dusk it had been a mysterious place of flickering lights and shadows, hiding who-knows-what behind half-seen walls. Daylight revealed the area for what it was—a miscellaneous collection of rundown shacks, sand-block warehouses, and the remains of the ancient shuttles that had brought the Founders down to New Earth.

At the very end of Artist's Way loomed the Craftsman's Guildhall, built just before the Merchants' War, still showing the scars of the rioting. At four stories, it towered over the rest of the buildings, marking the division between Artist's Sector and Striver's Hill. You'd think the Craftsmen would have covered up the wear-and-tear, but they'd left the broken window ledges and turrets as they'd been when the final contracts were signed to end the fighting. In defiance, I guess. Or because no one would pay to fix them.

Beyond the Guildhall, Artists' Way forked. One road led up Striver's Hill to the sprawling houses of the more successful Craftsmen, people like Rafe Urbine, who actually made a good living out of what they created. Beyond that lay the foothills of the Mineral Mountains, the road to the mines and small farms that produced the veg and fowl that fed the citizens of Lorr.

I took the other path, the one that led to the river. Now I could see what I'd missed the first time I'd passed through —sheds put together from salvaged scraps of ancient shuttles, standard sand-block houses, and one or two brick buildings set back, away from the road. I could see some Craftsmen at work through the open doors of the sheds and old ware-houses that had been turned into small factories. One had an array of two-wheels outside the door, another a row of clay jars ready for the smoking kiln.

I wasn't alone on the road. A veg-vendor's pedicart fol-lowed me from Artist's Way, the driver bellowing the qual-ity of her goods. From the other direction came a cart pulled by a belligerent goat.

"Oyo!" I recognized the goat-driver—Inger, from the farm across from the Urbine Studio. "How's business?"

"Not bad." She stopped at the gate to the two-wheel shop. "Are you Eyeing? I heard Urbine's female apprentice met a sorry end."

"I found her," I admitted. "There's a Service of Con-solation tomorrow at the Garden Way Meeting-House if you're interested in attending. You might pass the word along with your dairy products."

She shrugged. "That young female wasn't here long enough to merit consolation. She kept to the studio, never said as much as 'How's business' to those who live nearby."

"Snobby?"

"Not that. Just not interested." Inger turned her atten-tion to some customers who had emerged from the two-wheel shop. As always in Lorr, business comes before anything else.

I walked on, trying to see the place as Audra had. She'd left a comfortable house in Garden for the bleak room in Artist's. She'd abandoned a safe career as an Academic for the chancy life of a Craftsman. She'd tried to make friends of the other apprentices and had been rebuffed, but she persisted. And she'd professed an interest in beings that weren't supposed to exist.

I stopped in front of the Urbine Studio. In daylight, I could see its deficiencies as a dwelling. Two stories, nothing fancy, standard sand-block. I got a whiff of the septic tank, a sign this was one of the last buildings yet to be connected to Lorr's main drains. Marta's scornful words resonated. This was really "roughing it" for someone like Audra, used to the amenities of Garden, where each house had its own solar panels for heat and tie-ins to the electric for light.

I briefly thought of stopping at the studio, then caught a scent of something. Something that didn't belong in the river.

I stepped carefully along the path that wound down to the riverbank and tried to match it to the scene Audra had depicted. Something *was* wrong.

She had shown the water swirling. There were no eddies at this point, just a steady stream. The plants were wrong, too. There were trees here, spindly branches bending towards the water, missing from the picture. The reeds along the bank grew straight, not bending as she had shown. The path ended at the very edge of the bank, but not quite the way she had depicted it.

This was not the scene she had drawn.

My eye was caught by a flash of red floating in the reeds. I found a branch broken from one of the trees, and used it to pull what turned out to be a body to the shore. I knew before I saw the face.

Chezan would never find the acclaim he craved. He'd boasted once too often, to the wrong person.

This had to stop!

I pulled the body onto the bank and trudged back to the goat farm to summon the Guards. No doubt this would be put down to one more drunken artist stumbling into the river.

I knew better. I had no proof, but I would find it. And I would get justice for Audra, and Jox…and for Chezan.

I walked back up the road and waited for Inger to return from her rounds.

"Oyo!" I called as she drew near. "There's something in the river. I'm not sure what it is. Maybe you can help get it out?"

She looped the reins of her goat's harness over the gatepost and followed me to the river's edge, where I pointed at the flash of red, caught in the reeds. She found the same branch I had, and between us, we hauled Chezan onto the bank.

She drew back, her face a mask of horror. "That's…"

"I know. I can't believe it, either. We had food together last night, and now…"

The two of us contemplated the sorry mess that had once been a cynical artist who drank too much rice wine and talked too freely.

"Better go for the Guards," I said. "I'll stay until they show up, then I'll go over to the studio to let that cook know she'll have one less for dinner."

Inger grimaced and trotted off, leaving me to puzzle out what to do next.

I tried to work out the timing. It had been full dark when Chezan left me on Foodie Alley. He'd disappeared into the crowd. Had someone seen him talking with me? Or was this simply someone getting rid of loose ends?

He must have come back here, met someone—who? And then? Chezan hadn't just stumbled into the river because he was too muzzy with rice wine to tell where the path ended. He was muzzy when he left me, but not totally blanked.

Had someone in that mob seen the two of us together and decided to stop his mouth before he said too much?

I waited until I saw Inger's goatcart approaching, accompanied by two Guards. I waved them down.

"He's there." I pointed. "I'll tell the servant at the Urbine Studio. She can inform Guildmaster Urbine."

I left the Guards to their sad task and headed to the studio. I had to look over Chezan's belongings before the Guards got there.

Hildy the cook was as belligerent as before, slicing some veg into a bowl. "Eye Drach? What do you want?"

"Something's happened to Chezan. He's in the river, looks like he drowned."

"No loss, that one. He must have fallen in, full of alcohol as he always was."

"When did you see him last?"

"Yesterday. He woke late, dressed, and left at noon."

"Did he say where he was going?"

"Why tell me? None of that lot care for a mere servant. I cook, but they never bother to tell me when to serve, or how many will be here. I am handing in my notice at the end of Winterfest. Let that Marta do the cooking!" She slammed the knife into her cutting board and dumped the veg into a pot on the stove. "And don't ask me to collect his things, either. They can sit and rot, for all I care. He never did."

"What things? Clothes, sketchbook?"

Hilda scowled. "All sorts. He's been dossing down in the workroom after Audra came and took over the bedroom upstairs. Who's going to pick them up? I won't keep them."

"I'll have a look. Maybe there's something that'll tell us who to send them to. He said he had family in Pangkot."

"He said a lot of things," Hildy groused. "Most of them weren't true."

She turned back to her task, and I moved into the workroom. Edard's blobby flower painting sat there, propped on an easel, and the amorphous clay shape Marta was supposedly working on.

I saw a pallet in a far corner, with a bundle next to it. Chezan's? I unrolled the bundle to uncover a vivid green jacket and trou, a green scarf long enough to be used as a headwrap, and a weird stringy mass of henna-red hair…a wig?

Was Chezan my mysterious female follower?

He was scrawny, short, could pass for female under a padded jacket and trou. No one had seemed able to remember the face between the red hair and the green outfit.

Chezan could have been the one who shoved me under the carrier, or tried to get me with the dart. But why? Was he on his own, or taking orders? And if so…who from?

I chewed over this as I slogged back to Artist's Way. The Guards' skimmer passed overhead as I reached the main road. I ducked into the nearest clet-shop to avoid it, ordered chai, and considered the changed circumstances.

If Chezan was the one who'd tried to kill me twice, he wasn't very good at it. He'd missed the vital spot with the dart in Garden, and I'd scrambled out of the way of the carriers. He wasn't a trained Assassin, so he must have been under orders, but, again, whose? Not Fee M'Farr's. He'd made that clear, and his wrath when he found out someone was acting without authorization on his patch would be fearsome. The Fatsos could and would take revenge.

I sipped chai—not a bad brew, for a small shop—and wondered who wanted me dead. Why now? And did this tie in with Audra Martino's sad fate? Or was there some other reason?

I finished the chai, took a deep breath, and steeled myself for what was sure to be an emotional end to a frenzied day.

The afternoon was drawing to a close, the sun dipping to the western horizon. I had to get over to Garden before it got too dark to see anything. I hustled to the Grand Boulevard, where I picked up the carrier bumbling its way around the Central Plaza. Now, all I had to do was expose the murderer…and avoid being killed in the process.

xi

There was a mass of pedishaws and two-wheels in front of the Meeting-House. The drivers parked their vehicles in the space behind the building; the two-wheels were neatly slotted into a rack next to the door.

Eduardo Martino and Geri were waiting in front to greet their guests—Eduardo genial, his wife furious.

"This is wrong!" she declared as soon as she saw me. "The Service of Consolation is not a public spectacle! It is a moment for the family to contemplate their loss, and let the spirit go. Why have you insisted on this…this entertainment?"

Eduardo tried to calm her down. "Audra touched many people's lives besides ours, and our house in Garden won't hold all of them."

Assorted serious-looking persons joined them, mostly in the dark boiler-suits deemed appropriate by Techs for formal occasions. Martino clan, I assumed. Most of them had the Construction Guild sigil, a crossed hammer and saw, on their sleeves.

I greeted Eduardo with a nod, ignoring Geri. "Looks like you'll have a good showing. Audra would be pleased to see so many people here to keep her in memory."

Geri glared at me. "The Martino family is here, but who are all these other people? I don't know them."

Instructor Segretti descended from a pedishaw, followed by Britta. Eduardo made the introductions.

"Instructor Segretti, thank you for coming. I know you were close to Audra. And…?" He turned to Britta.

I explained, "This is Britta Drach, Audra's friend from the Advanced Academy."

Britta and Segretti nodded to Eduardo and Geri as Guildmaster Urbine descended from another pedishaw, followed by Marta. He also greeted Eduardo with a nod.

"Eye Drach told me you were having the Service of Consolation here. I give you my sympathy, Guildsman. Audra was a rare talent. Her work will keep her spirit in memory."

Eduardo and Urbine gripped hands as coworkers would.

"Thank you for being here. What happened—"

"Terrible, terrible. Such a waste!"

Urbine joined the group being led into the Meeting-House by Construction apprentices commandeered for the occasion.

"Only one more person needed, and then we can start." I looked skyward.

"I hope you know what you're doing," Edouard muttered.

So did I. I was no Brain, I couldn't commandeer a squad of Guards or bully a gang of suspects into a room, and I really hate public speaking. I prefer to insinuate myself into the situation and hint at a solution. But this time, things had gone too far. I had no choice.

I breathed a little easier as a Guards skimmer descended. Atterson emerged, fairly breathing fire.

"What do you think you're playing at, Drach? I've just come from—"

"I don't think, I know. I know what happened to Audra. I know who put her into the river, and why."

"Take it to the magistrate!"

"Not without solid proof, and that I don't have... not yet. But I will. Just trust me for a little while longer, and you'll have answers."

Geri glared at her sibling. "You didn't have to come, Sara. I'm sure you had more important business to attend to."

"I owe it to Audra," Atterson told her.

Geri and Eduardo marched into the Meeting-House, followed by Atterson and me.

Now I had them all here, I just hoped this would work.

xii

The Service of Consolation was held in the central hall, a bare room with only plain wooden benches for seating, electrics for lighting, and a lectern in front of the icons of the Founders at the far end. Their images included Captain Augusta Polaris, stern-faced, haughty, bearing the burden of keeping this sliver of Humanity alive long enough to greet the next ship, whenever it

230

came; and Tech Leader Fergus MacFarlaine, grinning roguishly, ready to challenge anyone and anything that stood in his way. There are furious debates as to whether or not they cohabited, and whether the result is still in the gene pool.

The Lector came forward. A short, stout male with a round face and pale hair in wisps around his pink scalp, he wore the dark jacket-and-trou set of the low-level Admin. He took his place at the stand in front of the crowd, who settled into the folding chairs supplied by the Guild for meetings such as this.

He began with the standard reading from the *Words of the Founders*. "The body is a shell, a husk, but the spirit lives on in the memory of those who come after."

Then, quiet, during which everyone was supposed to consider their connections to the deceased.

"Those who wish to may now speak of the departed," the Lector announced.

Silence stretched out as the assorted mourners, presumably, gathered thoughts into words. Finally, someone broke the stillness.

"Audra was a good girl," Geri quavered. "She could have been anything…" She choked and said no more.

Britta stood up bravely. "She was my friend. We studied the beings of the sea together. We attended classes, wrote essays. She was a seeker of knowledge. I will miss her."

Rafe Urbine stood. "She came to my studio as an apprentice. She had a great talent for portraying the world as it is."

Silence fell again. I looked around to see if anyone else had anything to add. Then I took the place at the lectern.

"Some of you already know me," I said. "Pola Drach, Independent Eye. I didn't know Audra as a living being. I found her body in the cave under the bridge, beside the river. I was asked to look into the circumstances of her demise, and I have discovered certain facts, which I must reveal now.

231

"She did not go into the river voluntarily. She was pushed."

Hubbub, whispered comments, and Atterson took a step forward.

I held up a hand. "The question is, why? What did Audra do make herself an enemy?" I looked around the hall. "Who hated her that much? Perhaps she rejected someone's advances, someone who wanted a deeper bond than Audra was prepared to give." I stared directly at Britta.

She rose in righteous anger. "I never would do such a thing! Never!"

"I didn't say you did." I scanned the group. "You weren't at the Urbine Gallery on the night in question. On the other hand, Instructor Segretti *was* there, and could have followed Audra when she left with the other apprentices."

Segretti exploded. "You cannot say I was there!"

"There is a register of attendees. Your name is on it."

"I may have dropped by to see what Audra did after she left the Academy, out of curiosity. But I certainly did not follow her out of the gallery. I saw her leave with the other apprentices, but I had no reason to kill her. She had broken all ties with the Academy, and with my studies."

"That's right, she did. But she'd read the South Coast version of your book, and seen the original drawings. You provided different material, direct from the old ship records stored in the Big Black Box," I countered. "The ones from the surveys taken before the First Landing.

"Because the drawings from the Port Chicago version of that book were very different from what Audra came up with. And Jox Custo's plea for the oceans included the regret that the great sea reptiles have nearly been wiped out. Only a very few remain, according to his pamphlets, and those few may not reproduce fast enough to continue the species.

"That's what has the Administration and the Academy in a twist—the claim that the information in the Lorr edition of *The Voyages of Captain Drogo Drach* is untrue. That the book

232

is fiction, not factual, and is therefore being misrepresented. If that got out, Instructor Segretti, your name and reputation wouldn't be worth a Hinterland rock."

Segretti turned purple with rage, sputtering insults.

"But you weren't on that bridge, and you didn't shove Audra into the river," I soothed him. "You had better things to do than counter claims your book was false. You wouldn't even talk to Jox, let alone refute his accusations of fraud. You left that in the hands of the Scribe's Guild and the Academy. You just went on with your experiments on small sea creatures."

"Where is this leading?" Eduardo demanded.

"Just clearing the air." I looked around the hall, searching for a head of bright-red hair. And there she was, lurking behind Rafe Urbine, edging towards the door.

"You see, Audra Martino was a unique person, with a very unique gift," I went on. "As one of the other apprentices in the Urbine studio put it, 'If she saw it, she could draw it'. Very clearly and distinctly, too. Exactly as it was, whether it was a collection of objects, or a living person…or a landscape, a small space between the reeds on the edge of the river.

"And that's why someone had to get rid of her. Because she saw something she wasn't supposed to see, and she drew it, very clearly. She drew a picture of the riverbank, and she included the small pellets someone had dropped when they received them in a shipment…Stop her!"

Marta had darted out the door.

"Get her!" I yelled. I hustled down the aisle between the benches while everyone babbled behind me. I reached the door just in time to see Marta on a two-wheel pedaling towards the Central Plaza and the crowds. She could lose herself in the traffic, she could catch a carrier. She was getting away!

Nothing for it. I hadn't been on a two-wheel in a while, but I couldn't let Marta go. I grabbed the nearest one off the rack in front of the Meeting-House, hoisted myself onto the saddle and followed her.

The setting sun cast long shadows over the people returning to their Garden homes, some on two-wheels, some on three-wheels, one or two pedishaws. Marta veered between the walkers and riders, taking advantage of the slight downward slope to speed up. I held onto the handles of my two-wheel. Somewhere behind me I heard someone yell "Stop!" I didn't. I just hoped the owner of the two-wheel would be forgiving when I returned it.

Marta reached the junction between Garden and Academy Way, gaining speed as she went. I grimly kept pace, focused on that red hair weaving between Academics in their mixed-up garb and Dark Ones in blue uniforms. I ignored the curses and cries of the people in our way.

Behind me, I heard someone shouting about the stolen two-wheels. I fought to keep my two-wheel balanced as I sped past the buildings of the Academy, and then the Temple of Healing. Up ahead I could now see the little bridge that marked the border between Industrial and Fishmarket.

Marta plunged over the sluggish stream as I wobbled down the middle of the road, trying to avoid pedishaws and other two- and three-wheels. I had to catch her before she got into Fishmarket, with its twisted roads and dead-end courts.

I rumbled over the bridge, and caught sight of her again, heading straight down Fishmarket Way. There were few vehicles on the road here, and the pedestrians scampered out of our way, so I was able to catch up, increasing speed as the road took a downward turn.

We reached the heart of Fishmarket with its scent of exotic spices and the smell of frying fish in oil and, somewhere underneath, the aroma of water-plants; the clang-clang and clink-clink of the gongs and bells of worshipers at the temples of Buda-Ganesha and Mara Deva; and over it all, the incessant chatter of languages I didn't understand. Males in baggy trou and loose shirts, females in gauzy skirts and veils filled the road. Marta had to slow down to avoid hitting them, and I pedaled harder to catch up with her.

She swerved off Fishmarket Way into an alley between two sand-block houses. I followed, bouncing along on the dirt path, skidding on slippery patches, and somehow still managing not to fall.

She turned again down a sloping path. I could smell the river, hear the rushing water ahead of me, the waves lapping the riverbank. Those sounds drew me onward.

The road ended in a small clearing, a patch of reeds. Where was Marta? I didn't see her two-wheel. Had I missed her? Was she lurking in the brush, waiting for me? I opened my jacket to get at my bludgeon.

I gazed at the clearing and realized this was it. This was where Audra had been, the exact place where she had seen something in the river…and something else on the ground.

A faint sound behind me. Squelch of a foot in the damp earth of the path. I grabbed my bludgeon and whirled around, raising it just in time to block the person behind me, who was trying to strike with a well-sharpened dart.

"Marta!" I yelled. "This won't do you any good. I found Chezan, the Guards are already on their way. You won't get away with another death." I spat out an obscenity as I shifted away from the maddened female.

She came at me again, jabbing at my exposed neck. I twisted away, trying to deflect her arm without breaking any bones. I wanted her alive, to make a full confession.

She lunged, gripping my jacket, one hand flailing with the dart, the other clawing at my eyes. I grabbed the hand with the dart and twisted her wrist to make her drop it. She still hung onto my jacket, though, grabbing for my neck.

We swayed together on the riverbank, slipping on the pebbles and muck left by the retreating tide. I felt my feet give way. She pushed me down, fell on top of me, trying to force my head into the mud.

We rolled over and over, neither of us able to get an advantage, closer and closer to the riverbank. I managed to wriggle out of her grip, grabbed a nearby tree to haul myself erect. She slid down the bank, scrabbling wildly for a handhold to keep away from the water streaming down to the ocean. She kicked out, but with only one foot. The other was held by something large, something bulbous. Something with arms lined with circular suckers.

She screamed in terror. grabbing at the slender stalks of the reeds, getting no traction.

"Let me help you!" I tried to catch one of her flailing hands.

Behind me, someone crashed through the reeds.

"You'll never get her by yourself." Someone large in a black sleeveless jacket, his bulging bare arms covered with tats, slid down the bank and grabbed for her other hand.

I didn't ask Brutus what he was doing there. I was just glad he was.

The two of us pulled together., but what was in the water was stronger than me, stronger than Brutus. Marta slipped under the water, came up sputtering, and sank again. Writhing tentacles enfolded her as she screamed something in a language I didn't understand.

We pulled harder, but it was no use. The tide had caught her, as well as whatever was pulling her down. My hands were slippery with the muck from the riverbank, and Brutus couldn't hold her by himself. Slowly, inexorably, she was pulled out of our grip into the middle of the stream, and vanished under the water

I collapsed onto the ground, panting. There was nothing I could do but stare into the water. Brutus squatted next to me, doing the same and shaking his head.

"What are you doing here?" I finally got enough breath to ask.

"I was late to the Service, like you asked, and I saw you chase that female with the red hair. You took a two-wheel, and that's not right, so I followed you. It's my duty." He sounded apologetic. "You stole, and you're not in the Guild."

"True. I'll return the two-wheel, no harm done to it. What about her?" I stared at the water. I caught a brief glimpse of red hair just above the surface, in the distance. Then it was gone, along with whatever had dragged her down.

Brutus frowned. "I think I know her. She comes to puja for Kali Mara. Sometimes. And I've seen her in Entertainment Row. She listened to the fella who yells about rodents coming to get us."

"And she's the one who gives out the pellets," I said. "But not the usual ones, the ones that are supposed to enable enlightenment. The strong ones, the ones that agitate the brain cells."

"But…why?"

"Coin," I said bitterly. "She took coin for the super-pellets. The other side of the deal was Chezan, the other apprentice in Urbine's studio. His family supply the pharmaceuticals for the Dark Ones. One of them must have enhanced the formula, and gave it to him to distribute. The pellets got into Lorr at your puja rituals."

I heard more crashing through the reeds and brush. A roar, and a plume of sand and pebbles, and a skimmer hovered just beyond the clearing. Atterson emerged to join Brutus and me.

"Have I interrupted something?"

"Not what you think." I struggled to my feet with some help from Brutus. "The one who did for Chezan is gone." I gestured toward the river. "She stabbed Audra with that poisoned dart of hers, then pushed her into the river. I think whatever *that* is…" I waved at the water, now gently rippling its way towards the ocean. "Brutus calls it Kali Mara. It may even be a kraken. But whatever it is, it saw Marta shove Audra into the river. It tried to get Audra out, but it was too late. Audra was drugged, and couldn't breathe, couldn't struggle out of the water, and…died."

"And you saw this…Kali Mara?"

Brutus nodded. "We did."

I added, "If the magistrates ask, we'll have to tell the truth. But the magistrates won't ask, will they." It wasn't a question.

"They'll find her body tomorrow, somewhere downstream," Atterson declared. "She was a suspect. A representative of the Administration went after her, she tried to escape, the tide got her. That's what's going into my report. Chief Polaris will accept it."

"And Chezan?"

"A drunken artist takes a walk by the river and loses his footing. It was bound to happen. His family will be informed." Atterson looked me over again. "And that's how it will be entered in the records in the Big Black Box."

"And Jox?" I wouldn't, couldn't let that go. "Marta got him, too. He was on the Waterfront after she left Audra. She couldn't be sure he hadn't seen her with Audra. She must have fed him a pellet, or dropped it in his drink, the way Chezan did with me at Smokey Joe's."

"Jox Custo was old. He was weakened from years of deprivation. The pellet simply completed the work of Nature." Atterson wouldn't give up.

"And you'll just let that go?"

"I have to. Orders." That was all she could say. She turned back to where her skimmer was hovering, "And there is no point in pushing the issue. Justice has been done. Let it go, Drach! Let it go."

Brutus helped me back to the path toward Fishmarket Way. "One more thing," he said. "The one who's been after you?"

"That was Marta, probably under orders from Selva Delrey. They never give up, those Delreys, but I'm still here. Let Fee M'Farr deal with it. He doesn't like anyone moving in on his territory, no matter who."

"You've got to come with me," Atterson said. "You're bruised, you may have been nicked by that poison, and you need medical attention."

"I'm also covered in mud and wet to the bone," I countered. "I'm not fit to be seen. Get me to my digs, let me wash and change, and I'll give you all you need for your report."

"And I'll return the two-wheel," Brutus said. "Take care of yourself, Pola Drach."

Kindness from a Fatso? But I'll take what I can get.

I let Atterson take me back to Foodie Alley. She let me slosh off the muck and put on a dry jacket. Then she hauled me into the nearest Dark Ones' Shrine for emergency treatment before dragging me off to the Guardhouse for a thorough interrogation.

I got treated for the various contusions, took some pain pellets, and after the deposition caught a pedishaw to Smokey Joe's. I needed a brew, and I wanted to let Basher know what was going on before he got some garbled report that I was flat on my back…again.

xiv

Smokey Joe's was relatively quiet at that hour, too late for the midday rush, too early for the night owls. Basher Bob was at his usual seat, with Velda at his side. He took in my disheveled appearance with a rueful shrug.

"Next time, get me in," he commented, as I hitched myself onto a stool next to him.

"No time," I explained.

"I was there," Brutus added.

Velda gave me a *ya really mean it?* look.

"Brutus was on duty," I said. "Watching out at the Service of Consolation for the Fatsos. There was an Unsanctioned assassin loose in Lorr, but that's been taken care of."

Velda looked me over. "By you?"

I nodded modestly. "By me… with some help from unexpected sources." I left it at that.

"How did you figure out it was the redhead?" Brutus asked.

"She drew my attention from the first," I said. "She kept talking about Audra as if she was already gone. Others still expected her to turn up."

239

"But why the Pangkoti? And where did the pinkies come from?" Brutus's face contorted with the effort of thinking.

"My best guess is Chezan's personal life didn't suit his Pangkoti family. He hangs out at the Green Dragon with the joyboys. Too familiar, by Upper Tier Pangkoti standards. Marta worked that angle, got him to pass the pellets from Hinterland to his joyboy buddies. Admin and the Dark Ones should be able to work things out from there." I took a swig of brew.

"So, you're going to leave it to the Admin?" Basher sounded skeptical.

"I have to," I said. But I didn't have to like it.

TRUTH AND
CONSEQUENCES

I SPENT THE NEXT TWO WEEKS CLEARING UP THE RECORDS and paying off my debts before the Years-End ceremonies that mark the official start of Winterfest. Eduardo Martino came to my office to wind up our accounts.

As he sat in the wooden chair, I expounded on what I'd been able to figure out while I was recovering from my mud bath.

"It was Marta and Chezan working together, until Chezan got too mouthy and Marta panicked. She was under orders, couldn't afford exposure. She must have followed him to the river, gave him a shove, and let the tide do the rest."

"What happened to Audra?" Eduardo demanded. "If Marta pushed her into the river, how did she get out?"

"I can't say for sure, but I think Audra looked into the river from the bridge and saw the…Kali Mara. She went down to the riverbank for a better look. Marta had spotted her on Entertainment Row after Chezan met his joyboy friends at the Green Dragon. She followed her to the bridge, then waited until she came down. That's when she shoved Audra into the river.

"The being called Kali Mara, trying to help, dragged her out of the water and into that little cave under the bridge. Audra was drugged, couldn't call out. She…went…alone, cold and forgotten."

I tried not to choke. An Independent Eye can't afford emotional involvement.

"But…why?" Eduardo asked.

"My guess? Partly envy and hatred of Audra's talent, but mostly coin. Audra had stumbled on Marta's business in pellets, financed by Selva Delrey's interest in Pangkot pharmaceuticals. Marta was Selva's creature, working through the Urbine Gallery, funneling information back to the lodge in Hinterland and getting orders and coin in return."

"Why attack Audra, though? She'd done nothing to provoke her."

"Audra didn't understand what was going on. She was an innocent when it came to people. She'd followed Marta down to the river a time or two and seen her distributing the pellets. Maybe some of them fell on the ground, maybe the youngsters who grabbed them were careless, but there they were, obvious to anyone who saw them. Audra always remembered every detail of what she saw.

"When Urbine told them to depict a dream, Audra couldn't imagine one. So, she did the scene at the river and included those pellets Marta doled out. Once Marta saw that, Audra was doomed. If anyone recognized what they were, attention would focus on the Urbine studio, and Marta couldn't have that."

I handed Eduardo my itemized bill, including extra coin for wear-and-tear on my body and clothing. He scowled, but paid it. I put the coin into my pouch. It would settle my account with Fletcher and to pay my rent to Jake and Holly.

"One more thing," I said, before Eduardo could leave. "I'd like one of Audra's sketches. Ask Urbine for the ones he removed from her sketchbook before he sent it on to you."

"Why would he do that?"

"Coin again," I said. "He can flog those drawings for plenty, since there won't be any more, and Audra's work was already getting major reviews on Post Four. You might want to have a word with Guildmaster Urbine, just to make sure you get a suitable share of any coin Audra's work brings in."

Eduardo looked grim. I didn't envy Guildmaster Urbine when next the two of them met.

I was about to close the office when the door opened, and Captain Atterson marched in.

"To what do I owe this honor? You're paid up," I told her.

"I thought you should know how my investigation turned out. The Guards found a stash of the pellets in Marta's room, hidden between the bedboards. They took them to the Dark Ones boffins for analysis.

"They seem to be some kind of fungus derivative, previously unknown. Origin also unknown, but could be something from the Southern Continent by way of Pangkot. A major warning has gone out from the Temple of Healing, signed by the Abbot of the Order himself, banning any use or distribution of said pellets."

"For all the good it will do," I muttered. The one way to get something into Fashion is to make people think it's bad for you. "What about Chezan? I'm not sure if that's something Marta did, or if he really did fall into the river drunk."

"The Pangkoti? According to Dark Kelvin, he drowned. He may have been helped into the river by a shove between the shoulders, but he had plenty of alcohol in his blood and water in his lungs. Without further evidence, it's being listed as a sorry accident. His remains will be shipped back to Pangkot, with the sincere apologies of the City of Lorr to his very prominent family."

"Who won't want to make a fuss about it. From what he said, their attitude will be 'Good riddance'. And I think the attacks on me had nothing to do with pellets or Audra, just Marta, with an assist from Chezan.

"That's what had me baffled. I didn't see how Marta could have shoved me under the carrier and fed pellets to Jox at the same time. It was Chezan who put on the red wig and flashy green jacket and trou. He followed me to Garden and the Central Plaza while Marta handled Jox. Only, he wasn't really up to it, kept missing the mark. Marta was the real assassin, working for Selva."

"Selva Delrey." Atterson made it sound like a curse. "We can't touch her in Hinterland."

"I'm sure Fee M'Farr will take care of it. Between his buddies at the mines and his operatives in Hinterlands, Selva will be taken out. He really doesn't like anyone muscling in on his territory, especially not amateurs. If anyone's going to be assassinated, he wants his Guild to do it."

Atterson nodded. "And one more thing. We found out where that Prophet came from. Turns out he had a Delrey connection, but it wasn't Selva. The name he goes under in Hinterland is Raspa Turin, and he's not exactly a Swindler. There really is a plot of land set aside for a sanctuary from whatever is coming at us in that Third Ship, financed by Old Gregor Delrey."

"What? I thought he was gone!"

With a shrug, Atterson headed for the door. "I have a report to make. What do I tell the Chief?"

"Tell Regina Polaris I did what I thought would benefit Lorr," I said, and let it go at that.

Neither of us mentioned Kali Mara, or whatever it was that had dragged Marta into the river.

"And don't worry about that two-wheel," Atterson added. "I made it clear you were in pursuit of a fugitive from justice, under orders from the Guards. You'll get off with a fine, but don't do it again. You have been officially warned!"

And off she went, leaving me to give Holly my yearly rental on the office.

I was about to do just that when I got a surprise visitor.

"Hannes! How'd you find me?"

"I asked the big fella that guards the bridge. He told me where you kept an office. I just wanted to tell you, I'm going home. The Seaman's Guild took care of Jox's remains, saw they were properly disposed of. I've got a deck place on a puffer leaving tomorrow for South Coast. I have to tell Mam what happened to Jox."

"It was Marta," I told him. "She saw someone in the mist when she pushed Audra into the river. She thought it was Jox—"

"But it was me," Hannes said. "Jox was following me, and told me not to chase females in Lorr. I went back to our stand…" he stopped. "If I hadn't…"

"Don't think that way," I tried to soothe him. "Jox was old, his heart wasn't up to what Marta dropped into his drink. The best way to honor him is to continue his fight for clean oceans."

Hannes brightened. "I'll do that. And the others, they've got places at the Advanced Academy. They'll keep it up, too."

"Take care," I said. "And have a profitable journey."

I had one more interruption when Holly popped her head in via the inner door.

"Pola? Messenger with some notices for you. And when you're finished, Jake's going to give it a rest. We're going down to the bridge to watch the flotilla go by. Coming with us?"

"Give me a minute." I took the folded messages.

One notice to pay up the last of my taxes before Year-End. One more invite to the Gala. And a note from Britta Drach, inviting me to a Winterfest Gathering at her new digs in Industrial.

She'd managed to wangle a set of rooms in one of the houses between the Temple of Healing and the Science Building, was sharing with the other two Norland females, and wanted to celebrate her new posting as Academic Assistant to Instructor Segretti.

This was one invitation I decided to accept. I'd give her the Lorr edition of *The Voyage of Drogo Drach* for Winterfest. I didn't know whether she already had a copy, but I didn't want it. I'll keep the one Jox gave me. the true one. And it wouldn't be a bad idea to establish a contact within the Advanced Academy. You never know when you might need some information.

ii

I decided I'd done enough work for the day. I locked up, went through the inner door, followed Holly and Zeta into Clothier's Alley. They joined the throng heading down the Grand Boulevard to the river. I stopped by the newsposts for one last check before the dark closed in.

Post Two had a notice from the Dark Ones and the Admin, in very large Lorran letters and Pangkoti pictographs, warning against the use of dangerous pharmaceuticals, especially pink ones.

Post Four had a notice that the Urbine Studio was opening to apprentices, under the management of Craftsman Edard, offering instruction in skills of painting and drawing, with guaranteed showing of work at the Urbine Gallery. A separate notice announced a showing of the works of the late Chezan. Word on the Grand Boulevard was that those paintings were going for vast sums. No mention of whose pockets those sums would wind up in. after said paintings were sold.

I joined the crowd at the Flatlands Bridge to watch the river parade. A fleet of colorfully decorated barges were lined up, ready to carry notables down to the high cliff, the edge of Flatlands, the spot where the very first shuttle landed when the First Ship finally made landfall.

First came the band, brass instruments blaring away. Then a barge with the Elite Squad of Guards in dress uniforms—

246

one from Pangkot, red and yellow banners waving, gongs clashing; one from South Coast, drummers drumming. Finally, the official craft for Lorr itself, with the Chief Administrator and the Guildmasters' Councilors beneath a hovering airship, proving that Lorr ruled New Earth on land and sea and air.

All were lit with flickering torches, bright on the river against a darkening sky. Over all rode Gold and Silver moons in half-phase, looking as if they were pasted on the sky.

"Pretty, isn't it?"

I turned to find Sara Atterson at my elbow. "Aren't you supposed to be on the Guards' barge?"

"I'm on duty. Someone has to keep an eye on the Waterfront."

"Even at Winterfest?"

She shrugged. "I'll get some time when the Chief gets back to see Geri and Eduardo. Winterfest will be...empty... without Audra."

A voice called to her, and she left me to listen to the music.

Someone at my elbow joined in the song in a surprisingly sweet tenor.

> There's a star somewhere in the open sky.
> Rise up, Spacer, and follow;
> A home for us, a place to fly.
> Rise up, Spacer, and follow.

I turned to see who was singing.

"Brutus?"

You'd think by the look of him, he'd be one of those booming bassos, but what came out of his mouth was high and clear, right on pitch.

"I saw you by the bridge. I thought..." He stopped, then started again. "There's some of us fellas, we're having a Winterfest gathering at Smokey Joe's. We've got a back room, asked that busker and his deb to sing with us, and the old-ster with the beard. He knows lots of the old songs and wants to learn some of ours." Brutus glanced at me expectantly. "Wanna come along?"

I tried to look pleased. "I don't sing." I moved off the bridge, heading back to Entertainment Row. Brutus followed me, insistent.

"You could listen."

"Brutus…" I began, but he cut me off.

"Y'know, Drach, we got off bad, but you're all right. You got me out of a bad spot, put in the good word with the Master Assassin. And it ain't as if you don't know what you'll get, so how about it?" He ended on an expectant note.

Founder's Faith! What is it that makes me attractive to the worst human males in Lorr? First Dark Kelvin, now this character!

"I'm not really ready for Winterfest."

By this time, we'd reached Smokey Joe's. Brutus shrugged. "You'd have fun," he promised.

"Maybe," I said. "You go in, enjoy your Winterfest treats. Sing one for me. Maybe next time."

I stood outside Smokey Joe's. I could hear the laughter and cheerful voices inside. I could join them, be one with the crowd. Basher and Velda would watch my back, Brutus and his Fatsos would sing,

But bad things happen to me at Winterfest gatherings. And there was Ficus, waiting for me at my digs…

I looked down the river. The barges had reached the end of their journey. I watched the sparks of light move up to the beacon.

Suddenly, a flash of light. A flame in the darkness, light-ing the way for the ship that never came…or would it? *Was* there a Third Ship somewhere in that blackness? Did Old Earth still exist, one of those tiny pinpricks of light in the night sky? Or was New Earth truly that last bastion of Hu-manity?

I sighed and slogged back down Entertainment Row to my digs. Ficus was waiting for its clet and water and bone-meal.

Tomorrow, I'll go back to guarding Lorr. One soul, one case at a time.

ACKNOWLEDGMENTS

Thanks to Cecillia Eng for the use of lines from her song "Earth That Was"

Thanks to Eileen Watkins, for beta-reading and editing

Songs parodied: "Eastbound and Down", Jerry Reed, 1977; "Rise Up, Shepherd", traditional carol

About the Author

ROBERTA ROGOW got her start writing for *Star Trek* fanzines in the mid-1970's. She mostly writes historical fiction, although she sometimes twists the history. Her most recent stories take place in a Manhattan Island that was settled by Spanish Moors instead of by Dutch Traders—*Last of the Mohegans* meets *Arabian Nights*, with a Danish accent—and, of course, on the distant planet of New Earth.

Roberta retired from a 37-year career as a children's librarian in 2008. The Pola Drach mysteries are a return to her SF fanfic roots. She now lives in New Jersey, and spends her time going to science fiction and mystery conventions when she is not writing mysteries or singing filk (science fiction folk music).

www.ingramcontent.com/pod-product-compliance
Lightning Source LLC
Chambersburg PA
CBHW032211030726
47494CB00020B/961